DECISION AT TRAFALGAR

Walker Adventure Novels by Richard Woodman

ARCTIC TREACHERY

THE BOMB VESSEL

DECISION AT TRAFALGAR

Richard Woodman

Walker & Co./New York

First published in the United States of America in 1987 by the Walker Publishing Company, Inc.

Library of Congress Cataloging-in-Publication Data

Woodman, Richard.
    Decision at Trafalgar.

    Reprint. Originally published: 1805. London :
J. Murray Publisher, 1985.
    1. Napoleonic Wars, 1800–1814––Fiction. 2. Trafalgar
(Cape), Battle of, 1805––Fiction. 3. Great Britain––
History, Naval––19th century––Fiction. I. Title.
PR6073.0617D43 1987   823'.914   87–21588
ISBN 0–8027–0993–1

    Printed in the United States of America

    10 9 8 7 6 5 4 3 2 1

For Liz and Brian Bell

Contents

PART ONE: BLOCKADE

1 The Club-Haul   3
2 The *Antigone*   13
3 The Spy Master   21
4 Foolish Virgins   30
5 Ruse de Guerre   40
6 The Secret Agent   47
7 The Army of the Coasts of the Ocean   57
8 Stalemate   66
9 Orders   75

PART TWO: BREAK-OUT

10 The Rochefort Squadron   83
11 The Snowstorm   92
12 The Look-out Frigate   98
13 Calder's Action   106
14 The Fog of War   113
15 Nelson   118
16 Tarifa   126

PART THREE: BATTLE

17 Santhonax   135
18 The Spectre of Nelson   145
19 Villeneuve   154
20 Nelson's Watch-Dogs   165
21 Trafalgar   174
22 Surrender and Storm   185
23 Gibraltar   196
24 The Martyr of Rennes   202
    Author's Note   208

DECISION AT TRAFALGAR

PART ONE

Blockade

'Let us be master of the Channel for six hours and we are masters of the world.'

NAPOLEON TO ADMIRAL LATOUCHE-TRÉVILLE   July 1804

'I do not say, my Lords, that the French will not come. I only say they will not come by sea.'

EARL ST VINCENT TO THE HOUSE OF LORDS   1804

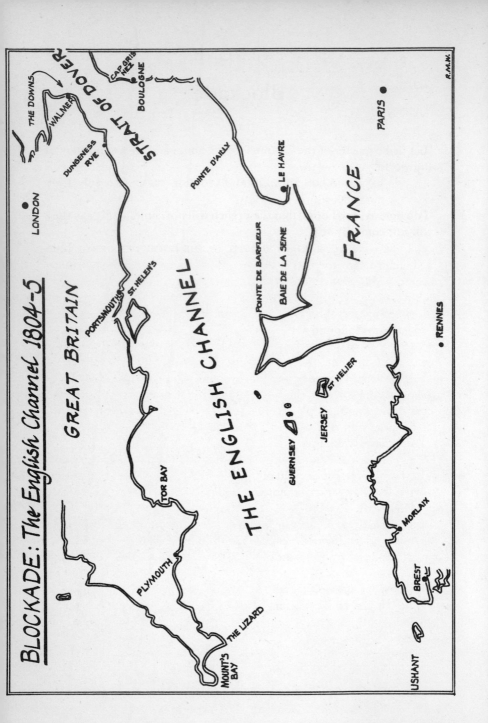

BLOCKADE: *The English Channel 1804–5*

GREAT BRITAIN

THE ENGLISH CHANNEL

FRANCE

STRAIT OF DOVER

THE DOWNS
WALMER
DUNGENESS
RYE
LONDON
PORTSMOUTH
ST. HELEN'S
TOR BAY
PLYMOUTH
THE LIZARD
MOUNT'S BAY

CAP GRIS NEZ
BOULOGNE
POINTE D'AILLY
LE HAVRE
PARIS
POINTE DE BARFLEUR
BAIE DE LA SEINE
GUERNSEY
ST. HELIER
JERSEY
RENNES
MORLAIX
BREST
USHANT

R.M.W.

The Club-Haul

'Sir! Sir!'

Midshipman Frey threw open the door of the captain's cabin with a precipitate lack of formality. The only reply to his urgent summons from the darkness within was the continuous creaking of the frigate as she laboured in the heavy sea.

'Sir! For God's sake wake up, sir!'

The ship staggered as a huge wave broke against her weather bow and sluiced over the rail into her waist. It found its way below by a hundred different routes. Outside the swinging door the marine sentry swore, fighting the impossibility of remaining upright. Frey stumbled against the leg of a chair overset by the violence of the ship's movement. He found the cabin suddenly illuminated as a surge of white water hissed up under the counter and reflected the pale moonlight through the stern windows. Mullender, the captain's steward, would catch it for not dropping the sashes if one of the windows was stove in, the boy thought irrelevantly as he shoved the chair aside and groped to starboard where, over the aftermost 18-pounder gun, the captain's cot swung.

'Sir! *Please* wake up!'

Frey hesitated. Pale in the gloom, Captain Nathaniel Drinkwater's legs stuck incongruously out of the cot. Still in breeches and stockings they seemed appendages not consonant with the dignity of a post-captain in the Royal Navy. Frey reached out nervously then drew back hurriedly as the legs began to flail of their own accord, responding to the squealing of the pipes at the hatchways and the sudden cry for all hands taken up by the sentries at their unstable posts about the ship.

'Eh? What the devil is it? Is that you, Mr Frey?'

The cot ceased its jumping and Captain Drinkwater's face, haggard with fatigue, peered at the midshipman. 'Why was I not called before?'

'I had been calling you for some time . . .'

'What's amiss?' The captain's tone was sharp.

'Mr Quilhampton's respects . . .'

'What is it?'

3

'We've to tack, sir. Immediately, sir. Mr Quilhampton apprehends we are embayed!'

'God's bones!' The sleep drained from Drinkwater's face with the dawning of comprehension. Beyond the bulkhead the ship had come to urgent life with the dull thunder of a hundred pairs of feet being driven on deck by the bosun's mates.

'My hat and cloak, Mr Frey. On deck at once, d'you hear me!' Drinkwater forced his feet into his buckled shoes and tugged on his coat, stumbling to leeward as the frigate lurched again. He shoved past the midshipman and swore as his shin connected with the overset chair-leg. He swore a second time as he bumped into the marine sentry sliding across the desk in an attempt to avoid part of the larboard watch tumbling up from the berth-deck below via the after-ladder.

By the time Frey had collected the captain's hat and cloak he emerged onto an almost deserted gun-deck. The purser's dips glimmered, casting dull gleams on the fat, black breeches of the double-lashed 18-pounder cannon and the bright-work on the stanchions. A few round shot remained in the garlands, but most had been dislodged and rolled down to leeward where they rumbled up and down amid a dark swirl of water. Mr Frey paused in the creaking emptiness of the berth-deck.

'All hands means you too, younker. Get your arse on deck instanter, God damn you!'

Frey doubled up the ladder with a blaspheming Lieutenant Rogers at his heels. The first lieutenant had only roused himself from a drunken slumber with the greatest difficulty. He did not like being shown up in front of the whole ship's company and Frey's belated appearance served to cover his tardiness.

The first thing Drinkwater noticed when he reached the upper deck was the strength of the wind. He had gone below less than two hours earlier with the ship riding out a south-westerly gale under easy sail on the larboard tack. Hill, the sailing master, had observed their latitude earlier as being ten leagues south of the Lizard and the ship was holding a course of west-north-west. Even allowing for considerable leeway Drinkwater could not see that Mr Quilhampton's fears were justified. He had left orders to be called at eight bells when, with both watches, they could tack to the southward and hope to come up with the main body of the Channel Fleet under Admiral Cornwallis somewhere west of Ushant.

Quilhampton's face was suddenly in front of him. The strain of

4

anxiety was plain even in the moonlight; clear too was the relief at Drinkwater's appearance.

'Well, Mr Q?' Drinkwater shouted at the dripping figure.

'Sir, a few minutes ago the scud cleared completely. I'm damned certain I saw land to leeward . . . or something confounded like it.'

'Have you seen the twin lights of the Lizard?' Drinkwater shouted, a worm of uncertainty uncoiling itself in his belly.

'Half an hour ago we couldn't see much, sir. Heavy, driving rain . . .'

'Then it cleared like this?'

'Aye, sir, and the wind veered a point or two . . .'

It was on Drinkwater's tongue to ask why Quilhampton had not called him, but it was not the moment to remonstrate. He crossed quickly to the binnacle, aware by the grunts of the helmsmen that they were having the devil of a time holding the frigate on course. A glance confirmed his fears. The veering wind had cast the ship's head to the north-west and if that latitude was in error he did not dare contemplate further.

'Thank you, Mr Frey.' He flung the boat-cloak over his shoulder and very nearly lost it in the violence of the wind. The scream of air rushing through the rigging had a diabolical quality that Drinkwater did not ever remember hearing before in a quarter-century of sea-service. He looked aloft. Both the fore and main topsails were hard-reefed and a small triangle of a spitfire staysail strained above the fo'c's'le. Even so the ship was over-canvased, almost on her beam ends as spume tore over her deck stinging the eyes and causing the cheeks to ache painfully.

'Look, sir! Look!'

Quilhampton's arm pointed urgently as he fought to retain his footing on the canting deck. Drinkwater slithered to the lee rail as the look-out took up the cry.

'Land! Land! Land on the lee bow!'

Rogers cannoned into him. 'She'll never stay in this sea, sir!'

Drinkwater smelt the rum on his stale breath, but agreed with him. 'Aye, Sam, and there's no room to wear.' He paused, gathered his breath and shouted his next order so there could be no mistake. 'We must club-haul!'

'Club-haul? Jesus!'

'Amen to that, Mr Rogers,' Drinkwater said sarcastically. 'Now, Mr Q. D'you get the mizen topmen and the gunners below to rouse out the top cable in the starboard tier. Open the port by number nine

5

gun and haul it forward outside all. Clap it on the starboard sheet-anchor. Ah, Mr Gorton,' Drinkwater addressed the second lieutenant who had come up with the master. 'Mr Gorton, you on the fo'c's'le with the bosun. Get Q's cable made fast and the anchor cleared away. I shall rely upon you to let the anchor go when I give the word.' Gorton turned away with Quilhampton and both officers hurried off.

'I hope your confidence ain't misplaced, sir.' Rogers stared after the figures of the two young men.

'Both demonstrated their resource in the Greenland Sea, Sam. Besides, I want you amidships to pass my orders in case they ain't heard.' Drinkwater refused to be drawn by Roger's touchiness respecting his two juniors. For all his obvious disabilities Drinkwater had dragged Lieutenant Rogers off the poop of an ancient bomb-vessel and placed him on the quarterdeck of one of the finest frigates in the service, so he had little cause to complain of partiality. 'See that the men are at their stations and all ropes will run clear.' That at least was something Rogers would do superbly and with a deal of invective to spur the men's endeavours.

'Well, Mr Hill?'

'I've told two of my mates off into the hold to sound the well and Meggs is mustering a party at the pumps. If you open number nine port she'll be taking water all the while.'

'That,' replied Drinkwater shouting, 'is a risk we'll have to take.'

There was little either captain or master could do until the preparations were completed. The ship was rushing through the water at a speed that, under other circumstances, they would have been proud of.

'Is it Mount's Bay, d'you think?' Hill's concern was clear. He, too, was worried about that latitude. 'We haven't sighted the Lizard lights, sir.'

'No.' Drinkwater hauled himself gingerly into the leeward mizen rigging and felt the wind catch his body as a thing of no substance. He clung on grimly and stared out to starboard. The thin veil of cloud which showed the gibbous moon nearly at the full was sufficient to extend a pale light upon the waves as the wind tore their breaking crests to shreds and sent the spume downwind like buckshot. With the greatest difficulty he made out what might have been the grey line of a cliff out on the starboard beam. He could only estimate its distance with difficulty. Perhaps a mile, perhaps not so much.

Then the moon sailed into a clear patch of sky. It was suddenly very bright and what Drinkwater saw caused his mouth to go dry.

6

A point or two on their starboard bow, right in their track as they sagged to leeward, rose a huge grey pinnacle of rock. In the moonlight its crags and fissures stood out starkly, and at its feet the breakers pounded white. But in the brief interval in the cloud Drinkwater became aware of something else. Atop the rock, perched upon its highest crag, a buttress and wall reared sheer from the cliff. Immediately he knew their position and that the danger to the ship and her company was increased a hundredfold. For beneath the ancient abbey on St Michael's Mount, stretching round onto their windward bow, the breakers pounded white upon the Mountamopus shoal.

There are few periods of anxiety greater in their intensity than that of a commander whose ship is running into peril, waiting for his people to complete their preparations. On the one hand experience and judgement caution him not to attempt a manoeuvre until everything is ready; upon the other instinct cries out to be released into immediate action. Yet, as the sweat prickled between his shoulder blades, Drinkwater knew that to act hastily was to court disaster. If the ship failed in stays there would be no second chance. It was useless to speculate upon the erroneous navigation that had brought them to this point, or why Rogers stank of rum, or, indeed, whether the two were connected. All these thoughts briefly crossed his mind in the enforced hiatus that is every captain's lot once orders have been given.

He looked again at the mount. The moon had disappeared now under a thick mantle of cloud, but they were close enough for its mass to loom over them, an insubstantial-looking lightening of the darkness to leeward, skirted about its base by the breakers that dashed spray half-way up its granite cliffs. This sudden proximity made his heart skip and he looked along the waist where men had been clustered in a dark group, hauling on the messenger that pulled the heavy cable along the ship's side. He could imagine their efforts being thwarted by the protruberances of the channels, the dead-eyes, the bead-blocks and all the other rigging details that at this precise moment seemed so much infernal nuisance. God, would they never finish?

The wind shrieked mercilessly and the frigate lay over so that he felt a terrible concern for that open gun-port into which, without a shadow of doubt, the sea would be sluicing continuously. He was unable to hear any noise above the storm and hoped that the pumping party were hard at it.

'Ready, sir!'

7

After the worry the word came aft and took him by surprise. It was Rogers, his face a pale blur of urgency abruptly illuminated as, again, the cloud was torn aside and the moon shone brightly. The light fell on the frigate, the sea and St Michael's Mount, sublime in its terrifying majesty.

'Stations for stays!' He left Rogers to bawl the order through the speaking trumpet, took Hill by the elbow and forced him across the deck. 'We'll take the wheel, Mr Hill. It'll need the coolest heads tonight.' He sensed Hill's bewilderment as to what had gone wrong with the navigation.

Captain and sailing master took over the head-wheel, the displaced quartermasters moving across the deck to assist the gunners to haul the main-yard.

'Ease down the helm, Mr Hill!' Drinkwater could feel the vibration of the hull as it rushed through the water, transmitted up from the rudder through the stock and tiller via the tiller ropes which creaked with the strain upon them. The ship lay over as she began to turn into the wind. A sea hit her larboard bow and threw her back a point. Drinkwater watched the angled compass card serenely illuminated by the yellow oil lamp, quietly obeying the timeless laws of natural science amid the elemental turmoil of the wind and sea.

Drinkwater raised his voice: 'Fo'c's'le there! Cut free the anchor! Let the cable run!'

Rogers took up the cry, bawling the first part forward and the latter part below to the party at the gun-port and by the cable-compressors. Drinkwater was dimly aware of a flurry of activity on the fo'c's'le and the hail that the anchor was gone. Behind him one of the two remaining helmsmen muttered, 'Shit or bust, mateys!'

'I hope it holds,' said Hill.

'It'll hold, Mr Hill. 'Tis sand and rock. The rock may part the cable in a moment or two but she'll hold long enough.' He wished he possessed the confidence he expressed. He could feel the cable rumbling through the port, there was no doubt about that strange sensation coming up through the thin soles of his shoes. Rogers was crouched at the companionway and suddenly straightened.

'Half cable veered, sir!'

Sixty fathoms of thirteen-inch hemp. Not enough, not yet. Drinkwater counted to three, then: 'Nip her!'

'I believe,' said Drinkwater to cover the extremity of his fear that in the next few seconds the anchor might break out or the cable part,' I believe at this point when staying, both the French and the Spanish

8

invoke God as a matter of routine.'

'Not such a bad idea, sir, beggin' yer pardon,' answered one of the helmsmen behind him.

And then the ship began to turn. For a moment he thought she might go the wrong way, for he had let go the lee anchor and that from a port well abaft the bow.

'Hard over now, my lads . . .' He began to spin the wheel, aware that the anchor and cable were snubbing the ship round into the wind and thus assisting them. With the courses furled there were no tacks and sheets to raise and she was suddenly in the eye of the wind. There was a thunderous clap which sent a tremble through the hull as the fore-topsail came aback and juddered the whole foremast to its step in the kelson.

'Main-topsail haul!' Thank God for his crew, Drinkwater thought. They were only a few days out of Chatham and might have had a crew that were raw and unco-ordinated, but he had drafted the entire company from the sloop *Melusine*, volunteers to a man. The main and mizen yards came round. So too did the ship, she was spinning like a top, her bow rising and her bowsprit stabbing at the very moon as she passed through the wind. The main-topsail filled with a crack that sent a second mighty tremor through the ship.

'We've done it, by God!' yelled Rogers.

'Cut, man! Cut the bloody cable!'

With the ship cast upon the other tack they had only a few seconds before the action of the anchor would pull the ship's head back again, but the backed fore-topsail was paying her off.

'Haul all!'

The foreyards came round and Rogers came aft and reported the cable cut. Drinkwater caught a glimpse of rock close astern, of the hollow troughs of a sea that was breaking in shallow water.

He handed the wheel back to the quartermasters. 'Keep her free for a little while. We are not yet clear of the shoals.'

'Aye, aye, sir.'

'Ease the weather braces, Mr Rogers.'

They made the final adjustments and set her on a course clear of the Mountamopus as a dripping party came up from the gun-deck and reported the port closed. Relief was clear on every face. As if cheated in its intention, the storm swept another curtain of cloud across the face of the moon.

'You may splice the main-brace, Mr Rogers, then pipe the watch below. My warmest thanks to the ship's company.'

Drinkwater turned away and headed for the companionway, his cabin and cot.

'Three cheers for the cap'n!'

'Silence there!' shouted Rogers, well knowing Drinkwater's distaste for any kind of show. But Drinkwater paused at the top of the companionway and made to raise his hat, only to find he had no hat to raise.

Squatting awkwardly to catch the light from the binnacle, Mr Frey made the routine entry on the log slate for the middle watch: *Westerly gales to storm. Ship club-hauled off St Michael's Mount, Course S.E. Lost sheet anchor and one cable.* He paused, then added on his own accord and without instruction: *Ship saved.*

The weather had abated somewhat by dawn, though the sea still ran high and there was a heavy swell. However, it was possible to relight the galley range and it was a more cheerful ship's company that set additional sail as the wind continued to moderate during the forenoon.

Drinkwater was on deck having slept undisturbed for four blessed hours. His mind felt refreshed although his limbs and, more acutely, his right shoulder which had been mangled by wounds, ached with fatigue. It was almost the hour of noon and he had sent down for his Hadley sextant with a view to assisting Hill and his party establish the ship's latitude. The master was still frustrated over his failure of the day before, for he could find no retrospective error in his working.

On waking Drinkwater had reflected upon the problem. He himself did not always observe the sun's altitude at noon. Hill was a more than usually competent master and had served with Drinkwater on the cutter *Kestrel* and the sloop *Melusine*, proving his ability both in the confined waters of the Channel and North Sea, and also in the intricacies of Arctic navigation.

As Mullender gingerly lifted the teak box lid for Drinkwater to remove the instrument he caught the reproach in Hill's eyes.

'It wants about four minutes to apparent noon, sir,' said Hill, adding with bitter emphasis, 'by my reckoning.'

Drinkwater suppressed a smile. Poor Hill. His humiliation was public; there could be few on the ship that by now had not learned that their plight last night had been due to a total want of accuracy in the ship's navigation.

Hill assembled his party. Alongside him stood three of the ship's six midshipmen and one of the master's mates. Lieutenant Quilhampton was also in attendance, using Drinkwater's old quadrant given him by the captain. Drinkwater remembered that Quilhampton and he had been discussing some detail the previous day and that the lieutenant had not taken a meridian altitude. Nor had Lieutenant Gorton. Drinkwater frowned and lifted his sextant, swinging the index and bringing the sun down to the horizon. The pale disc shone through a thin veil of high cloud and he adjusted the vernier screw so that it arced on the horizon. He peered briefly at the scale, replaced the sextant to his eye and noted that the sun continued to rise slowly as it moved towards its culmination.

'Nearly on, sir,' remarked Hill who had been watching the rate of rise slow down. The line of officers swayed with the motion of the ship, a picture of concentration. The sun ceased to rise and 'hung'. Its brief motionless suspension preceeded its descent into the period of post-meridian and Hill called, 'On, sir, right on!'

'Very well, Mr Hill, eight bells it is.'

By the binnacle the quartermaster turned the glass, the other master's mate hove the log and eight bells was called forward where the fo'c's'le bell was struck sharply. The marine sentinels were relieved, dinner was piped and a new day started on board His Britannic Majesty's 36-gun, 18-pounder, frigate *Antigone* as she stood across the chops of the Channel in search of Admiral Cornwallis and the Channel Fleet.

'Well, Mr Hill,' Drinkwater straightened from his sextant, 'what do we make it?' Drinkwater saw Hill bending over his quadrant, his lips muttering. A frown puckered his forehead, something seemed to be wrong with the master's instrument.

To avoid causing Hill embarrassment Drinkwater turned to the senior of the midshipmen: 'Mr Walmsley?'

Midshipman Lord Walmsley cast a sideways look at the master, swallowed and answered, 'Er, thirty-nine degrees, twenty-six minutes, sir.'

'Poppy cock, Mr Walmsley. Mr Frey?'

'Thirty-nine degrees six minutes, sir.' Drinkwater grunted. That was within a minute of his own observation.

'Mr Q?'

'And a half, sir.'

The two master's mates and Midshipman the Honourable Alexander Glencross agreed within a couple of minutes. Drinkwater turned to Mr Hill: 'Well, Mr Hill?'

Hill was frowning. 'I have the same as Lord Walmsley, sir.' His voice was puzzled and Drinkwater looked quickly at his lordship who had already moved his index arm and was lowering his instrument back into the box between his feet. It suddenly occurred to Drinkwater what had happened. Hill habitually muttered his altitude as he read it off the scale and Walmsley had persistently overheard and copied him. Yesterday, without Quilhampton and Drinkwater, Hill would have believed his own observation, apparently corroborated by Walmsley, and dismissed those of his juniors as inaccurate.

Drinkwater made a quick calculation. By adding the sum of the corrections for parallax, the sun's semi-diameter and refraction, then taking the result from a right angle to produce the true zenith distance, he was very close to their latitude. They were almost upon the equinox so the effect of the sun's declination was not very large and there would be a discrepancy in their latitudes of some twenty miles. Hill's altitude would put them twenty miles *south*, where they had thought they were yesterday.

'Very well, gentlemen. We will call it thirty-nine degrees, six and a half minutes.'

They bent over their tablets and a few minutes later Drinkwater called for their computed latitudes. Again only Walmsley disagreed.

'Very well. We shall make it forty-nine degrees, eleven minutes north . . . Mr Hill, you appear to have an error in your instrument.'

Hill had already come to the same conclusion and was fiddling with his quadrant, blushing with shame and annoyance. Drinkwater stepped towards him.

'There's no harm done, Mr Hill,' he said privately, reassuring the master.

'Thank you, sir. But imagine the consequences . . . last night, sir . . . we might have been cast ashore because I failed to check . . .'

'A great deal might happen *if*, Mr Hill,' broke in Drinkwater. 'There is too much hazard in the sea-life to worry about what did not happen. Now bend your best endeavours to checking the compass. We have an error there too, or I suspect you would have tumbled yesterday's inaccuracy yourself.'

The thought seemed to brighten Hill, to shift some of the blame and lighten the burden of his culpability. Drinkwater smiled and turned away, fastening his grey eyes on the senior midshipman.

'Mr Walmsley,' he snapped, 'I wish to address a few words to you, sir!'

Chapter 2

The 'Antigone'

Captain Nathaniel Drinkwater turned his chair and stared astern to where patches of sunlight danced upon the sea, alternating with the shadows of clouds. The surface of the sea heaved with the regularity of the Atlantic swells that rolled eastwards in the train of the storm. In the wake of the *Antigone* herself half a dozen gulls and fulmars quartered the disturbed water in search of prey. Further off a gannet turned its gliding flight into an abrupt and predatory dive; but Drinkwater barely noticed these things, his mind was still full of the interview with Lord Walmsley.

Drinkwater had inherited Lord Walmsley together with most of the other midshipmen from his previous command. They had already been on board when he had hurriedly joined the *Melusine* for her voyage escorting the Hull whaling fleet into the Arctic Ocean the previous summer. The officer responsible for selecting and patronising this coterie of 'young gentlemen', Captain Sir James Palgrave, had been severely wounded in a duel and prevented from sailing in command of the *Melusine*. Now Drinkwater rather wished Walmsley to the devil along with Sir James whose wound had mortified and who had paid with his life for the consequences of a foolish quarrel. Walmsley was an indolent youngster, spoiled, vastly over-confident and of a character strong enough to dominate the cockpit. Occasionally charming, there was no actual evil in him, though Drinkwater would have instinctively written *bad* against his character had he been asked, if only because Lord Walmsley did not measure up to Drinkwater's exacting standards as an embryonic sea-officer. The fact was that his lordship did not give a twopenny damn about the naval service or, Drinkwater suspected, Captain Nathaniel Drinkwater himself. The captain was, after all, only in command of one of the many cruisers attached to the hastily raked-up collection of ships that made up the Downs Squadron. Lord Walmsley knew as well as Captain Drinkwater that, whatever hysteria was raised in the House of Commons about the menace of invasion across the Strait of Dover, it would not be Admiral Lord Keith's motley collection of vessels that stopped it but the might of the Channel Fleet under Admiral Cornwallis. Since Cornwallis's squadrons were bottling up the French in

Brest it seemed unlikely that Keith's ships would be achieving anything more glorious than commerce harrying and a general intimidation of the north coast of France. It was well known that Keith himself did not want his job and that he considered his own post to be that usurped by the upstart Nelson: holding the key to the Mediterranean outside Toulon.

Drinkwater sighed; when the Commander-in-Chief of the station made common knowledge of his dissatisfaction, was it any wonder that a young kill-buck like Walmsley should adopt an attitude of indifference? What was more, Walmsley had influence in high places. This depressing reflection irritated Drinkwater. He turned, rose from his chair and, taking a key from his waistcoat pocket, unlocked his wine case. He took out one of the two cut-glass goblets and lifted the decanter. The port glowed richly as he held the glass against the light from the stern windows. Resuming his seat he hitched both feet up on the settee that ran from quarter to quarter across the stern and narrowed his eyes. Damn Lord Walmsley! The young man was a souring influence among a group of reefers who, if they were not exactly brilliant, were not without merit. Midshipman Frey, for instance, just twelve years old, had already seen action off the coast of Greenland, was proving a great asset as a seaman and had also demonstrated his talents as an artist. Drinkwater was not averse to advancing the able, and had already seen both Mr Quilhampton and Mr Gorton get their commissions and placed them on his own quarterdeck as a mark of confidence in them, young though they were. Messrs Wickham and Dutfield were run-of-the-mill youngsters, willing and of a similar age. The Honourable Alexander Glencross was led by Lord Walmsley. The sixth midshipman was even younger than Frey, a freckled Scot named Gillespy forced upon him as a favour to James Quilhampton. In his pursuit of Mistress Catriona MacEwan, poor Quilhampton had sought to press his suit by promising the girl's aunt to find a place for the child of another sister. Little Gillespy was therefore being turned into a King's sea-officer to enhance Quilhampton's prospects as a suitable husband for the lovely Catriona. Drinkwater had had a berth for a midshipman and James had pleaded his own case so well that Drinkwater found himself unable to refuse his request.

'I believe Miss MacEwan is kindly diposed towards me, sir,' Quilhampton had said, 'but her festering aunt regards me as a poor catch . . .' Drinkwater had seen poor Quilhampton's eyes fall to his iron hook which he wore in place of a left hand. So, from friendship and pity, Drinkwater had agreed to the boy joining the ship. As for Gillespy, he had so far borne his part well, despite being constantly sea-sick since *Antigone* left the Thames, and had spent the first half-dozen of his watches on deck lashed to a carronade slide. Drinkwater wondered what effect Walmsley and Glencross might have on such malleable clay.

'Damn 'em both!' he muttered; he had more important things to think about and could ill-afford his midshipmen such solicitude. They must take their chance like he had had to. Whatever his misgivings over the reefers, he was well served by his officers, Hill's error notwithstanding. That had been an unfortunate mistake and principally due to the badly fitted compass that was, in turn, a result of the chaotic state of the dockyards. They had found the error in the lubber's line small in itself, but enough to confuse their dead-reckoning as they steered down the Channel with a favourable easterly wind. That was an irony in itself after two months of the foulest weather for over a year; gales that had driven the Channel Fleet off station at Brest and into the lee of Torbay.

'Disaster', he muttered as he sipped the port, 'is always a combination of small things going wrong simultaneously . . .' And, by God, how close they had come to it in Mount's Bay! He consoled himself with the thought that no great harm had been done. Although he had lost an anchor and cable, the club-haul had not only welded his ship's company together but shown them what they were themselves capable of. 'It's an ill wind,' he murmured, then stopped, aware that he was talking to himself a great deal too much these days.

'Now I want a good, steady stroke.' Tregembo, captain's coxswain regarded his barge crew with a critical eye. He had hand-picked them himself but since Drinkwater had read himself in at *Antigone*'s entry the captain had not been out of the ship and this was to be the first time they took the big barge away. He knew most of them, the majority had formed the crew of *Melusine*'s gig, but they had never performed before under the eyes of an admiral or the entire Channel Fleet.

He grunted his satisfaction. 'Don't 'ee let me down. No. Nor the cap'n, neither. Don't forget we owe him a lot, my lads,' he glowered round them as if to quell contradiction. There was a wry sucking of teeth and winking of eyes that signified recognition of Tregembo's partiality for the captain. 'No one but Cap'n Drinkwater 'd've got us out o' Mount's Bay an' all three masts still standing . . . just you buggers think on that. Now up on deck with 'ee all.' Tregembo followed the boat's crew up out of the gloom of the gun-deck.

Above, all was bustle and activity. Tregembo looked aft and grinned to himself. Captain Drinkwater stood where, in Tregembo's imagination, he always stood, at the windward hance, one foot on the slide of the little brass carronade that was one of a pair brought from the *Melusine.* Ten minutes earlier the whole ship had been stirred by the hail of the masthead look-out who had sighted the topgallants of the main body of the Channel Fleet cruising on Cornwallis's rendez-vous fifty miles west of Ushant. In the cabin below, Mullender was fussing over Drinkwater's brand new uniform coat with its single gleaming epaulette, transferred now to the right shoulder and denot-ing a post-captain of less than five years seniority. Mullender at last satisfied himself that no fluff adhered to the blue cloth with a final wipe of the piece of wool flag-bunting, and lifted the stained boat-cloak out of the sea-chest. He shook his head over it, considering its owner would benefit from a new one and cut a better dash before the admiral to boot, but, with a single glance out of the stern windows, considered the weather too fresh to risk a boat journey without it. Gold lace tarnished quickly and the protection of the cloak was essential. Drawing a sleeve over the knap on the cocked hat, Mullen-der left the cabin. He had been saving the dregs of four bottles to celebrate such a moment and retired to his pantry to indulge in the rare privilege of the captain's servant.

Drinkwater lowered his glass for the third time, then impatiently lifted it again. This time he was rewarded by the sight of a small white triangle just above the horizon. In the succeeding minutes others rose over the rim of the earth until it seemed that, for half of the visible circle where sea met sky, the white triangles of sails surrounded them. Beneath each white triangle the dark hulls emerged with their lighter strakes and chequered sides. The gay colours of flag signals and ensigns enlivened the scene and *Antigone* buzzed as officers and men pointed out ships they recognised, old friends or scandalous hulks that were only kept afloat by the prayers of their crews and the diabolical links their commanders enjoyed with the devil himself.

' 'Ere, ain't that the bloody *Himmortalitee?*' cried an excited seaman, and an equally effusive Hill agreed.

'Aye, Marston, that is indeed the *Immortalité*, and a damned fine ship she was when I was in her as a master's mate.'

'Gorn to the devil, Mister 'Ill, now we oldsters ain't there to watch. She used to gripe like a stuck porker in anything of a blow . . .'

'God damn it the *Belleisle*, by all that's holy . . .'

'And the *Goliath* . . .'

Drinkwater tolerated the excitement as long as it did not mar the efficiency of the *Antigone*. One of the look-out cruisers broke away and hauled her yards to intercept them.

'Permission to hoist the private signal, sir?' James Quilhampton crossed the deck, touching his hat.

'Very well, Mr Q.' Drinkwater nodded and lifted his glass, watching the frigate close hauled on the wind as she moved to intercept the new arrival. She was a thing of loveliness on such a morning and was sending up her royals to cut a dash and impress the *Antigone*'s company with her handiness and discipline. The two frigates exchanged recognition and private signals.

'Number Three-One-Three, sir. *Sirius*, thirty-six, Captain William Prowse.'

'Very well.' Drinkwater stood upon the carronade slide and waved his hat as the two cruisers passed on opposite tacks.

'The flagship's two points to starboard, sir,' the ever-attentive Quilhampton informed him.

'Very well, Mr Q, ease her off a little.' He wondered how *Antigone* appeared from *Sirius* as the look-out frigate tacked in her wake and hauled her own yards, swinging round to regain station. Drinkwater cast a critical eye aloft and then along the deck. Tregembo was mustering the barge's crew in the waist before ordering them into the boat. Although he was far from being a wealthy officer, he had managed a degree of uniformity for his boat's crew due to the large number of slops he had acquired in two previous ships. Over their flannel shirts and duck trousers the men wore cut-down greycoats that gave the appearance of pilot jackets, while upon their heads Tregembo had placed warm seal-skin caps, part of the profit of the *Melusine*'s voyage among the ice-floes of the Arctic seas. It was a piece of conceit in which Drinkwater took a secret delight.

He was proud of the frigate too. Notwithstanding the deplorable state of the dockyards and the desperate shortage of every necessity for fitting out ships of war caused by Lord St Vincent's reforms, she was cause for self-congratulation. The First Lord's zeal in rooting out corruption might have long-term benefits, but for the present the disruptions and shortages had made the commissioning of men-of-war a nightmare for their commanders. Drinkwater recognised his good fortune. The dreadful condition of *Melusine* on her return from the Arctic had removed her from active service and they had managed to take out of her a quantity of stores which, with what the dockyard at Chatham allowed, had enabled them to get *Antigone* down to Blackstakes for her powder in good time. Best of all he had employed seamen in her fitting out and not the convict labour St Vincent advocated. Besides, the ship herself had been in good condition. Built by the French in Cherbourg only nine years earlier, she had been captured in the Red Sea in September 1798 by a party of British seamen that included Drinkwater himself. His appointment to this particular ship was, he knew, a mark of favour from the First Lord. Originally armed with twenty-six long 24-pounder cannon, she had been taken with most of her guns on shore and the Navy Board had seen fit to reduce her force to conform with other frigates of the Royal Navy. Now she mounted twenty-six black 18-pounder long guns upon her gun-deck, two long 9-pounder bow-chasers upon her fo'c's'le together with eight stubby 36-pounder carronades. On her quarter-deck were eight further long nines and the two brass carronades that had formerly gleamed at the hances of *Melusine*.

Drinkwater grunted his satisfaction as Hill reported the flagship a league distant and gave his permission for sail to be shortened. There were occasions when he regretted not being able to handle the ship in the day-to-day routines but on an occasion such as the present one it gave him equal pleasure to watch the officers and men go about their duty, to remark on the performance of individuals and to note the weaker officers and petty officers in the ship. There was also the necessity to observe the whale-men he had pressed from the Hull whalers *Nimrod* and *Conqueror*; in particular a man named Waller, formerly the commander of the *Conqueror*, who had only escaped hanging by Drinkwater's clemency.* Waller was expiating treason before the mast as a common seaman and Drinkwater kept an eye on him. He had had Rogers, the first lieutenant, split all the whale-men into different messes so that they could not confer or form any kind of a combination. For a minute he was tempted to send Waller with the two score of pressed men taken aboard from the *Nore* guardship as replacements for the Channel Fleet. But he could not abandon his responsibilities that easily. It was better to keep Waller under his own vigilant eye than risk him causing trouble elsewhere in the fleet. The rest behaved well enough. Good seamen, most had come from the *Melusine* where they had originally been volunteers during the short-lived Peace of Amiens.

* See *The Corvette*

18

'Hoist the signal for dispatches, sir?'

Drinkwater turned to find the diminutive Mr Frey looking up at him. He nodded. 'Indeed yes, Mr Frey, if you will be so kind.' He smiled at the boy who grinned back. All in all, reflected Drinkwater, he was one of the most fortunate of all the post-captains hereabouts, and he cast his eyes round the horizon where ship after ship of the British fleet cruised under easy sail in three great columns with the frigates cast out ahead, astern and on either flank.

Drinkwater sniffed the fresh north-westerly breeze and felt invigorated by the delightful freshness of the morning. The storm of two nights previously had cleared the air. Even here, a hundred miles off the Isles of Scilly where already the first crocuses would be breaking through the soil, spring was in the air. He nodded at Rogers who walked over to him.

'Mornin', Sam.'

'Good morning, sir. Sail's shortened and the barge is ready for lowering.'

Drinkwater regarded his first lieutenant, remembering their previous enmity aboard the *Hellebore* when they had been wrecked after an error of judgement made by Samuel Rogers, and of their successes together in the Baltic in the old bomb-vessel *Virago*. Rogers was a coarse and vulgar man, no scientific officer and only a passable navigator, but he was a competent seaman and his valour in action was too valuable an asset to be lightly set aside merely because he lacked social accomplishments. Besides, in his present situation he would have precious little opportunity to worry over such a deficiency. He was, Drinkwater knew, perfect as a first luff; the very man the hands loved to hate, who was indifferent to that hatred and who could take the blame for all the hardships, mishaps and injustices the naval service would press upon their unfortunate souls and bodies.

'She's looking very tiddly, Sam. Fit for an admiral's inspection already. I congratulate you.'

Rogers gave him a grin. 'I heard about your appetite for tiddly ships after the *Melusine*, sir.'

Drinkwater grinned back. 'She was a damned *yacht*, Sam. You should have heard the gunroom squeal when I cut off her royal masts and fitted a crow's nest to con her through the ice.'

'She was different from the old *Virago* then?'

'As chalk is from cheese . . .'

They were interrupted by Lieutenant Quilhampton. 'Flag's signalling, sir: "Captain to come aboard".'

19

'Very well. Bring the ship to under the admiral's lee quarter, Mr Q . . . Sam be so good as to salute the flag while I shift my coat.'

'Aye, aye, sir.' The two officers began to carry out their orders as Drinkwater hurried below to where an anxious Mullender had coat, hat, cloak and sword all ready for him.

The Spy Master

Admiral Sir William Cornwallis rose from behind his desk and motioned Drinkwater to a chair. His flag-lieutenant took the offered packet of Admiralty despatches and handed them to the admiral's secretary for opening.

'A glass of wine, Captain?' The flag-lieutenant beckoned a servant forward and Drinkwater hitched his sword between his legs, laid his cocked hat across his lap and took the tall Venetian goblet from the salver. 'Thank you. I have two bags of mail for the fleet in my barge and a draft of forty-three men for the squadron . . .'

'I shall inform the Captain of the Fleet, sir. Sir William, your permission?'

'By all means.' The admiral bent over the opened dispatches as the flag-lieutenant left the cabin. The servant withdrew and Drinkwater was left with Cornwallis, his immobile secretary and another man, a dark stranger in civilian clothes, who seemed to be regarding Drinkwater with some interest and whose evident curiosity Drinkwater found rather irksome and embarrassing. He avoided this scrutiny by studying his surroundings. The great cabin of His Britannic Majesty's 112-gun ship *Ville de Paris* was a luxurious compartment compared with his own. As a first-rate line of battleship the *Ville de Paris* was almost a new ship, built as a replacement for Rodney's prize, the flagship of Admiral De Grasse, taken at the Battle of Saintes in the American War and so badly knocked about that she had foundered on her way home across the stormy Atlantic. It was an irony that a ship so named should bear the flag of the officer responsible for keeping the French fleet bottled up in Brest. Drinkwater did not envy the admiral his luxury: the monotony of blockade duty would have oppressed him. Even in a frigate attached to the inshore squadron cruising off Ushant, the perils of tides and rocks would far outweigh the risk of danger from the enemy coupled as they were with the prevailing strong westerly winds. As his old friend Richard White constantly wrote and told him, he was lucky to have avoided such an arduous and thankless task. There were a few who had carved out a glorious niche for themselves with brilliant actions. Pellew, for instance, in the *Indefatigable* and with *Amazon* in company had caught the French battleship *Droits de l'Homme,* harried her all night and forced her to become embayed in Audierne Bay where she was wrecked. The thought of embayment still caused him a shudder and he recollected that Pellew's triumph had also caused the loss of *Amazon* from the same cause. No, for the most part the maintenance of this huge fleet with its frigates and its supply problems was simply to keep Admiral Truguet and the principal French fleet capable of operating in the Atlantic, securely at its moorings in Brest Road. By this means Napoleon would not be able to secure the naval supremacy in the Channel that he needed to launch his invasion. Whatever the monotony of the duty there was no arguing its effectiveness. All the same Drinkwater was not keen to be kept under the severe restraint of commanding a frigate on blockade.

There was a rustle as Cornwallis lowered the papers and leaned back in his seat. He was a portly gentleman of some sixty years of age with small features and bright, keen blue eyes. He smiled cordially.

'Well, Captain Drinkwater, you are not to join us I see.'

'No, Sir William. I am under Lord Keith's command, attached to the Downs Squadron but with discretionary orders following the delivery of those dispatches.' He nodded at the contents of the waterproof packet which now lay scattered across Cornwallis's table.

'Which are . . . ?'

'To return to the Strait of Dover along the French coast, harrying trade and destroying enemy preparations for the invasion.'

'And not, I hope, wantonly setting fire to any French villages en route, Captain?' It was the stranger in civilian dress who put this question. Drinkwater opened his mouth to reply but the stranger continued, 'Such piracy is giving us a bad name, Captain Drinkwater, giving the idea of invasion a certain respectability among the French populace that might otherwise be not over-enthusiastic about M'sieur Bonaparte. Hitherto, whatever the enmities between our two governments, the people of the coast have maintained a, er, certain friendliness towards us, eh?' He smiled, a sardonic grin, and held up his glass of the admiral's claret. 'The matter of a butt or two of wine and a trifle or two of information; you understand?'

Drinkwater felt a recurrence of the irritation caused earlier by this man, but Cornwallis intervened. 'I am sure Captain Drinkwater understands perfectly, Philip. But Captain, tell us the news from London. What are the fears of invasion at the present time?'

'Somewhat abated, sir. Most of the news is of the problems surrounding Addington's ministry. The First Lord is under constant attack from the opposition led by Pitt . . .'

'And we all know the justice of Billy Pitt's allegations, by God,' put in the stranger with some heat.

Drinkwater ignored the outburst. 'As to the invasion, I think there is little fear while you are here, sir, and the French fleet is in port. I believe St Vincent to be somewhat maligned, although the difficulties experienced in fitting out do support some of Mr Pitt's accusations.' Drinkwater judged it would not do him any good to expatiate on St Vincent's well-meaning but near-disastrous attempts to root out corruption, and he did owe his own promotion to the old man's influence.

Cornwallis smiled. 'What does St Vincent say to Mr Pitt, Captain?'

'That although the French may invade, sir, he is confident that they will not invade by sea.'

Cornwallis laughed. 'There, at least, St Vincent and I would find common ground. Philip here is alarmed that any relaxation on our part would be ill-timed.' Then the humour went out of his expression and he fell silent. Cornwallis occupied the most important station in the British navy. As Commander-in-Chief of the Channel Fleet he was not merely concerned with blockading Brest, but also with maintaining British vigilance off L'Orient, Rochefort and even Ferrol where neutral Spain had been coerced into allowing France to use the naval arsenals for her own. In addition there was the immense problem of the defence of the Channel itself, still thought vulnerable if a French squadron could be assembled elsewhere in the world, say the West Indies, and descend upon it in sufficient force to avoid or brush aside the Channel Fleet. On Cornwallis's shoulder fell the awesome burden of ensuring St Vincent's words were true, and Cornwallis had transformed the slack methods of his predecessor into a strictly enforced blockade, earning himself the soubriquet of 'Billy Blue' from his habit of hoisting the Blue Peter to the foremasthead the instant his flagship cast anchor when driven off station by the heavy gales that had bedevilled his fleet since the New Year. It was clear that the responsibility and the monotony of such a task were wearing the elderly man out. Drinkwater sensed he would have liked to agree with the current opinion in London that the threat of invasion had diminished.

'Did you see much of the French forces or the encampments, Captain?' asked the stranger.

'A little above Boulogne, sir, but I was fortunate in having a favourable easterly and was ordered out by way of Portsmouth and so favoured the English coast. I took aboard the Admiralty papers at Portsmouth.'

'It is a weary business, Captain Drinkwater,' Cornwallis said sadly, 'and I am always in want of frigates . . . by heaven 'tis a plaguey dismal way of spending a life in the public service!'

'Console yourself, Sir William,' the stranger put in at this show of bile, and with a warmth of feeling that indicated he was on exceptionally intimate terms with the Commander-in-Chief. 'Consider the wisdom of Pericles: "If they are kept off the sea by our superior strength, their want of practice will make them unskilful and their want of skill, timid." Now that is an incontestable piece of good sense, you must admit.'

'You make your point most damnably, Philip. As for Captain Drinkwater, I am sure he is not interested in our hagglings . . .'

The allusion to Drinkwater's junior rank, though intended to suppress the stranger, cut Drinkwater to the quick. He rose, having no more business with the admiral and having securely lodged his empty glass against the flagship's roll. 'I would not have you think, Sir William, that I am anxious to avoid any station or duty to which their Lordships wished to assign me.'

Cornwallis dismissed Drinkwater's concern. 'Of course not, Captain. We are all the victims of circumstance. It is just that I feel the want of frigates acutely. The Inshore Squadron is worked mercilessly and some relief would be most welcome there, but if Lord Keith has given you your orders we had better not detain you. What force does his Lordship command now?'

'Four of the line, Sir William, five old fifties, nine frigates, a dozen sloops, a dozen bombs and ten gun-brigs, plus the usual hired cutters and luggers.'

'Very well. And he is as anxious as myself over cruisers I doubt not.'

'Indeed, sir.'

Drinkwater moved towards the door as Cornwallis's eyes fell again to the papers. These actions seemed to precipitate an outburst of forced coughing from the stranger. Cornwallis looked up at once.

'Ah, Philip, forgive me . . . most remiss and I beg your pardon. Captain Drinkwater, forgive me, I am apt to think we are all acquainted here. May I introduce Captain Philip D'Auvergne, Duc de Bouillon.'

Drinkwater was curious at this grandiose title. D'Auvergne was grinning at his discomfiture.

24

'Sir William does me more honour than I deserve, Captain Drinkwater. I am no more than a post-captain like yourself, but unlike yourself I do not have even a gun-brig to command.'

'You are a supernumerary, sir?' enquired Drinkwater.

Both Cornwallis and D'Auvergne laughed, implying a knowledge that Drinkwater was not a party to.

'I should like you to convey Captain D'Auvergne back to his post at St Helier, Captain, as a small favour to the Channel Fleet and in the sure knowledge that it cannot greatly detain you.'

'It will be an honour, Sir William.'

'Very well, Captain,' said D'Auvergne, 'I am ready. Keep in good spirits, Sir William. It will be soon now if it is ever to occur.'

Unaware to what they alluded, Drinkwater asked: 'You have no baggage, Captain D'Auvergne?'

D'Auvergne grinned again. 'Good Lord no. Baggage slows a man, eh?' And the two men laughed again at a shared joke.

The meal had been a tense affair. Captain Drinkwater had become almost silent and Drinkwater had remained curious as to his background and his function, aware only that he enjoyed a position of privilege as Cornwallis's confidant. The only clue to his origin was in his destination, St Helier. Drinkwater knew there were a hundred naval officers with incongruous French-sounding surnames who hailed from the Channel Islands. But Cornwallis had called St Helier D'Auvergne's 'post', whatever that meant, and it was clear from his appetite that he had not lived aboard ship for some time or he would have been a little more sparing with Drinkwater's dwindling cabin stores. The decanter had circulated twice before D'Auvergne, with a parting look at the retreating Mullender, leaned forward and addressed his host.

'I apologise for teasing you, Drinkwater. The fact is Cornwallis, like most of the poor fellows, is worn with the service and bored out of his skull by the tedium of blockade. Any newcomer is apt to suffer the admiral's blue devils. 'Tis truly a terrible task and to have been a butt of his irritability is to have rendered your country a service.'

'I fear,' said Drinkwater with some asperity, 'that I am still being used as a butt, and to be candid, sir, I am not certain that I enjoy it over much.'

The snub was deliberate. Drinkwater had no idea of D'Auvergne's seniority though he guessed it to be greater than his own. But he was damned if he was going to sit at his own table and listen to such stuff from a man drinking his own port! Drinkwater had expected D'Auvergne to bristle, rise and take his leave; instead he leaned back in his chair and pointed at Drinkwater's right shoulder.

'I perceive you have been wounded, Captain, and I know you for a brave officer. I apologise doubly for continuing to be obscure . . . Mine is a curious story, but I am, as I said, a post-captain like yourself. I served under Lord Howe during the American War and was captured by the French. Whilst in captivity I came to the notice of the old Duc de Bouillon with whom I shared a surname, although I am a native of the Channel Islands. His sons were both dead and I was named his heir after a common ancestry was discovered . . .' D'Auvergne smiled wryly. 'I might have been one of the richest men in France but for a trifling matter of my estates having been taken over by their tenants.' He made a deprecatory gesture.

'You might also have lost your head,' added Drinkwater, mellowing a little.

'Exactly so. Now, Drinkwater, that wound of yours. How did you come by that?'

Since his promotion to post-captain and the transfer of his epaulette from his left to his right shoulder, Drinkwater had thought his wound pretty well disguised. Although he still inclined his head to one side in periods of damp weather when the twisted muscles ached damnably, he contrived to forget about it as much as possible. He was certainly not used to being quizzed about it.

'My shoulder? Oh, I received the fragment of a mortar shell during an attack on Boulogne in the year one. It was an inglorious affair.'

'I recollect it. But that was your second wound in the right arm, was it not?'

'How the deuce d'you know that?'

'Ah. I will tell you in a moment. Was it a certain Edouard Santhonax that struck you first?'

'The devil!' Drinkwater was astonished that this enigmatic character could know so much about him. He frowned and the colour mounted to his cheeks. The relaxation he had begun to feel was dispelled by a sudden anger. 'Come, sir. Level with me, damn it. What is your impertinent interest in my person, eh?'

'Easy, Drinkwater, easy. I have no impertinent interest in you. On the contrary, I have always heard you spoken of in the highest terms by Lord Dungarth.'

'Lord Dungarth?'

'Indeed. My station in St Helier is connected with Lord Dungarth's department.'

'Ahhh,' Drinkwater refilled his glass, passing the decanter across the table, 'I begin to see . . .'

Lord Dungarth, with whom Drinkwater had first become acquainted as a midshipman, was the head of the British Admiralty's intelligence network. Drinkwater's personal relationship with the earl extended to a private obligation contracted when Dungarth had helped to spirit Drinkwater's brother Edward away into Russia when the latter was wanted for murder. The evasion of justice had been accomplished because he had killed a French agent known to Dungarth. Edward had in fact slaughtered Etienne de Montholon because he had found him in bed with is own mistress, but Dungarth's interest in Montholon had served to cover Edward's crime and protect Drinkwater's own career. It was an episode in his life that Drinkwater preferred to forget.

'What do *you* know of Santhonax?' he asked at last.

D'Auvergne looked round him. 'That he commanded this ship in the Red Sea; that you captured him and he subsequently escaped; that he was appointed a colonel in the French Army after transferring from the naval service; and that he is now an aide-de-camp to First Consul Bonaparte himself.'

'And your opinion of him?'

'That he is daring, brave and the epitome of all that makes the encampments of the French along the heights of Boulogne a most dangerous threat to the safety of Great Britain.'

Drinkwater's hostility towards D'Auvergne evaporated. The two had discovered a common ground and Drinkwater rose, crossing the cabin and lifting the lid of the big sea-chest in the corner. 'So I have always thought myself,' he said, reaching into the chest. 'Furthermore, I have this to show you . . .'

Drinkwater returned to the table with a roll of canvas, frayed at the edges. He spread it out on the table. The paint was badly cracked and the canvas damaged where the tines of a fork had pierced it. It was D'Auvergne's turn to show astonishment.

'Good God alive!'

'You know who she is?'

'Hortense Santhonax . . . with Junot's wife one of the most celebrated beauties of Paris . . . This . . .' He stared at the lower right hand corner, 'this is by David. How the devil did you come by it?'

Drinkwater looked down at the portrait. The red hair and the slender neck wound with pearls rose from a bosom more exposed than concealed by the wisp of gauze around the shoulders.

'It hung there, on that bulkhead, when we took this ship in the Red Sea. I knew her briefly.'

'Were you in that business at Beaubigny back in ninety-two?'

Drinkwater nodded. 'Aye. I was mate of the cutter *Kestrel* when we took Hortense, her brother and others off the beach there, *émigrés* we thought then, escaping from the mob . . .'

'Who turned their coats when their money ran out, eh?'

'That is true of her brother certainly. She, I now believe, never intended other than to dupe us.' He did not add that she had been Hortense de Montholon then, sister to the man his own brother Edward had murdered at Newmarket nine years later.

D'Auvergne nodded. 'You are very probably right in what you say. She and her husband are fervent and enthusiastic Bonapartists. I have no doubt that, if Bonaparte continues to ascend in the world, so will Santhonax.'

'This knowledge is learned from your station at St Helier, I gather?'

D'Auvergne smiled, the sardonic grin friendly now. 'Another correct assumption, Drinkwater.' He regarded his host with curiosity. 'I had heard your name from Dungarth in the matter of some enterprise or other. He is not given to idle gossip about all his acquaintances, as a gentleman in our profession cannot afford to be. But I perceive you have seen a deal of service . . .' he trailed off.

Drinkwater smiled back. 'My midshipmen consider me an ancient and tarpaulin officer, Captain D'Auvergne. Very little of my time has been spent in grand vessels like the one I have the honour to command at this time. I take your point about the need to guard the tongue, but I also take it that you have a clearing house on Jersey where information is collected?'

'Captain,' D'Auvergne said lightly, 'you continue to amaze with the accuracy of your deductions.'

The decanter passed between them and Drinkwater began to relax for the first time since the morning. The silence that fell between them was companionable now. After a pause D'Auvergne said, 'Knowing the confidence reposed in you by Lord Dungarth, I will venture to tell you that it is part of my responsibility to gather information through a network of agents in northern France. My operations are of particular interest to Sir William, for I am able to pass on a surprising amount of news concerning Truguet's squadron at Brest. Hence my unease at the prospect of you harrying the actual sea-borders of France. Harry their trade and destroy the invasion barges wherever you find them, but have a thought for the sympathies of sea-faring folk who have never had much loyalty for the government in Paris . . .'

'Or London, come to that,' Drinkwater added wryly. The two men laughed again.

'Seriously, Drinkwater, I believe we are at the crisis of the war and I am sad that the government is not united behind a determination to face facts. This inter-party wrangling will be our undoing. The French army is formidable, everywhere victorious, a whole population tuned to war. All we have to hope for is that Bonaparte might fall. There are indications of political upheavals in France. You have heard of the recent discovery of a plot to kill the First Consul; there are other reactions to him still fermenting. If they succeed I believe we will have a lasting peace before the year is out. But if Bonaparte survives, then not only will his position be unassailable but the invasion inevitable. The plans are already well advanced. Do not underestimate the power, valour or energy of the French. If Bonaparte triumphs he will have hundreds of Santhonaxes running at his horse's tail. Their fleet *must* be kept mewed up in Brest until this desperate business is concluded. This is the purpose of my visits to Cornwallis but I can see no harm in the captain of every cruiser being aware of the extreme danger we are in.' D'Auvergne leaned forward and banged the table for emphasis. 'Invasion and Bonaparte are the most lethal combination we have ever faced!'

Foolish Virgins

'Where away?'

Drinkwater shivered in the chill of dawn, peering to the eastward where Hill pointed.

'Three points to starboard, sir. Ten or a dozen small craft with a brig as escort.'

He saw them at last, faint interruptions on the steel-blue horizon, growing more substantial as every minute passed and the gathering daylight grew. Squatting, he steadied his glass and studied the shapes, trying to deduce what they might be. Behind him he heard the shuffle of feet as other officers joined Hill, together with a brief muttering as they discussed the possibility of an attack.

Drinkwater rose stiffly. His neck and shoulder ached in the chilly air. He shut the telescope with a snap and turned on the officers.

'Well, gentlemen. What d'you make of 'em, eh?'

'Invasion barges,' said Hill without hesitation. Drinkwater agreed.

' "*Chaloupes*" and "*péniches*", I believe they call the infernal things, moving eastwards to the rendezvous at Havre and all ready to embark what Napoleon Bonaparte is pleased to call the Army of the Coasts of the Ocean.'

'Clear for action, sir?' asked Rogers, his pale features showing the dark shadow of an unshaven jaw and reminding Drinkwater that daylight was growing quickly.

'No. I think not. Pipe up hammocks, send the hands to breakfast. Mr Hill, have your watch clew up the fore-course. Hoist French colours and edge down towards them. No show of force. Mr Frey, a string of bunting at the fore t'gallant yardarms. We are French-built, gentlemen. We might as well take advantage of the fact. Mr Rogers, join me for breakfast.'

As he descended the companionway Drinkwater heard the watch called to stand by the clew-garnets and raise the fore tack and sheet. Below, the berth-deck erupted in sudden activity as the off-duty men were turned out of their hammocks. He nodded to the marine sentry at attention by his door and entered the cabin. Rogers followed and both men sat at the table which was being hurriedly laid by an irritated Mullender.

'You're early this morning, sir,' grumbled the steward, with the familiar licence allowed to intimate servants.

'No, Mullender, you are late . . . Sit down, Sam, and let us eat. The morning's chill has made me damned hungry.'

'Thank you. You do intend to attack those craft, don't you?'

'Of course. When I've had some breakfast.' He smiled at Rogers who once again looked at though he had been drinking heavily the night before. 'D'you remember when we were in the *Virago* together we were attacked off the Sunk by a pair of luggers?'

'Aye . . .'

'And we beat 'em off. Sank one of them if I remember right. The other . . .'

'Got away,' interrupted Rogers.

'For which you have never forgiven me . . . ah, thank you, Mullender. Well I hope this morning to rectify the matter. Let's creep up and take that little brig. She'd make a decent prize, mmm?'

'By God, I'll drink to that!' Comprehension dawned in Roger's eyes.

'I thought you might, Sam, I thought you might. But I want those bateaux as well.'

They attacked the skillygolee enthusiastically, encouraged by the smell of bacon coming from the pantry where Mullender was still muttering, each occupied with their private thoughts. Rogers considered a naval officer a fool if he did not risk everything to make prize-money. Since he had never had the chief command of a ship, he thought himself very hard done by over the matter. The event to which Drinkwater had alluded was a case in point. Both knew that they had been fortunate to escape capture when they were engaged by a pair of lugger privateers off Orfordness when on their way to Copenhagen. But whereas Drinkwater appreciated his escape, Rogers regretted they had not made a capture, even though the odds against success had been high. The *Virago* had been a lumbering old bomb-vessel whose longest-range guns were in her stern, an acknowledgement that an enemy attack would almost certainly be from astern! But a pretty little brig-corvette brought under the guns of the *Antigone* would be an entirely different story. With such an overwhelming superiority Drinkwater would not hesitate to attack and the outcome was a foregone conclusion. Nevertheless Rogers found himself hoping the brig would have a large crew, so that he might distinguish himself and perhaps gain a mention in *The Gazette*.

Drinkwater's thoughts, on the other hand, were only partially concerned with the brig. It was the other vessels he was thinking of. They were five leagues south-east of Pointe de Barfleur, on the easternmost point of the Cotentin Pensinsula. The convoy of invasion craft were on passage across the Baie de la Seine bound for their rendezvous at Le Havre. It was here that the French were assembling vessels built further west, prior to dispersing them along the Pas de Calais, at Étaples, Boulogne, Wimereux and Ambleteuse, in readiness for the embarkation of the army destined to conquer Great Britain and make the French people masters of the world.

Perhaps Drinkwater's experiences of the French differed from those of his colleagues who were apt to ridicule the possibility of ultimate French victory; perhaps Captain D'Auvergne had alerted him to the reality of a French invasion; but from whatever cause he did not share his first lieutenant's unconditional enthusiasm. What Rogers saw as a possible brawl which should end to their advantage, Drinkwater saw as a matter of simple necessity. It was up to him to destroy in detail before the French were able to overwhelm in force. There had been much foolish talk, and even more foolish assertions in the newspapers, of the impracticality of the invasion barges. There had been mention of preposterous notions of attack by balloon, of great barges driven by windmills, even some crack-pot ideas of under-water boats which had had knowledgable officers roaring with laughter on a score of quarter-decks, despite the fact that such an attack had been launched against Admiral Howe in New York during the American War. Drinkwater was apt to regard such arrogant dismissal of French abilities as extremely unwise. From what he had observed of those *chaloupes* and *péniches* there was very little wrong with them as sea-going craft. That alone was enough to make them worthy targets for His Majesty's frigate *Antigone*.

'Beg pardon, sir.'

'Yes, Mr Wickham, what is it?' Drinkwater dabbed his mouth with his napkin and pushed back his chair.

'Mr Hill's compliments, sir, and the wind's falling light. If we don't make more sail the enemy will get away.'

'We cannot permit that, Mr Wickham. Make all sail, I'll be up directly.'

Rogers followed him on deck and swore as soon as he saw the distance that still remained. Hill crossed the deck and touched his hat.

'Stuns'ls, sir?'

'If you please, Mr Hill, though I doubt we'll catch 'em now.'

32

Drinkwater looked round the horizon. Daylight had revealed a low mist which obscured the sharp line of the horizon. Above it the sun rose redly, promising a warm day with mist and little wind. Already the sea was growing smooth, its surface merely undulating, no longer rippling with the sharp though tiny crests of a steady breeze. Hardly a ripple ran down *Antigone*'s side: the wind had suddenly died away and Drinkwater now detected a sharp chill. Beside him Rogers swore again. He turned quickly forward.

'Mr Hill!'

'Sir?'

'Belay those stuns'ls. All hands to man yard and stay tackles, hoist out and launch!' He turned to Rogers. 'Get the quarter-boats away, Sam, there's fog coming. You're to take charge.'

Rogers needed no second bidding. Already alert, the ship's company tumbled up to sway out the heavy launch with its snub-nosed carronade mounted on a forward slide. It began to rise jerkily from the booms amidships as, near at hand, the slap of bare feet on the deck accompanied a hustling of men over the rail and into the light quarter-boats hanging in the davits. Among the jostling check shirts and pigtails, the red coats and white cross-belts of the marines mustered with an almost irritating formality.

'Orders, sir?' Mr Mount the lieutenant of marines saluted him.

'Mornin', Mr Mount. Divide your men up 'twixt quarter-boats and launch. Mr Rogers is in command. I want those invasion craft destroyed!'

'Very well, sir.' Mount saluted and spun round: 'Sergeant, your platoon in the starboard quarter-boat. Corporal Williams, your men the larboard. Corporal Allen, with me in the launch!'

The neat files broke up and the white-breeched, black-gaitered marines scrambled over the rails and descended into the now waiting boats. Drinkwater looked at the enemy. The invasion craft had already vanished but the brig still showed, ghostly against the insubstantial mass of the closing fog.

'Mr Hill! A bearing of the brig, upon the instant!'

'Sou'-east-a-half-south, sir!'

'Mr Rogers!' Drinkwater leaned over the rail and bawled down at the first lieutenant in the launch. 'Steer sou'-east-a-half-south. We'll fire guns for you but give you fifteen minutes to make your approach.'

He saw Rogers shove a seaman to one side so that he could see the boat compass and then the tossed oars were being lowered, levelled and swung back.

'Give way together!'

The looms bent with sudden strain and the heavy launch began to move, followed by the two quarter-boats. In the stern of each boat sat the officers in their blue coats with a splash of red from the marines over which the dull gleam of steel hung until engulfed by the fog.

'Now we shall have to wait, Mr Hill, since all the lieutenants have left us behind.'

'Indeed, sir, we will.'

Drinkwater turned inboard. There was little he could do. Already the decks were darkening from condensing water vapour. Soon it would be dripping from every rope on the ship.

'I had hoped the sun would rise and burn up this mist,' he said.

'Aye, sir. But 'tis always an unpredictable business. The wind dropped very suddenly.'

'Yes.'

The two men stood in silence for a few minutes, frustrated by being unable to see the progress of the boats. After a little Hill pulled out his watch.

'Start firing in five minutes, sir?'

'Mmmm? Oh, yes. If you please, Mr Hill.' They must give Rogers every chance of surprise but not allow him to get lost. Drinkwater would not put it past a clever commander to launch a counter-attack by boat, anticipating the very action he had just taken in sending a large number of his crew off.

'Send the men to quarters, Mr Hill, all guns to load canister on ball, midshipmen to report the batteries they are commanding when ready.' He raised his voice. 'Fo'c's'le there! Keep a sharp look-out!'

'Aye, aye, sir!'

'Report anything you see!'

'Aye, aye, sir!'

He turned aft to where the two marine sentries stood, one on either quarter, the traditional protection for the officer of the watch. It was also their duty to throw overboard the lifebuoy for any man unfortunate enough to fall over the side. 'You men, too. Do you keep a sharp look-out for any approaching boats!'

He fell to a restless pacing, aware that the fog had caught him napping, a fact which led him into a furious self-castigation so that the report of the bow chaser took him by complete surprise.

The boom of the bow chaser every five minutes was the only sound to be heard apart from the creaks and groans from *Antigone*'s fabric that constituted silence on board ship. Even that part of the ship's company left on board seemed to share some of their captain's anxiety. They too had friends out there in the damp grey fog. The haste with with the boats had been hoisted out had allowed certain madcap elements among the frigate's young gentlemen to take advantage of circumstances. In manning the guns, Drinkwater had learned, most of the midshipmen had clambered into boats, and those who had not done so were now regretting their constraint.

Lord Walmsley had gone, followed by the Honourable Alexander Glencross, both under Rogers in the launch. Being well acquainted with his temperament, Drinkwater knew that Rogers would have – what was the new expression? – turned a blind eye, that was it, to such a lack of discipline. Wickham had also gone in the boats, carting off little Gillespy. Dutfield had not been on deck and Frey had too keen a sense of obligation to his post as signal midshipman to desert it without the captain's permission, even though the lack of visibility rendered it totally superfluous. As a consequence Drinkwater had posted Hill's two mates, Caldecott and Tyrrell, in the waist and in charge of the batteries.

'Gunfire to starboard, sir!'

The hail came from the fo'c's'le where someone had his arm stretched out. Drinkwater went to the ship's side and cocked his head outboard, attempting to pick up the sound over the water and clear of the muffled ship-noises on the deck. There was the bang of cannon and the crackle of small-arms fire followed by the sound of men shouting and cursing. It did nothing to lessen Drinkwater's anxiety but it provoked a burst of chatter amidships.

'Silence there, God damn you!' The noise subsided. Side by side with Hill, Drinkwater strained to hear the distant fight and to interpret the sounds. The cannon fire had been brief. Had Rogers attacked the brig successfully? Or had the brig driven *Antigone*'s boats off? If so was Rogers pressing his attack against the invasion craft? And what had happened to little Gillespy and Mr Q? Anxiety overflowed into anger.

'God damn this bloody fog!'

As though moved by this invective there was a sudden lightening in the atmosphere. The sun ceased to be a pale disc, began to glow, to burn off the fog, and abruptly the wraiths of vapour were torn aside revealing *Antigone* becalmed upon a blue sea as smooth as a millpond. Half a mile away the brig lay similarly inert and without the aid of a glass Drinkwater could see her tricolour lay over her taffrail.

35

A cheer broke out amidships and beside him Hill exclaimed, 'She's ours, by God!' But uncertainty turned to anger as Drinkwater realised what Rogers had allowed to happen. He swept the clearing horizon with his Dolland glass.

'God's bones! What the hell does Rogers think he's about . . . Mr Hill!'

'Sir?'

'Hoist out my barge . . . and hurry man, hurry!'

Drinkwater swept the glass right round the horizon. There were no other ships in sight. But beyond the brig the convoy of *chaloupes* and *péniches* was escaping, quite unscathed as far as he could tell. In a lather of impatience Drinkwater sent Frey below for his sword and pistols.

'You will remain here, Mr Frey, to assist Mr Hill . . . Hill, you are to take command until Mr Rogers returns. I will take Tyrrell with me.' Frey opened his mouth to protest, then shut it again as he caught sight of the baleful look in his captain's eyes.

As he hurried into the waist, Drinkwater heard Hill acknowledge his instructions and then he was down in the barge and Tregembo was ordering the oars out and they were away, the oar looms bending under Tregembo's urging. He looked back once. *Antigone* sat upon the water, her sails slack and only adding to the impression of confusion that the morning seemed composed of. He forced himself to be calm. Perhaps Rogers had had no alternative but to attack the brig. Drinkwater knew enough of Roger's character to guess that the fog would have given him a fair excuse to ignore the invasion craft.

They were approaching the brig now. They pulled past three or four floating corpses. Someone saw their approach and then Rogers was leaning over the rail waving triumphantly.

'Pass under the stern,' Drinkwater said curtly to Tregembo, and the coxswain moved the tiller. Drinkwater stood up in the stern of the boat.

'Mr Rogers,' he hailed, 'I directed you to attack the invasion craft!'

Rogers waved airily behind him. 'Mr Q's gone in pursuit, sir.' The first lieutenant's unconcern was infuriating.

'You may take possession, Mr Rogers, and retain the quarter-boat. Direct Gorton and Mount to follow me in the launch!'

Roger's crestfallen look brought a measure of satisfaction to Drinkwater, then they were past the brig and Drinkwater realised he had not even read her name as they had swept under her stern windows.

Tregembo swung the boat to larboard as the invasion craft came into view.

Smaller than the brig and clearly following some standing order of the brig's commander, they had made off under oars as soon as Roger's attack materialised. They were about a mile and a half distant and were no longer headed away from the brig. Seeing they were pursued by only a single boat they had turned, their oars working them round to confront their solitary pursuer. Mr Quilhampton's quarter-boat still pressed on, about half a mile from the French and a mile ahead of Drinkwater.

'Pull you men,' he croaked, his mouth suddenly dry; then, remembering an old obscenity heard years ago, he added, 'pull like you'd pull a Frenchman off your mother.'

There was an outbreak of grins and the men leaned back against their oars so that the looms fairly bent under the strain and the blades flashed in the sunshine and sparkled off the drops of water that ran along them, linking the rippled circles of successive oar-dips in a long chain across the oily surface of the sea. Drinkwater looked astern. The white painted carvel hull of the big launch was following them, but it was much slower. Drinkwater could see the black maw of the carronade muzzle and wished the launch was ahead of them to clear the way. The thought led him to turn his attention to the enemy. Did they have cannon? They would surely be designed to carry them in the event of invasion but were they fitted at the building stage or at the rendezvous? He was not long in doubt. A puff of smoke followed by a slow, rolling report and a white fountain close ahead of Quilhampton's boat gave him his answer. And while he watched Quilhampton adjust his course, a second fountain rose close to his own boat. For a second the men wavered in their stroke, then Tregembo steadied them. An instant later half a dozen white columns rose from the water ahead.

Beside him Tyrrell muttered, 'My God!' and Drinkwater realised the hopelessness of the task. What could three boats do against ten, no twelve, well-armed and, Drinkwater could now see, well-manned boats armed with cannon. One carronade was going to be damn-all use.

'Stand up and wave, Mr Tyrrell.'

'I beg pardon, sir?'

'I said stand up and wave, God damn you! Recall Quilhampton's boat before we are shot to bits!'

'Aye, aye, sir.' Tyrrell stood and waved half-heartedly.

'I said wave, sir, like this!' Drinkwater jumped up and waved his hat above his head furiously. Someone at the oars in Quilhampton's boat saw him.

'Swing the boat round, Tregembo, I'm breaking off the attack.'

'Aye, ayr, zur,' Tregembo acknowleged impassively and the barge swung round.

He waved again, an exaggerated beckoning, until Quilhampton's boat foreshortened in its turn. 'Pull back towards the launch.' He sat down, relieved. Ten minutes later the three boats bobbed together in a conferring huddle while, nearly a mile away, the French invasion craft had formed two columns and were pulling steadily eastwards.

'Well they've lost a brig, sir,' said Mount cheerfully. A ripple of acknowledgement went round the boat crews, a palliative to their being driven off by the French.

'Very true, Mr Mount, and doubtless we'll all be enriched thereby, but the smallest of those *péniches* can carry fifty infanty onto an English beach and you have just seen how well they can hold off the boats of a man-of-war. If the French have a few days of calm in the Channel it will not matter how many of their damn brigs are waiting to be condemned by the Prize Court, if the Prize Court ain't able to sit because a French army's hammering on the doors.' He paused to let the laboured sarcasm sink in. 'In carrying out an attack with a single boat you acted foolishly, Mr Q.' Quilhampton's face fell. Drinkwater rightly assumed Rogers had ordered him forward, but that did not alter the fact that Drinkwater had nearly lost a boat-load of men, not to mention a friend. It was clear that Quilhampton felt his public admonition acutely and Drinkwater relented. After all, there was no actual harm done and they *had* taken a brig, as Mount had pointed out.

'We have *all* been foolish, Mr Q, unprepared like the foolish virgins.'

This mitigation of his earlier rebuke brought smiles to the men in the boats as they leaned, panting on their oar looms.

'But I still have not given up those invasion craft. By the way, where's Mr Gorton?'

'Er . . . he was wounded when we boarded the brig, sir.' Quilhampton's eyes did not meet Drinkwater's.

'God's bones!' Drinkwater felt renewed rage rising in him and suppressed it with difficulty. 'Pull back to the ship and look lively about it.'

He slumped back in the stern of the barge, working his hand across his jaw as he mastered anger and anxiety. He was angry that the attack had failed to carry out its objective, angry that Gorton was wounded, and angry with himself for his failure as he wondered how the devil he was going to pursue the escaped invasion craft. And the parable he had cited to Quilhampton struck him as having been most applicable to himself.

Ruse de Guerre

Captain Drinkwater's mood was one of deep anger, melancholy and self-condemnation. He stood on the quarterdeck of the 16-gun brig *Bonaparte*, a French national corvette whose capture should have delighted him. Alas, it had been dearly bought. Although surprised by the speed of Rogers's attack, the French had been alerted to its possibility. Two marines and one seaman had been killed, and three seamen and one officer severely wounded. In the officer's case the stab wound was feared mortal and Drinkwater was greatly distressed by the probability of Lieutenant Gorton's untimely death. Unlike many of his colleagues, Drinkwater mourned the loss of any of his men, feeling acutely the responsibility of ordering an attack in the certain knowledge that some casualities were bound to occur. He was aware that the morning's boat expedition had been hurriedly launched and that insufficient preparation had gone into it. The loss of three men was bad enough, the lingering agony of young Gorton particularly affected him, for he had entertained high hopes for the man since he had demonstrated such excellent qualities in the Arctic the previous summer. It was not in Drinkwater's nature to blame the sudden onset of fog, but his own inadequate planning which had resulted not only in deaths and woundings but in the escape of the invasion craft whose capture or destruction might have justified his losses in his own exacting mind.

But he had been no less hard on Rogers and Mount. He had addressed the former in the cabin, swept aside all protestations and excuses in his anger, and reduced Rogers to a sullen resentment. It simply did not seem to occur to Rogers that the destruction of the invasion craft was of more significance than the seizure of a French naval brig.

'God damn it, man,' he had said angrily to Rogers, 'don't you *see* that you could have directed the quarter-boats to attack the brig, even as a diversion! Even if they were driven off! You and Mount in the launch could have wrought havoc among those *bateaux* in the fog, coming up on them piecemeal. The others would not have opened fire lest they hit their own people!' He had paused in his fury and then exploded. 'Christ, Sam, 'twas not the brig that was important!'

Well it was too late now, he concluded as he glared round the tiny quarterdeck. Rogers was left behind aboard *Antigone* with a sheet of written orders while Drinkwater took over the prize and went in pursuit of the invasion craft.

'Tregembo!'

'Zur?'

'I want those prisoners to work, Tregembo, work. You understand my meaning, eh? Get those damned sweeps going and keep them going.'

'Aye, aye, zur.' Tregembo set half a dozen men with ropes' ends over the prisoners at the huge oars.

It was already noon and still there was not a breath of wind. The fog had held off, but left a haze that blurred the horizon and kept the circle of their visibility under four miles. Somewhere in the haze ahead lay the *chaloupes* and the *péniches* that Drinkwater was more than ever determined to destroy. He had taken the precaution of removing the brig's officers as prisoners on board *Antigone* and issuing small arms to most of his own volunteers. In addition he had a party of marines under a contrite Lieutenant Mount (who was eager to make amends for his former lack of obedience). Drinkwater had little fear that the brig's men would rise, particularly if he worked them to exhaustion at the heavy sweeps.

He crossed the deck to where Tyrrell stood at the wheel.

'Course south-east by east, sir,' offered the master's mate.

Drinkwater nodded. 'Very well. Let me know the instant the wind begins to get up.'

'Aye, aye, sir.'

He turned below, wondering if he would find anything of interest among the brig's papers and certain that Rogers had not thought of looking.

The wind came an hour after sunset. It was light for about half an hour and finally settled in the north and blew steadily. Drinkwater ordered the sweeps in and the prisoners below.

'Mr Frey.'

'Sir?' The midshipman came forward eagerly, pleased to have been specially detailed for this mission and aware that something of disgrace hung over the events of the morning.

'I want you to station yourself in the foretop and keep a close watch ahead for those invasion craft. From that elevation you may see the light from a binnacle, d'you understand?'

'Perfectly sir.'

'Very well. And pass word for Mr Q.'

Quilhampton approached and touched his hat. 'Sir?'

'I intend snatching an hour or two's sleep, Mr Q. You have the deck. I want absolute silence and no lights to be shown. Moonrise ain't until two in the mornin'. You may tell Mount's sentries that one squeak out of those prisoners and I'll hold 'em personally responsible. We may be lucky and catch those invasion *bateaux* before they get into Havre.'

'Let's hope so, sir.'

'Yes.' Drinkwater turned away and made for the cabin of the brig where, rolling himself in his cloak and laying his cocked pistols beside him, he lay down to rest.

He was woken from an uneasy sleep by Mr Frey and rose, stiff and uncertain of the time.

'Eight bells in the first watch, sir,' said Frey.

Drinkwater emerged on deck to find the brig racing along, leaning to a steady breeze from the north, the sky clear and the stars glinting like crystals. Quilhampton loomed out of the darkness.

'I believe we have 'em, sir,' he pointed ahead, 'there, two points to starboard.'

At first Drinkwater could see nothing; then he made out a cluster of darker rectangles, rectangles with high peaks: lugsails.

'Straight in amongst 'em, Mr Q. Get the men to their quarters in silence. Orders to each gun-captain to choose a target carefully and, once the order is given, fire at will.' Fatigue, worry and the fuzziness of unquiet sleep left him in an instant.

' 'Ere's some coffee, sir.'

'Thank you, Franklin.' He took the pot gratefully. Night vision showed him the dark shadow of Franklin's naevus, visible even in the dark.

' 'S all right, sir.'

Drinkwater swallowed the coffee as the men went silently to their places. The brig's armament was of French 8-pounders; light guns but heavy enough to sink the *chaloupes* and *péniches*.

'Haul up the fore-course, Mr Q. T'gallants to the caps, if you please.'

'Rise fore-tacks and sheets there! Clew-garnets haul!' The orders passed quietly and the fore-course rose in festoons below its yard.

'T'gallants halliards . . .'

The topgallant sails fluttered, flogged and kicked impotently as

42

their yards were lowered. The brig's speed eased so as to avoid over-running the enemy.

Drinkwater hauled himself up on the rail and held onto the forward main shroud on the starboard side. *Bonaparte* had eased her heel and he could clearly see the enemy under her lee bow.

'Make ready there! Mr Frey, stand by to haul the fore-yards aback.'

The sudden flash of a musket ahead was followed by a crackle of fire from small arms. The enemy had seen them but were unable to fire cannon astern.

'Steady as you go . . .'

'Steady as she goes, sir.'

He saw the dark blob of a *chaloupe* lengthen as it swung round to fire a broadside, saw its lugsails enlarge with the changing aspect, saw them flutter as she luffed.

'Starboard two points! Gun-captains, fire when you bear.'

There was a long silence, broken only by shouts and the popping of musketry. A dull thud near Drinkwater's feet indicated where at least one musket ball struck the *Bonaparte*. The *chaloupe* fired its broadside, the row of muzzles spitting orange, and a series of thuds, cracks and splintering sounded from forward. Then they were running the *chaloupe* down. He could see men diving overboard to avoid the looming stem of the brig as it rode over the heavy boat, split her asunder and sank her in passing over the broken hull. Along the deck the brig's guns fired, short barking coughs accompanied by the tremble of recoil and the reek of powder. Another boat passed close alongside and Drinkwater felt the hat torn from his head as musket balls buzzed round him.

'Mind zur.' Like some dark Greek Olympic hero Tregembo hefted a shot through the air and it dropped vertically into the boat. Next to him Quilhampton's face was lit by the flash of the priming in a scatter gun and the bell-muzzle delivered its deadly charge amongst the boat's crew as they drew astern, screaming in the brig's wake.

'Down helm!'

'Fore-yards, Mr Frey!'

The *Bonaparte* came up into the wind and then began to make a stern board as Drinkwater had the helm put smartly over the other way. Amidships the men were frantically spiking their guns round to find new targets. Individual guns fired, reloaded and fired again with hardly a shot coming in return from the invasion craft that lay in a shattered circle around them. Mount's marines were up on the rails and leaning against the stays, levelling their muskets on any dark spot

43

that moved above the rails of the low hulls, so that only the cry of the wounded and dying answered the British attack.

'Cease fire! Cease fire!'

The reports of muskets and cannon died away. Drinkwater counted the remains of the now silent boats around them. He could see nine, with one, possibly two, sunk.

'I fear one has escaped us,' he said to no one is particular.

'There she is, sir!' Frey was pointing to the southwards where the dark shape of a sail was just visible.

'Haul the fore-yards there, put the ship before the wind, Mr Q.'

Bonaparte came round slowly, then gathered speed as they laid a course to catch the departing *bateau*. From her size Drinkwater judged her to be one of the larger *chaloupes canonnières*, rigged as a three-masted lugger. For a little while she stood south and Drinkwater ordered the fore-course reset in order to overhaul her. But it was soon obvious that the French would not run, and a shot was put across her bow. She came into the wind at once and the *Bonaparte* was hove to again, a short distance to windward.

'What the devil is French for "alongside"?' snapped Drinkwater.

'Try *accoster*, sir.'

'Hey, *accoster, m'sieur, accoster*!' They saw oar blades appear and slowly the two vessels crabbed together. 'Mr Mount, your men to cover them.'

'Very well, sir . . .' The marines presented their muskets, starlight glinting dully off the fixed bayonets. There was a grinding bump as the *chaloupe* came alongside. The curious, Drinkwater among them, stared down and instantly regretted it. Drinkwater felt a stinging blow to his head and jerked backwards as it seemed the deck of the vessel erupted in points of fire.

He staggered, his head spinning, suddenly aware of forty or fifty Frenchmen clambering over the rail from which the complacent defenders had fallen back in their surprise.

'God's bones!' roared Drinkwater suddenly uncontrollably angry. He lugged out his new hanger and charged forward. 'Follow me who can!' He slashed right and left as fast as his arm would react, his head still dizzy from the glancing ball that had scored his forehead. Blood ran thickly down into one eye but his anger kept him hacking madly. With his left hand he wiped his eye and saw two marines lunging forward with their bayonets. He felt a sudden anxiety for Frey and saw the boy dart beneath a boarding pike and drive his dirk into a man already parrying the thrust of a bayonet.

44

' 'Old on, sir, we're coming!' That was Franklin's voice and there was Tregembo's bellow and then he was slithering in what remained of someone, though he did not know whether it was friend or foe. His sword bit deep into something and he found he had struck the rail. He felt a violent blow in his left side and he gasped with the pain and swung round. A man's face, centred on a dark void of an open mouth, appeared before him and he smashed his fist forward, dashing the pommel of his hanger into the teeth of the lower jaw. The discharge of his enemy's pistol burnt his leg, but did no further damage and Drinkwater again wiped blood from his eyes. He caught his breath and looked round. Something seemed to have stopped his hearing and the strange absence of noise baffled him. Around him amid the dark shapes of dead or dying men, the fighting was furious. Quilhampton felled a man with his iron hook. Two marines, their scarlet tunics a dull brown in the gloom, their white cross-belts and breeches grey, were bayonetting a French officer who stood like some blasphemous crucifix, a broken sword dangling from his wrist by its martingale. A seaman was wrestling for his life under a huge brute of a Frenchman with a great black beard while all along the deck similar struggles were in progress. Drinkwater recognised the struggling seaman as Franklin from the dark, distinctive strawberry birthmark. Catching up his sword he took three paces across the deck and drove the point into the flank of the giant.

The man turned in surprise and rose slowly. Drinkwater recovered his blade as the giant staggered towards him, ignoring Franklin who lay gasping on the deck. The giant was unarmed and grappled forward, a forbidding and terrifying sight. There was something so utterly overpowering about the appearance of the man that Drinkwater felt fear for the first time since they had gone into action. It was the same fear a small boy feels when menaced by a physical superior. Drinkwater's sword seemed inadequate to the task and he had no pistols. He felt ignominious defeat and death were inevitable. His legs were sagging under him and then his hearing came back to him. The man's mouth was open but it was himself that was shouting, a loud, courage-provoking bellow that stiffened his own resolve and sent him lunging forward, slashing at the man's face with his sword blade. The giant fell on his knees and Drinkwater hacked again, unaware that the man was bleeding to death through the first wound he had inflicted. The giant crashed forward and Drinkwater heard a cheer. What was left of his crew of volunteers encircled the fallen man, like the Israelites round Goliath.

The deck of the *Bonaparte* remained in British hands.

Antigone leaned over to the wind and creaked as her lee scuppers drove under water. Along her gun-deck tiny squirts of water found their way inboard through the cracks round the gun-ports. In his cabin Drinkwater swallowed his third glass of wine and finally addressed himself to his journal.

It is not, he wrote at last, *the business of a sea-officer to enjoy his duty, but I have often derived a satisfaction from achievement, quite lacking in the events of today. We have this day taken a French National brig-corvette of sixteen 8-pounder long guns named the* Bonaparte. *We have also destroyed twelve invasion bateaux, two of the large class mounting a broadside of light guns, taken upwards of sixty prisoners and thereby satisfied those objectives set in launching the attack at dawn. Yet the cost has been fearful. Lieutenant Gorton's wound is mortal and nineteen other men have died, or are likely to die, as a result of the various actions that are, in the eyes of the public, virtually un-noteworthy. Had we let the enemy slip away, the newspapers would not have understood why a frigate of* Antigone's *force could not have destroyed a handful of boats and a little brig. It was clear the enemy had prepared for the possibility of attack, that the brig was to bear its brunt while the bateaux escaped, and, that, at the end, we were nearly overwhelmed by a ruse de guerre that might have made prisoners of the best elements aboard this ship, to say nothing of extinguishing forever the career of myself. Even now I shudder at the possible consequences of their counter-attack succeeding.*

He laid his pen down and stared at the page where the wet gleam of the ink slowly faded. But all he could see was the apparition of the French giant and remember again how hollow his legs had felt.

The Secret Agent

As April turned into a glorious May, Lieutenant Rogers continued to smart from Drinkwater's rebuke. It galled him that even the news that the *Bonaparte* had been condemned as a prize and purchased into the Royal Navy – thus making him several hundred pounds richer – failed to raise his spirits. There were few areas in which Rogers evinced any sensitivity, but one was in his good opinion of himself, and it struck him that he had come to rely upon his commander's reinforcement of this. Such hitherto uncharacteristic reliance upon another further annoyed him, and to it he began to add other causes for grievance. Drinkwater's report had said little, certainly nothing that would elevate his first lieutenant and place him on the quarter-deck of the prize as a commander. In fact Drinkwater had sent the prize into Portsmouth with the wounded under the master's mate Tyrrell, so, apart from his prize money, Rogers had dismissed the notion that he could expect anything further from the capture. In addition to this it seemed that the impetus to *Antigone*'s cruise had gone, that no further chance of glory, advancement, or simply resuming his normal relationship with Drinkwater would offer itself to him. He took refuge in the only action left to him as first lieutenant; he harried the crew. *Antigone*'s people were employed constantly in a relentless series of drills. They shifted sails, exercised at small-arms and cutlasses, and sent down the topgallant and topmasts. To kill any residual boredom they even got the heavy lower yards across the rails a-portlast. When Drinkwater drily expressed satisfaction, Rogers demurred respectfully and repeated the evolution until it was accomplished to his own satisfaction.

For his part, Drinkwater accepted this propitiation as evidence of Rogers's contrition, and his own better nature responded so that the difference between them gradually diminished. Besides, news of Gorton's slow death at Haslar Hospital seemed to conclude the incident.

Towards the end of April they had spoken to the 18-gun brig-sloop *Vincejo* on her way to the westward, with orders to destroy the coastal trade off south Brittany. Her commander had come aboard and closeted himself with Drinkwater for half an hour. Their discussion was routine and friendly. After Wright's departure Drinkwater was able to confirm the speculations of the officers and explain that their late visitor was indeed the John Wesley Wright who, as a lieutenant, had escaped from French custody in Paris with Captain Sir Sydney Smith. He also mentioned that Wright was far from pleased with the condition of his ship, its armament, or its manning, and this seemed to divert the officers into a discussion about the '*Vincey Joe*', an old Spanish prize, held to be cranky and highly unsuitable for its present task.

Drinkwater kept to himself the orders Wright had passed him and the knowledge that Wright, like himself twelve years earlier, had been employed by Lord Dungarth's department in the landing and recovery of British agents on the coast of France. The orders Wright had brought emanated from Lord Dungarth via Admiral Keith, and prompted Drinkwater to increase his officers' vigilance in the interception and seizure of French fishing boats. Hitherto fishermen had been largely left alone. They were, as D'Auvergne had pointed out, the chief source of claret and cognac in England, and were not averse to parting with information of interest to the captains of British cruisers. But their knowledge of the English coast and its more obscure landing places, the suitability of their boats to carry troops and their general usefulness in forwarding the grand design of invasion had prompted an Admiralty order to detain them and destroy their craft. In this way *Antigone* passed the first weeks of a beautiful summer.

It was from their captures, and from the dispatch luggers and cutters with which Lord Keith kept in touch with his scattered cruisers, that Drinkwater and his officers learned of the consequences of the attempt made by discontented elements in France to assassinate Napoleon Bonaparte. The Pichegru-Cadoudal conspiracy had implicated both wings of French politics and been exposed in the closing weeks of the previous year. It had taken some time to round up the conspirators and had culminated in the astounding news that Bonaparte's gendarmes had illegally entered the neighbouring state of Baden and abducted the young Duc D'Enghien. The duke had been given a drum-head court-martial which implicated the Bourbons in the plot against Bonaparte, and summarily shot in a ditch at Vincennes. Drinkwater's reaction to the execution of D'Enghien combined with the orders he had received from Wright to extend *Antigone*'s cruising ground further east towards Pointe d'Ailly.

'Standing close inshore like this,' Drinkwater overheard Rogers grumbling to Hill as he sat reading with his skylight open, 'we're not going to capture a damn thing. We're more like a bloody whore trailing her skirt up and down the street than a damned frigate. I wish we were in the West Indies. Even a fool of a Frenchman isn't going to put to sea with us sitting here for all to see.'

'No,' said Hill reflectively, and Drinkwater put down his book to hear what he had to say in reply. 'But it could be that that is just what the Old Man wants.'

'What? To be seen?'

'Yes. When I was in the *Kestrel*, cutter, back in ninety-two we used to do just this waiting to pick up a spy.'

'Wasn't our Nathaniel aboard *Kestrel* then?'

'Yes,' said Hill, 'and that cove Wright has been doing something similar more recently.'

'Good God! Why didn't you mention it before?'

Drinkwater heard Hill laugh. 'I never thought of it.'

In the end it was the fishing boat that found them as Drinkwater intended. She came swooping over the waves, a brown lugsail reefed down and hauled taut against the fresh westerly that set white wave-caps sparkling in the low sunshine of early morning. Drinkwater answered the summons to the quarterdeck to find Quilhampton backing the main-topsail and heaving the ship to. He levelled his glass on the approaching boat but could make nothing of her beyond the curve of her dark sail, apart from an occasional face that peered ahead and shouted at the helmsman. A minute or two later the boat was alongside and a man in riding clothes was bawling in imperious English for a chair at a yardarm whip. The men at the rail looked aft at Drinkwater.

He nodded: 'Do as he asks, Mr Q.'

As soon as the stranger's feet touched the deck he dextrously extricated himself from the bosun's chair, moved swiftly to the rail and whipped a pistol from his belt.

'What the devil are you about, sir?' shouted Drinkwater seeing the barrel levelled at the men in the boat.

'Shootin' the damned Frogs, Captain, and saving you your duty!' The hammer clicked impotently on a misfire and the stranger turned angrily. 'Has anyone a pistol handy?'

Drinkwater strode across the deck. 'Put up that gun, sir, d'you hear me!' He was outraged. That the stranger should escape from an enemy country and then shoot the men who had risked everything to bring him off to *Antigone* seemed a piece of quite unnecessary brutality.

'Here, take this.' Drinkwater turned to see Walmsley offering the stranger a loaded pistol.

'Good God! What, *you* here, Walmsley! Thank you . . .'

'Put up that gun, sir!' Drinkwater closed the gap between him and the spy and knocked up the weapon. The man spun round. His face was suffused with rage.

'A pox on you! Who the deuce d'you think you are to meddle in my affairs?'

'Have a care! I command here and you'll not fire into that boat!'

'D'you know who I am, damn you?'

'Indeed, Lord Camelford, I do; and I received orders to expect you some days ago.' He dropped his voice as Camelford looked round as though to obtain some support from Walmsley. 'Your reputation with pistols precedes you, my Lord. I must insist on your surrendering even those waterlogged weapons you still have in your belt.' He indicated a further two butts protruding from Camelford's waistband.

Camelford's face twisted into a snarl and he leaned forward, thrusting himself close to Drinkwater. 'You'll pay for your insolence, Captain. I do not think you know what influence I command, nor how necessary it was that I despatched those fishermen . . .'

'After promising them immunity to capture if they brought you offshore I don't doubt,' Drinkwater said, matching Camelford's anger. 'No fisherman would have risked bringing you off and under my guns without such assurance. It's common knowledge that we have been taking every fishing boat we can lay our hands on . . .'

'And now look, you damned fool, those two got clean away . . .' Camelford pointed to where the brown lugsail leaned away from the rail, full of wind and hauling off from *Antigone*'s side as her seamen stood and witnessed the little drama amidships.

'And you have kept your word, my Lord,' Drinkwater said soothingly, 'and now shall we go to my cabin? Put the ship on a course of north north-east, Mr Q. I want to fetch The Downs without delay.'

'Who the hell is he?' Rogers asked Hill as first lieutenant and master stood on the quarterdeck supervising their preparations for coming to an anchor in The Downs. 'D'you know?'

'Yes. Don't you recall him as Lieutenant Pitt? Vancouver left him ashore at Hawaii back in ninety-four for insubordination . . .'

'Is he the fellow that shot Peterson, first luff of the *Perdrix*, in, what, ninety-eight?'

'The same fellow. And the court-martial upheld his defence that Peterson, though senior, had refused to obey a lawful order . . .'

'Having the name Pitt helped a great deal, I don't doubt,' said Rogers. 'He resigned after it though, a regular kill-buck by the look of it. I thought Drinkwater was going to have a fit when he came aboard.'

'Oh he'll get away with almost anything. He's related to Lord Grenville by marriage, Billy Pitt by blood, and, I believe, to Sir Sydney Smith. I daresay it's due to the latter pair that he's been employed as an agent. I wonder what he was doing in France?'

'Mmmm. It must take some stomach to act as a spy over there,' Rogers's tone was one of admiration as he nodded in the direction of the cliffs of Gris Nez.

'Oh yes. Undoubtedly,' mused Hill, 'but I wonder what exactly . . .' The conversation broke off as a thunderous-looking Drinkwater came on deck.

'Are we ready to anchor, Mr Rogers?'

'Aye, sir, as near as . . . all ready, sir.' Rogers saw the look in Drinkwater's eye and went forward.

'Very well, bring-to close to the flagship, Mr Hill, then clear away my barge!'

Drinkwater had had a wretched time with the obnoxious Camelford. In the end he had virtually imprisoned the spy in his own cabin with a few bottles and spent most of the time on deck. Actually avoiding a ridiculous challenge from the man's deliberate provocation tested his powers of self-restraint to the utmost. He found it hard to imagine what on earth a person of Camelford's stamp was doing on behalf of the British government in France. After they had anchored, Drinkwater went below and found Camelford slumped in his own chair, the portrait of Hortense Santhonax spread on the table before him. He opened his mouth to protest at the ransacking of his effects but Camelford slurred:

'D'you know this woman, Captain Drinkwater?'

'The portrait was captured with the ship,' Drinkwater answered non-committally.

'I asked if you know her.'

'I know who she is.'

'If you ever meet her or her husband, Captain, do what I wanted to

51

do to those fishermen. Shoot 'em both!'

Drinkwater sensed Camelford was in earnest. Whatever the man's defects, he was, at that moment, making an effort to be both conciliatory and informative. Besides, experience had taught Drinkwater that agents recently liberated from a false existence surrounded by enemies were apt to behave irrationally, and news of Santhonax or his wife held an especial fascination for him. He grinned at Camelford.

'In *his* case I doubt if I'd hesitate.'

'You know Edouard Santhonax too, then?'

Drinkwater nodded. 'He was briefly my prisoner on two occasions.'

'Did you know Wright was captured in the Morbihan?'

'Wright? Of the *Vincejo*?'

'Yes. He was overwhelmed in a calm by a number of gunboats and forced to surrender. They put him in the Temple and cut his throat with a rusty knife.' Camelford tapped the cracked canvas before him. 'Her husband visited the Temple the night before, with a commission from the Emperor Napoleon . . .'

'The *Emperor* Napoleon?' queried Drinkwater, bemused by this strange and improbable story.

'Hadn't you heard, Captain?' Camelford leaned back. 'Oh my goodness no, how could you? Bonaparte the First Consul is transfigured, Captain Drinkwater. He is become Napoleon, Emperor of the French. A plebiscite of the French people has raised him to the purple.'

Following Camelford's welcome departure, Drinkwater was summoned to attend Lord Keith. As he kicked his heels aboard Keith's flagship, the *Monarch*, Drinkwater learned that not only had Napoleon secured his position as Emperor of the French but his own patron, Earl St Vincent, had been dismissed from the Admiralty. The old man refused to serve under William Pitt who had just been returned as Prime Minister in place of Addington. Pitt had said some harsh things about St Vincent when in opposition and had replaced him as First Lord of the Admiralty with Lord Melville. But Drinkwater's thoughts were not occupied with such considerations for long. His mind returned to the image of Wright lying in the Temple prison with his throat cut and the shadowy figure of Edouard Santhonax somewhere in the background. He wondered how accurate Camelford's information was and what Camelford was doing in France. Was it possible that a man of Camelford's erratic character had been employed to do what Cadoudal and Pichegru had failed to do: to assassinate Napoleon Bonaparte? The only credible explanation for that hypothesis was that Camelford had been sent into France in a private capacity. Drinkwater vaguely remembered Camelford had avoided the serious consequences of his duel with Peterson. If that had been due to family connections, was it possible that someone had put him up to an attempt on the life of Bonaparte? Pitt himself, for instance, to whom Camelford was related and who had every motive for wishing the Corsican Tyrant dead.

There was some certainty nagging at the back of Drinkwater's mind, something that lent credibility to this extraordinary possibility. And then he remembered D'Auvergne's obscure remark to Cornwallis. Something about 'it would be soon if it was ever to be'. At the time he had connected it with D'Auvergne's passionate conviction that invasion was imminent; now perhaps the evidence pointed to Camelford having been sent into France to murder Napoleon. D'Auvergne's involvement in such operations could have made him a party to it. He was prevented from further speculation by the appearance of Keith's flag-lieutenant.

'The admiral will see you now, sir.'

He looked up, recalled abruptly to the present. Tucking his hat under his arm, Drinkwater went into the great cabin of the *Monarch*, mustering in his mind the mundane details of his need of firewood, fresh water and provisions. His reception was polite but unenthusiastic; his requisitions passed to Keith's staff. The acidulous Scots admiral asked him to take a protégé of his as lieutenant in place of Gorton and then instructed Drinkwater that his presence had been requested by the new Prime Minister, then in residence at Walmer Castle.

Drinkwater answered the summons to Walmer Castle with some misgivings. It chimed in uncomfortably with his train of thought while he had been waiting to see Keith and he could only conclude Pitt wished to see him in connection with the recent embarkation of his cousin, Camelford. It was unlikely that the interview would be pleasant and he recalled Camelford's threats when he had prevented the shooting of the fishermen.

The castle was only a short walk from Deal beach. Many years ago he had gone there to receive orders for the rendezvous that had brought Hortense and then Edouard Santhonax into his life. On that occasion he had been received by Lord Dungarth, head of the

Admiralty's intelligence service. To his astonishment it was Dungarth who met him again.

'My dear Nathaniel, how very good to see you. How are you?'

'Well enough, my Lord.' Drinkwater grinned with pleasure and accepted the offered glass of wine. 'I hope I find you in health?'

Dungarth sighed. 'As well as can be expected in these troubled times, though in truth things could not be much worse. Our hopes have been dashed and Bonaparte has reversed the Republic's principles without so much as a murmur from more than a handful of die-hards. Old Admiral Truguet has resigned at Brest and Ganteaume's taken over, but I believe this imperial nonsense will combine the French better than anything, and that shrewd devil Bonaparte knows it . . . But I did not get you here to gossip. Billy Pitt asks for you personally. You did well to get Camelford back in one piece.'

'It was nothing, my Lord . . .'

'Oh, I don't mean embarking him. He's a cantankerous devil; I'm surprised he hasn't challenged half your officers. His honour, what there is of it, is a damned touchy subject.'

'So I had gathered,' Drinkwater observed drily.

Dungarth laughed. 'I'm sure you had. Anyway his capture would have been an embarrassment, particularly with the change of government.'

'You said "our hopes have been dashed", my Lord; might I assume that Bonaparte was not intended to live long enough to assume the purple?'

Dungarth's hazel eyes fixed Drinkwater with a shrewd glance. 'Wouldn't you say that Mr Pitt serves the most excellent port, Nathaniel?'

Drinkwater took the hint. 'Most excellent, my Lord.'

'And most necessary, gentlemen, most necessary . . .' A thin, youngish man entered the room and strode to the decanter. Drinkwater noticed that his clothes were carelessly worn, his stockings, for instance, appeared too large for him. He faced them, a full glass to his lips, and Drinkwater recognised the turned-up nose habitually caricatured by the cartoonists. 'So this is Captain Drinkwater, is it?'

'Indeed,' said Dungarth, making the introductions, 'Captain Drinkwater; the Prime Minister, Mr Pitt.'

Drinkwater bowed. 'Yours to command, sir.'

'Obliged, Captain,' said Pitt, inclining his head slightly and studying the naval officer. 'I wish to thank you for your forbearance. I think you know to what I allude.'

'It is most considerate of you, sir, to take the trouble. The service was a small one.' Drinkwater felt relief that the incident was to be made no more of.

Pitt smiled over the rim of his glass and Drinkwater saw how tired and sick his boyish face really was, prematurely aged by the enormous responsibilities of high office.

'He was the only midshipman that remained loyal to Riou when the *Guardian* struck an iceberg in the Southern Ocean,' said Pitt obliquely, as though this extenuated Camelford's behaviour. Drinkwater recalled Riou's epic struggle to keep the damaged *Guardian* afloat for nine weeks until she fetched Table Bay. The thought seemed to speak more of Riou's character than of Camelford's. 'Lord Dungarth assures me', Pitt went on, 'that I can rely upon your absolute discretion.'

So, Drinkwater mused as he bowed again and muttered, 'Of course, sir', it seemed that he *had* guessed correctly and that Pitt himself had sent his cousin into France to end Bonaparte's career. But he was suddenly forced to consider more important matters.

'Good,' said Pitt, refilling his glass. 'And now, Captain, I wish to ask you something more. How seriously do you rate the prospects of invasion?'

The enormity of the question took Drinkwater aback. Even allowing for Pitt's recent resumption of office it seemed an extraordinary one. He shot a glance at Dungarth who nodded encouragingly.

'Well, sir, I do not know that I am a competent person to answer, but I believe their invasion craft capable of transporting a large body of troops. That they are encamped in sufficient force is well known. Their principal difficulty is in getting a great enough number of ships in the Strait here to overwhelm our own squadrons. If they could achieve that . . . but I am sure, sir, that their Lordships are better placed to advise you than I . . .'

'No, Captain. I ask *you* because you have just come in from a Channel cruise and your opinions are not entirely theoretical. I am told that the French cannot build barges capable of carrying troops. I do not believe that, so it is *your* observations that I wished for.'

'Very well, sir. I think the French might be capable of combining their fleet effectively. Their ships are not entirely despicable. If fortune gave them a lucky start and Nelson . . .' he broke off, flushing.

'Go on, Captain. "If Nelson . . ." '

'It is nothing, sir.'

'You were about to say: "if Nelson maintains his blockade loosely

55

enough to entice Latouche–Tréville out of Toulon for a battle, only to lose contact with him, matters might result in that combination of their fleets that you are apprehensive of." Is that it?'

'It is a possibility talked of in the fleet, sir.'

'It is a possibility talked of elsewhere, sir,' observed Pitt with some asperity and looking at Dungarth. 'Nelson will be the death or the glory of us all. He let a French fleet escape him before Abukir. If he wasn't so damned keen on a battle, but kept close up on Toulon like Cornwallis at Brest . . .' Pitt broke off to refill his glass. 'So you think there is a chance of a French fleet entering the Channel?'

Drinkwater nodded. 'It is a remote one, sir. But the Combined Fleets of France and Spain did so in seventy-nine. They would have more chance of success if they went north about.'

'Round Scotland, d'you mean?'

'Yes, sir. There'd be less chance of detection,' said Drinkwater, warming to his subject and egged on by the appreciative expression on Dungarth's face. 'A descent upon the Strait of Dover from the North Sea would be quite possible and they could release the Dutch fleet en route. You could circumvent Cornwallis by . . .'

'A rendezvous in the West Indies, by God!' interrupted Pitt. 'Combine all your squadrons then lose yourself in the Atlantic for a month and reappear at our back door . . . Dungarth, d'you think it's possible?'

'Very possible, William, very possible, and also highly likely. The Emperor Napoleon has one hundred and seventy thousand men encamped just across the water there. I'd say that was just what he *was* intending.'

Pitt crossed the rich carpet to stare out of the window at the pale line of France on the distant horizon. The waters of the Strait lay between, blue and lovely in the sunshine beyond the bastions of the castle, dotted with the white sails of Keith's cruisers. Without turning round, Pitt dismissed Drinkwater.

'Thank you, Captain Drinkwater. I shall take note of your opinion.'

Dungarth saw him to the door. 'Thank you, Nathaniel,' the earl muttered confidentially, 'I believe your deductions to be absolutely correct.'

Drinkwater returned to his boat flattered by the veiled compliment from Dungarth and vaguely disturbed that his lordship, as head of the navy's intelligence service, needed a junior captain to make his case before the new Prime Minister.

The Army of the Coasts
of the Ocean

'Six minutes, Mr Rogers,' said Drinkwater pocketing his watch, 'very creditable. Now you may pipe the hands to dinner.'

The shifting of the three topsails had been accomplished in good time and the tide was just turning against them. They could bring to their anchor and dine in comfort, for there was insufficient wind to hold them against a spring ebb. It was a great consolation, he had remarked to Rogers earlier, that they could eat like civilised men ashore at a steady table, while secure in the knowledge that their very presence an anchor in the Dover Strait was sufficient to keep the French army from invading.

For almost seven weeks now, *Antigone* had formed part of Lord Keith's advance division, cruising ceaselessly between the Varne Bank and Cap Gris Nez, one of several frigates and sixty-fours that Keith kept in support of the small fry in the shallower water to the east. Cutters, luggers, sloops and gun-brigs, with a few bomb-vessels, kept up a constant pressure on the attempts by the French army to practice embarkation. Drinkwater knew the little clashes between the advance forces of the two protagonists were short, sharp and murderous. His disfigured shoulder was proof of that.

Having frequently stood close inshore at high water, Drinkwater had seen that the invasion flotilla consisted of craft other than the *chaloupes* and *péniches* with which he was already familiar. There were some large *prames*, great barges, one hundred feet long and capable of carrying over a hundred and fifty men. A simple elevation of the telescope to the green hills surrounding Boulogne was enough to convince Drinkwater that he had been right in expressing his fears to Pitt. Line after line of tents spread across the rolling countryside. Everywhere the bright colours of soldiers in formation, little squares, lozenges, lines and rectangles, all tipped with the brilliant reflections of sunlight from bayonets, moved under the direction of their drillmasters. Occasionally squadrons of cavalry were to be seen moving; wheeling and changing from line to column and back to line again. Drinkwater was touched by the fascination of it all. Beside him Frey would sit with his box of water-colours, annoyed and impatient with himself that he could not do justice to the magnificence of the scene.

At night they could see the lines of camp-fires, the glow of lanterns, and occasionally hear the bark of cannon from the batteries covering the beaches which opened fire on an insolent British cutter working too close inshore.

Now Drinkwater waited for the cable to cease rumbling through the hawse and for Hill to straighten up from the vanes of the pelorus as *Antigone* settled to her anchor.

'Brought up, sir.'

'Very well. Mr Hill, Mr Rogers, would you care to dine with me? Perhaps you'd bring one of your mates, Mr Hill, and a couple of midshipmen.'

Mullender had fattened a small pig in the manger on scraps and that morning pronounced it ready for sacrifice. Already the scent of roasting pork had been hanging over the quarterdeck for some time and Drinkwater had been shamed into sending a leg into the gun-room and another into the cockpit. Mullender had been outraged by this largesse, particularly when Drinkwater ordered what was left after his own leg had been removed to be sent forward. But it seemed too harsh an application of privilege to subject his men to the aroma of sizzling crackling and deny them a few titbits. Besides, their present cruising ground was so near home that reprovisioning was no problem.

A companionable silence descended upon the table as the hungry officers took knife and fork to the dismembered pig.

'You are enjoying your meal, Mr Gillespy, I believe?' remarked Drinkwater, amused at the ecstatic expression on the midshipman's face.

'Yes, sir,' the boy squeaked, 'thanking you sir, for your invitation . . .' He flushed as the other diners laughed at him indulgently.

'Well, Mr Gillespy,' added Rogers, his mouth still full and a half-glass of stingo aiding mastication and simultaneous speech, 'it's an improvement on the usual short commons, eh?'

'Indeed, sir, it is.'

'You had some mail today, Mr Q, news of home I trust?' Drinkwater asked, knowing three letters had come off in the despatch lugger *Sparrow* that forenoon.

'Yes, sir. Catriona sends you her kindest wishes.' James Quilhampton grinned happily.

'D'you intend to marry this filly then, Mr Q?' asked Rogers.

'If she'll have me,' growled Quilhampton, flushing at the indelicacy of the question.

'Can't see the point of marriage, myself,' Rogers said morosely.

'Oh, I don't know,' put in Hill. 'Its chief advantage is that you can walk down the street with a woman on your arm without exciting damn-fool comments from y'r friends.'

'Fiddlesticks!' Rogers looked round at the half-concealed smirks of Quilhampton and Frey. Even little Gillespy seemed to perceive a well-known joke. 'What the devil d'you mean, Hill?' demanded Rogers, colouring.

'That you cut out a pretty little corvette, trimmed fore and aft with ribbons and lace, with an entry port used by half the fleet in Chatham . . .'

'God damn it . . .'

'Now had you been *married* we would have thought it your wife, don't you see?'

'Why . . . I . . .'

'No, Hill, we'd never have fallen for that,' said James Quilhampton, getting his revenge. 'A married man would not have been so imprudent as to have carried so much sail upon his *bowsprit!*'

Upon this phallic reference the company burst into unrestrained laughter at the first lieutenant's discomfiture. Rogers coloured and Drinkwater came to his rescue.

'Take it in good part, Sam. I heard she was devilish pretty and these fellows are only jealous. Besides I've news for you. You need no longer stand a watch. I received notice this morning that Keith wants us to find a place for an élève of his, a Lieutenant Fraser . . .'

'Oh God, a Scotchman,' complained Rogers, irritated by Quilhampton and knowing his partiality in that direction. Mullender drew the cloth and placed the decanter in front of Drinkwater. He filled his glass and sent it round the table.

'And now, gentlemen . . . The King!'

Drinkwater looked round the table and reflected that they were not such a bad set of fellows and it was a very pleasant day to be dining, with the reflections of sunlight on the water bouncing off the painted deckhead and the polished glasses.

Two days later the weather wore a different aspect. Since dawn *Antigone* had worked closer inshore under easy sail, having been informed by signal that some unusual activity was taking place in the harbour and anchorage of Boulogne Road. By noon the wind, which had been steadily freshening from the north during the forenoon, began to blow hard, sending a sharp sea running round Cap Gris Nez and among the considerable numbers of invasion craft anchored under the guns of Boulogne's defences.

The promise of activity, either action with the enemy or the need to reef down, had aroused the curiosity of the officers and the watch on deck. A dozen glasses were trained to the eastward.

'Mr Frey, make to *Constitution* to come within hail.'

'Aye, aye, sir.' The bunting rose jerkily to the lee mizen topsail yard and broke out. Drinkwater watched the hired cutter that two days earlier had brought their new lieutenant. She tacked and lay her gunwhale over until she luffed under the frigate's stern. Drinkwater could see her commander, Lieutenant Dennis, standing expectantly on a gun-carriage. He raised a speaking-trumpet.

'Alert Captain Owen of the movement in the Road!' He saw Dennis wave and the jib of *Constitution* was held aback as she spun on her heel and lay over again on a board reach to the west where Owen in the *Immortalité* was at anchor with the frigate *Leda*. Owen was locally the senior officer of Keith's 'Boulogne division' and it was incumbent upon Drinkwater to let him know of any unusual movements of the French that might be taken advantage of.

'Well, gentlemen, let's slip the hounds off the leash. Mr Frey, make to *Harpy*, *Bloodhound* and *Archer* Number Sixteen: "Engage the enemy more closely".' The 18-gun sloop and the two little gun-brigs were a mile or so to the eastward and eager for such a signal. Within minutes they were freeing off and running towards the dark cluster of French *bateaux* above which the shapes of sails were being hoisted.

'Mr Hill, a man in the chains with a lead. Beat to quarters and clear for action, Mr Rogers.' He stood beside the helmsmen. 'Up helm. Lee forebrace there . . .'

Antigone eased round to starboard under her topsails and began to bear down on the French coast. The sun was already westering in a bloody riot of purple cloud and great orange streaks of mare's tails presaging more wind on the morrow. *Antigone* stood on, coming within clear visual range of the activity in the anchorage.

'Forty-four, forty-five brigs and – what've you got on that slate, Frey? – forty-three luggers, sir,' reported Quilhampton, who had been diligently counting the enemy vessels as the sun broke briefly through the cloud and shot rays of almost horizontal light over the sea, foreshortening distances and rendering everything suddenly clear. Then it sank from view and left the silhouettes of the *Immortalité*

60

and *Leda* on the horizon, coming in from the west.

The small ships were close inshore, the flashes from their guns growing brighter as daylight diminished and the tide turned. Owen made the signal for withdrawal and the *Antigone*, in company with the *Harpy, Bloodhound* and *Archer*, drew off for the night and rode out the rising gale at anchor three leagues offshore.

At daylight on the following day, 20th July, Drinkwater was awoken by Midshipman Dutfield. 'Beg pardon, sir, but Mr Fraser's compliments, sir, and would you come on deck.'

Drinkwater emerged into the thin light of early morning. The north-north-westerly wind was blowing with gale force. The Channel waves were steep, sharp and vicious and *Antigone* rode uncomfortably to her anchor. The flood tide was just away and the frigate lay across wind and tide, rolling awkwardly. But it was not this circumstance that the new lieutenant wished to draw to Drinkwater's attention.

'There, sir,' he pointed, 'just beyond the low-water mark, lines of fascines to form a rough wall with artillery . . . see!' Fraser broke off his description as the French gave evidence of their purpose. The flash of cannon from the low-water mark was aimed at the gun-brigs anchored inshore. Out of range of the batteries along the cliffs, they were extremely vulnerable to shot from a half-mile nearer. The French, as if demonstrating their ingenious energy, had made temporary batteries on the dry sands and could withdraw their guns as the tide made. What was more, shot fired on a flat trajectory so near the surface of the sea could skip like stones upon a pond. They'd smash a gun-brig with ease and might, with luck, range out much further.

'It's bluidy clever, sir.'

'Aye, Mr Fraser . . . but why today?' Drinkwater adjusted his glass and immediately had his answer. At the hour at which it was normal to see lines of infantry answering the morning roll-call he was aware of something very different about the appearance of the French camps. Dark snakes wound their way down towards the dip in the hills where the roofs and belfries of Boulogne indicated the port.

'By heaven, Mr Fraser, they're embarking!'

'In this weather, sir?'

'Wind or not, they're damned well on the move . . .' The two officers watched for some minutes in astonishment. 'There are a lot less *bateaux* in the anchorage this morning,' Drinkwater observed.

'Happen they've hauled them inshore to embark troops.'

61

'That must have been a ticklish business in this wind with a sea running.'

'Aye.'

As the tide made, Owen ordered his tiny squadron under weigh and once again *Antigone* closed the coast. By now the batteries along the tideline had been withdrawn and there was sufficient water over the shoals for the bigger frigates to move in after the sloops and gun-brigs.

At noon *Antigone* came within range of the batteries and Drinkwater opened fire. After the weeks of aimless cruising, the stench of powder and the trembling of the decks beneath the recoiling carriages was music in the ears of *Antigone*'s crew.

Their insolence was met by a storm of fire from the shore; it seemed that everywhere the ground was level the French had cannon. The practical necessity of having to tack offshore in the northerly wind allowed them to draw breath and inspect the ship for damage. There was little enough. A few holes in the sails and a bruised topgallant mast. Astern of them the gun-brigs and sloops were snapping around the two or three luggers that were trying to work offshore. The flood tide swept them northwards and, off Ambleteuse, Drinkwater gave orders to wear ship.

'Brace in the spanker there! Brace in the after-yards! Up helm!' The after-canvas lost its power to drive the frigate as Drinkwater turned her south.

'Square the headyards! Steady . . . steady as she goes!'

'Steady as she goes, sir.'

'Square the after-yards!'

Antigone steadied on her new course, standing south under her three topsails, running before the wind inside the shoals and parallel with the coast. It wanted an hour before high water but here the tide ran north for several hours yet and they could balance wind and tide, checking the ship's southward progress against the tide, and thus wreak as much havoc as they possibly could while the smoke from their own guns hung over their deck masking them from the enemy. The motion of the deck eased considerably.

'Mr Rogers! Shift over the starbowlines to assist at the larboard batteries. Every gun-captain to choose his target and fire as at a mark, make due allowance for elevation and roll. You may open fire!'

Drinkwater stared out to larboard. They were a mile from the cliffs at Raventhun and suddenly spouts of water rose on their beam. Drinkwater levelled his glass.

62

'Mr Gillespy!'

'Sir?'

'D'you see that square shape over there, where the ground falls away?'

The boy nodded. 'Yes, sir.'

'That's Ambleteuse fort. Be so kind as to point it out to Mr Rogers so that he may direct the guns.'

The little estuary that formed the harbour opened up on their beam as *Antigone* exchanged shot with the fort. Within the harbour they could see quite clearly a mass of rafted barges crammed with soldiers, rocking dangerously as the sharp waves drove in amongst them.

A shower of splinters sprouted abruptly from the rail where a ball struck home and more holes appeared in the topsails. Amidships the launch was hit by three shot within as many minutes and then they were passing out of range of the fort's embrasures. Rogers was leaping up and down from gun to gun, exhorting his men and swearing viciously at them when their aim failed. As the land rose again a battery of horse artillery could be seen dashing at the gallop along the cliff. Suddenly Drinkwater saw the officer leading the troop fling up his hand and the gunners rein in their horses.

'Mr Rogers! See there!' Rogers narrowed his eyes and stared through the smoke that cleared slowly in the following wind. Then comprehension struck him and he leant over the nearest gun and aimed it personally. The Frenchmen had got their cannon unlimbered and were slewing them round. They were shining brass cannon, field pieces of 8- or 9-pound calibre, Drinkwater estimated, and they were ready loaded. He saw white smoke flash from an almost simultaneous volley from the five guns and a second later the shot whistled overhead, carrying off the starboard quarter-boat davits and dumping the boat in the sea alongside, where it trailed in its falls amongst the broken baulks of timber.

Amidships Rogers was howling with rage as his broadside struck flints and chunks of chalk from the cliff a few feet below the edge. But his next shots landed among the artillerymen and they had the satisfaction of seeing the battery limbered up amid frantic cheers from the gunners amidships.

'We're too close inshore, sir. Bottom's shoaling.' Drinkwater turned to the ever-dutiful Hill who, while this fairground game was in progress, attended to the navigation of the ship.

'Bring her a point to starboard then.'

They were abeam of Wimereux now. Here too, there was a fort on the rocks at the water's edge, and below the fort two of the French invasion craft were stranded and going to pieces under the white of breakers. Drinkwater was suddenly aware that the cloud of powder smoke that rolled slowly ahead of the ship was obscuring his view. 'Cease fire! Cease fire!'

The smoke cleared with maddening slowness, but gradually it seemed to lift aside like a theatrical guaze, revealing a sight of confusion such as their own cannon could not achieve. They were less than two miles from Boulogne now, and under the cliffs and along the breakwaters of the harbour more than a dozen of the invasion barges lay wrecked with the sea breaking over them. Their shattered masts had fallen over their sides and men could be seen in the water around them.

They had a brief glimpse into the harbour as they crossed the entrance, a brief glimpse of chaos. It seemed as though soldiers were everywhere, moving like ants across the landscape. Yet, as *Antigone* crossed the narrow opening the guns of Boulogne were briefly silent, their servers witnesses of the drowning of over a thousand of their comrades. In this hiatus *Antigone* passed by, her own men standing at their guns, staring at the waves breaking viciously over rocking and overloaded craft, at men catching their balance, falling and drowning.

'I think there's the reason for the activity, sir,' said Fraser pointing above the town. 'I'll wager that's the Emperor himself.'

Drinkwater swung his glass and levelled it where Fraser pointed. Into the circle of the lens came an unforgettable image of a man in a grey coat, sitting on a white horse and wearing a large black tricorne hat. The man had a glass to his eye and was staring directly at the British frigate as it swept past him. As he lowered his own glass, Drinkwater could just make out the blur of Napoleon's face turning to one of his suite behind him.

'Napoleon Bonaparte, Emperor o' the French,' muttered Fraser beside him. 'He looks a wee bit like Don Quixote . . . Don Quixote *de la Manche . . .*'

Fraser's pun was lost in the roar of the batteries of Boulogne as they reopened their fire upon the insolent British frigate. Shot screamed all round them. Hill was demanding they haul further offshore and Rogers was asking for permission to re-engage. He nodded at both officers.

'Very well, gentlemen, if you would be so kind.' He turned for a final look at the man on the white horse, but he had vanished, obscured by the glittering train of his staff as they galloped away. 'The gale has done our work for us,' he muttered to himself, 'for the time being.'

Stalemate

'Will you damned lubbers put your backs into it and *pull!*'

Midshipman Lord Walmsley surveyed the launch's crew with amiable contempt and waved a scented handkerchief under his nose. He stood in the stern sheets of the big boat in breeches and shirt, trying to combat the airless heat of the day and urge his oarsmen to more strenuous efforts. Out on either beam Midshipmen Dutfield and Wickham each had one of the quarter-boats and all three were tethered to the *Antigone*. At the ends of their towropes the boats slewed and splashed, each oarsman dipping his oar into the ripples of his last stroke, so that their efforts seemed utterly pointless. The enemy lugger after which they were struggling lay on the distant horizon.

Walmsley regarded his companion with a superior amusement. Sitting with his little hand on the big tiller was Gillespy, supposedly under Walmsley's tutoring and utterly unable to exhort the men.

'It is essential, Gillespy, to encourage greater effort from these fellows,' his lordship lectured, indicating the sun-burnt faces that puffed and grunted, two to a thwart along the length of the launch. 'You can't do it by squeaking at 'em and you can't do it by asking them. You have to bellow at the damned knaves. Call 'em poxy laggards, lazy land-lubbing scum; then they get so God-damned angry that they pull those bloody oar looms harder. Don't you see? Eh?'

'Yes . . . my Lord,' replied the unfortunate Gillespy who was quite under Walmsley's thumb, isolated as he was in the launch.

The lesson in leadership was greeted with a few weary grins from the men at the oars, but few liked Mr Walmsley and those that were not utterly uncaring from the monotony of their task and being constantly abused by the senior midshipman of their division, resented his arrogance. Of all the men in the boat there was one upon whom Walmsley's arrogant sarcasm acted like a spark upon powder.

At stroke oar William Waller laboured as an able seaman. A year earlier he had been master of the Greenland whale-ship *Conqueror*, a member of the Trinity House of Kingston-upon-Hull and engaged in a profitable trade in whale-oil, whale-bone and the smuggling of furs from Greenland to France where they were used to embellish the gaudy uniforms of the soldiers they had so recently been cannonading upon the cliffs of Boulogne. It had been this illicit trade that had reduced him to his present circumstances. He had been caught red-handed engaged in a treasonable trade with a French outpost on the coast of Greenland by Captain Nathaniel Drinkwater.

Although well aware that he could have been hanged for what he had done, Waller was a weak and cunning character. That he had escaped with his life due to Drinkwater's clemency had at first seemed fortunate, but as time passed his present humiliations contrasted unfavourably with his former status. His guilt began to diminish in his own eyes as he transferred responsibility for it to his partner who had been architect of the scheme and had died for it. The greater blame lay with the dead man and Waller was, in his own mind, increasingly a victim of regrettable circumstances. When he had been turned among them, many of *Melusine*'s hands had been aware of his activities. They had shunned him and despised him, but Waller had held his peace and survived, being a first-rate seaman. But he had kept his own counsel, a loner among the gregarious seamen of his mess, and long silences had made him morose, driven him to despair at times. He had been saved by the transfer to the *Antigone* and a bigger ship's company. Among the pressed and drafted men who had increased the size of the ship's company to form the complement of a frigate, there had been those who knew nothing of his past. He had taught a few ignorant landsmen the rudiments of seamanship and there were those among the frigate's company that called him friend. He had drawn renewed confidence from this change in his circumstances. He let it be known among his new companions that he was well-acquainted with the business of navigation and that many of *Antigone*'s junior officers were wholly without knowledge of their trade. In particular Lord Wamlsley's studied contempt for the men combined with his rank and ignorance to make him an object of the most acute detestation to Waller.

On this particular morning, as Waller hauled wearily at the heavy loom of the stroke oar, his hatred of Walmsley reached its crisis. He muttered under his breath loudly enough for Walmsley and Gillespy to hear.

'Did you say something, Waller?'

Waller watched the blade of his oar swing forward, ignoring his lordship's question.

'I asked you what you said, Waller, damn you!'

Waller continued to pull steadily, gazing vaguely at the horizon.

'He didn't say nothing, sir,' the man occupying the same thwart said.

'I didn't ask you,' snapped Walmsley, fixing his eyes on Waller. 'This lubber, Mr Gillespy, needs watching. He was formerly the *skipper* of a damned whale-*boat* . . .' Walmsley laid a disparaging emphasis on the two words, 'a bloody merchant master who thought he could defy the King. And now God damn him he thinks he can defy you and I . . .'

Waller stopped rowing. The man behind him bumped into his stationary back and there was confusion in the boat.

'Give way, damn you!' Walmsley ordered, his voice low. Beside him little Gillespy was trembling. The oarsmen stopped rowing and the launch lost way.

'Go to the devil, you poxed young whoreson!' Waller snarled through clenched teeth. A murmur of approval at Waller's defiance ran through the boat's crew.

'Why you God-damn bastard!' Walmsley shoved Gillespy aside and pulled the heavy tiller from the rudder stock. In a single swipe he brought the piece of ash crashing into the side of Waller's skull, knocking him senseless, his grip on the oar-loom weakened and it swept up and struck him under the chin as he slumped into the bottom of the boat.

The expression on the faces of the launch's crew were of disbelief. Astern of them the towline drooped slackly in the water.

Drinkwater sat in the cool of his cabin re-reading a letter he had recently received from his wife Elizabeth, to see if he had covered all the points raised in it in his reply. The isolation of command had made the writing of his private journal and the committing of his thoughts to his letters an important and pleasurable part of his daily routine. Cruising so close to the English coast meant that Keith's ships were in regular contact with home via the admiral's dispatch-vessels. In addition to fresh vegetables and mail, these fast craft kept the frigates well supplied with newspapers and gossip. The hired cutter *Admiral Mitchell* had made such a delivery the day before.

He laid the letter down and picked up the new steel pen Elizabeth had sent him, dipping it experimentally in the ink-pot and regarding its rigid nib with suspicion. He pulled the half-filled sheet of paper towards him and resumed writing, not liking the awkward scratch and splatter of the nib compared with his goosequill, but aware that he would be expected to reply using the new-fangled gift.

Our presence in the Channel keeps Boney and his troops in their camps. Last week he held a review, lining his men up so that they presented an appearance several miles long . . .

He paused, not wishing to alarm Elizabeth, though from her letters he knew of the arrangements each parish was making to raise an invasion alarm and call out the militia and yeomanry.

It is said that Boney himself went afloat in a gilded barge and that he dismissed Admiral Bruix for attempting to draw a sword on him when he protested the folly of trying an embarkation in the teeth of a gale. What the truth of these rumours is I do not know, but it is certain that many men were drowned and some score or so of barges wrecked.

He picked up his pen and finished the letter, then he sanded, folded and sealed it. Mullender came into the cabin and, at a nod from Drinkwater, poured him a glass of wine. He leaned back contented. Beyond the cabin windows the Channel stretched blue, calm and glorious under sunshine. Through the stern windows the reflected light poured, dancing off the deckhead and bulkheads of the cabin and falling on the portraits of his family that hung opposite. He became utterly lost in the contemplation of his family.

His reverie was interrupted by a shouting on deck and a hammering at his cabin door.

Drinkwater sat in his best uniform, flanked by Lieutenant Rogers and Lieutenant Fraser. The black shapes of their three hats sat on the baize tablecloth, inanimate indications of formality. Before them, uncovered, stood Midshipman Lord Walmsley. Drinkwater looked at the notes he had written after examining Midshipman Gillespy. The boy had been terrified but Drinkwater and his two lieutenants had obtained the truth out of him, unwilling to make matters worse by having to consult individual members of the boat's crew. Gillespy had withdrawn now, let out before Walmsley was summoned to hear the surgeon's report.

Drinkwater had once entertained some hopes of the midshipman but this episode disgusted him. He himself had no personal feelings towards Waller beyond a desire to see him behave as any other pressed seaman on board and to see him treated as such. Walmsley knew of Waller's previous circumstances and Drinkwater assumed that this had led to his contemptuous behaviour.

He looked up at the young man. Walmsley did not appear unduly concerned about the formality of the present proceedings. Drinkwater recollected his acquaintance with Camelford and wondered if

69

Camelford's presence had set a portfire to this latent insolence and arrogance of Walmsley.

The silence of waiting hung heavily in the cabin. Following the incident in the launch, Drinkwater had had the boats hoisted inboard. Their progress to the west was no longer necessary since their chase, a lugger holding a breeze inshore, had long ago disappeared to the south-west. There was a knock at the door.

'Enter!'

'Come in, Mr Lallo. Pray take a seat and tell us what is the condition of Waller.'

The surgeon, a quiet, middle-aged man whose only vice seemed to be a messy reliance upon Sharrow's snuff, seated himself, sniffed and looked at Drinkwater. His didactic manner prompted Drinkwater to add: 'In words we all comprehend, if you please, Mr Lallo.'

Mr Lallo sniffed again. 'Well, sir,' he began, casting a meaningful look at the back of Lord Walmsley, 'the man Waller has taken a severe and violent blow with a heavy object . . .'

'A tiller,' put in Rogers impatiently.

'Just so, Mr Rogers. With a tiller, which has caused an aneurism . . . a distortion of the arteries and interrupted the flow of blood to the cere . . . to the brain . . .'

'You mean Waller's had a stroke?'

Lallo looked resentfully at Rogers and nodded. 'In effect, yes. He is reduced to the condition of an idiot.'

Drinkwater felt the particular meaning of the word in its real form. That Waller and his treason were no longer of any consequence struck him as an irony, but that a midshipman should have reduced him to that state by an over-indulgence of his authority was a reflection of his own powers of command. Drinkwater did not share Earl St Vincent's conviction that the men should respect a midshipman's coat if the object within was not worthy of their duty. He had always considered the training of his midshipmen a prime responsibility. With Walmsley he had failed. It did not matter that he had inherited his lordship from another captain. Nor, he reflected, could he hope that the processes of naval justice might redress something of the balance. The arrogance of well-connected midshipmen was nothing new in the navy, nor was the whitewashing of their guilt by courts-martial.

'Thank you, Mr Lallo. You do not entertain any hopes for Waller's eventual recovery then?'

'I doubt it, Captain Drinkwater. I believe him to have been a not unintelligent man, sir. He might be fit to attend the heads for the

remainder of his days, though he is like to be afflicted with ataxia.'
Lallo glared at the first lieutenant, defying him to require a further
explanation.

'Thank you, Mr Lallo. That will be all.'

After the surgeon had left, Drinkwater turned his full attention
upon Walmsley.

'Well, Mr Walmsley. Do you have anything to say?'

'I did my duty, sir. The man was insolent. I regret . . .'

'You *regret*! You regret hitting him so *hard*, I suppose. Eh?'

Walmsley swallowed. 'Yes, sir.'

'Lord Walmsley,' Drinkwater said, using the title for the first time,
'you are a young man with considerable ability, aware of your
position in society and clearly contemptuous of your present surroundings. It is my intention to punish you as you are a midshipman.
What you do after that as a gentleman is a matter for your own sense
of honour. You may go now.'

'May I not know my punishment?'

'No. You will be informed. Whatever you appear at the gaming
tables, you are, sir, only a midshipman on board this ship!'

Walmsley stood uncertainly and Drinkwater saw, for the first time,
signs that the young man's confidence was weakening. There was a
trembling about the mouth and a brightening of the eyes. Walmsley
turned away and the three officers watched him leave the cabin.

Next to him Drinkwater heard Lieutenant Fraser expel his breath
with relief. Drinkwater turned to him. 'Well, Mr Fraser, it is customary upon these occasions to ask the junior officer present to give his
opinion first.'

'Court-martial, sir . . .'

'But upon what charge, Fraser, for God's sake?' put in Rogers
intemperately and Drinkwater smelt the drink on him. 'No, sir, he's
too much influence for that. I doubt that'd do any of us any good.'
Rogers spoke with heavy emphasis and Drinkwater raised an eyebrow. 'Besides he's done no more than many, and Waller was an
insolent bastard at times. My advice, sir, is keep it in the ship.'

'Not a' bluidy mastheading, for God's sake, sir,' expostulated
Fraser who was showing signs of ability and perception far exceeding
the first lieutenant's.

'No, gentlemen,' Drinkwater cut in. 'Thank you both for your
opinions, so succinctly put,' he added drily. 'You are both right. The
matter should not go outside the ship, but I do not hold with officers
abusing their powers. Whatever Walmsley's expectations he is but a

71

midshipman, and a midshipman going to the bad. It is not my intention to encourage him further. As for his punishment, we shall marry him to the gunner's daughter.'

Drinkwater rose from the table and took up his hat. The two lieutenants scrambled to their feet.

'Pipe all hands to witness punishment, Mr Rogers!'

Drinkwater emerged on deck some few minutes later, the punishment book in his hand. It contained few entries since Drinkwater was reluctant to administer corporal punishment for any but serious offences and had adopted such measures as stoppage of grog and the wearing of a collar as a public humiliation, finding them much more appropriate and effective for the trivial offences usually committed. This morning, however, would be different.

He took his place at the head of the officers who stood in a half-circle, their swords by their sides. Behind them in three ranks, Mount's marines were paraded, a glittering assembly of scarlet, white and steel. The men were crowded in the waist, over the boats and the hammock nettings in the gangways. Word had got about that Walmsley was to be punished and the hands were in a state of barely suppressed glee. In the circumstances and in view of the offender's station, Drinkwater called him forward and read the usually curtailed preamble with formal gravity.

'Silence there!' barked Rogers as the hands murmured their delight when Walmsley stepped uncertainly forward. He had lost his cocksure attitude and was clearly very apprehensive. It occurred to Drinkwater that Walmsley might have imagined such a thing as this could never happen to him, that it was something that affected others not of his standing.

'Mr Walmsley, the enquiry held by myself and the officers of His Britannic Majesty's frigate under my command have examined and condemned your conduct this forenoon and found you guilty of behaviour both scandalous and oppressive. This crime, not being capital, shall be punished according to the Custom of the Navy under the Thirty-Sixth Article of War, as enacted by the King's most excellent Majesty, by and with the advice and consent of', Drinkwater paused and fixed his eyes on the abject Walmsley, 'the Lords Spiritual and Temporal and Commons in Parliament assembled.

'You are, Mr Walmsley, to be flogged over the breech of a gun.' He snapped the book closed. 'Mr Comley!' The boatswain stepped forward. 'Two dozen strokes, sir. And lay 'em on!'

Comley put his hand on Walmsley's shoulder and pushed him forward until he stood by the breech of one of the quarterdeck guns. A shove sent the young man over the cannon and Comley drew back his rattan. In the next few minutes the boatswain did not spare his victim.

Captain Drinkwater continued walking the windward side of the quarterdeck long after sunset. The blazing riot of scarlet had faded by degrees to a pale lemon yellow and finally to a duck-egg blue that remained slightly luminous as the stars in their constellations blazed overhead. The air remained warm although there was enough of a breeze to enable *Antigone* to be steered under her topsails, and she cruised slowly southwards.

Drinkwater thought over the events of the day, distressed by the incident in the boats and aware that he had dealt with it in the only just way. Walmsley had begged an interview with him which he had refused, and the sight of Waller lying inert in the care of Mr Lallo convinced him that he was right, that the longer the young man felt his punishment the better. Drinkwater sighed, worrying about the effect on the rest of the ship's company. The internal business of the ship was oppressing him, already the tedium of blockade, even in this relatively independent form of cruising, was making him irritable and the ship's company fractious. The fine summer weather and apparent inactivity of the French seemed to lend a quality of futility to their movements, although logic proclaimed the necessity of their presence, along with the other independent frigates and all the vessels of the various blockading squadrons. There was a quality of stalemate in the war and it was difficult to determine what would happen next. It seemed to Drinkwater that the equation was balanced, that even the weather, usually so impartial a player in the game, had assimilated some of this inertia and put no demands on his own skill or the energies of his people. It seemed an odd contrast to the previous summer when the changeable moods of the Greenland Sea kept them constantly about the business of survival.

He found himself longing for action. *Antigone* had missed the bombardment of Havre in late July and seen no more than some pedestrian chases after small fry which had achieved little. At the beginning of August had come the news that Admiral Ganteaume had attempted a break-out from Brest, but had turned back; so that the equation, showing for a moment signs of imbalance, had had its equilibrium re-established.

Drinkwater heard seven bells struck. Eleven o'clock. It was time he

73

took himself below. Mr Quilhampton, who had been confined to the lee quarterdeck in the down-draught from the main-topsail for his entire watch, looked after the retreating figure and clucked his tongue sympathetically.

'Poor fellow,' he muttered to himself, taking up the weather side and ordering Gillespy to heave the log, 'fretting over a pair of ne'er-do-wells!'

Orders

'All hands, ahoy! All hands, reef topsails!'

Drinkwater staggered as *Antigone* slammed into a sea. A burst of spray exploded over her weather bow and whipped aft, catching the officers on the quarterdeck in the face to induce the painful wind-ache in their cheeks. The equinox had found them at last and Drinkwater experienced a pang of sudden savage joy. He had been warned of the onset of the gale by the increasing ache in his neck and shoulder that pressaged damp weather. During the long, warm, dry days of that exceptional summer he had hardly been reminded of his wound, but now the illusions were gone, stripped aside in that first wet streak of winter that incommoded his officers and afforded him his amusement.

He clapped his hand to his hat as a gust more violent than hitherto laid the ship over. 'Mr Rogers!'

'Sir?'

'We'll reef in stays, Mr Rogers. See what the hands can do!' He saw Rogers's look of incredulity and grinned as the first lieutenant turned away.

'Hands, tack ship and reef topsails in one!' bawled Rogers through his speaking trumpet. It amused Drinkwater to see the variety of reactions his order provoked. Hill caught his eye with a twinkle, Quilhampton grinned in anticipation, while Lieutenant Fraser, still considering Drinkwater something of an enigma, looked suitably quizzical. The hands milled at their mustering points.

'Man the rigging! 'Way aloft, topmen!'

Drinkwater crossed the deck and stood by the helm. 'Keep her off the wind a half point, quartermaster.'

'Aye, aye, sir.'

Drinkwater felt the thrill of anticipation. There was no real need to put the ship upon the other tack at this precise moment, but the evolution of going about and reefing the topsails at the same moment was an opportunity for a smart frigate to demonstrate the proficiency of her ship's company. By the eagerness with which the topmen lay aloft, some of this had communicated itself to them. One could always count on an appeal to a professional seaman's skill.

'Deck there!' The masthead look-out was hailing. 'Sail four points on the weather bow, sir. Looks like a cutter!'

Drinkwater acknowledged the hail, his sense of satisfaction growing. They now had a reason for tacking and an audience, and Fraser was looking at Drinkwater as if wondering how he had known of the presence of the other vessel.

'Down helm!'

Next to Drinkwater the four men at the double wheel spun the spokes through their fingers. *Antigone* came upright as she turned into the wind, the rush of her forward advance slowed rapidly and the scream of the wind across her deck diminished.

'Clew down topsails! Mainsail haul! Trice up and lay out!'

This was the nub of the manoeuvre, for the main and mizen yards were hauled with the topmen upon them at the same moment as the topsail yards were lowered on their halliards, the braces tended, the bowlines slacked off and the reef-pendants hauled up. Apart from Drinkwater's orders to the helmsmen and the general commands to the deck conveying the progress of the manoeuvre, there was a host of subsidiary instructions given by the subordinate officers and petty officers at their stations at the pin rails, the braces, the halliards and in the bunts of the topsails aloft.

As the yards were lowered, the studding sail booms lifted and the main and mizen topsails flogged, folding upwards as the reef-pendants did their work. *Antigone* continued her turn, heeling over to her new course as the fore topsail came aback, spinning her head with increasing speed.

'Midships and meet her.' Drinkwater peered forward and upwards where he could see the foretopmen having the worst time of it, trying to reef their big topsail while it was still full of wind.

'Man the head-braces! Halliards there!'

Rogers watched for the hand signals of the mates and midshipmen aloft to tell him the earings were secured and the reef-points passed round the reduced portions of each topsail. Meanwhile *Antigone* crabbed awkwardly to leeward.

'Hoist away topsails! Haul all!'

Aloft the topsails rose again, stretched and reset, assuming the flat curve of sails close hauled against the wind as the forebraces hauled round their yards parallel with those on the main and mizen masts. On deck the halliards were sweated tight and the bowlines secured against the shivering of the weather leeches, belayed ropes were being coiled down and the topmen were sliding down the backstays,

76

chaffing each other competitively. *Antigone* stopped crabbing and began to drive forward again on the new tack. She butted into a sea and the spray came flying aft over the other bow.

'Steady,' Drinkwater ordered the helmsmen, peering into the binnacle at the compass bowl. 'Course Nor'west by west.'

'Steady, sir. Course Nor'west by west it is, sir.'

Rogers came aft and touched his hat. He was grinning back at Drinkwater. 'Ship put about on the larboard tack, sir, and all three topsails reefed in one.'

'Very creditable, Mr Rogers. Now you may pipe "Up spirits" and let us see what this cutter wants.'

Drinkwater glanced through the stern windows where the *Admiral Mitchell* danced in their wake. The lieutenant in command of her had luffed neatly under their lee quarter half an hour ago and skilfully tossed a packet of dispatches on board from her chains. She now lay waiting for him to digest the news they contained. He studied the written orders for some moments, put aside the private letters and newspapers, and summoned Lord Walmsley. To Drinkwater's regret Walmsley had not offered to resign, though Drinkwater knew he could afford to and had therefore taken steps to settle the midshipman elsewhere. The young man knocked and entered the cabin.

'Sir?' Walmsley had been rigidly formal since his punishment. The experience had been deeply engraved upon his consciousness, yet Drinkwater sensed beneath this formality a deep and abiding resentment. Walmsley was still not convinced that he had erred.

'Mr Walmsley, I have for some time been considering your future. I have been successful in obtaining for you another berth. Rear-Admiral Louis who has, as you know, hoisted his flag aboard the *Leopard* to assist Lord Keith in the Strait of Dover, has agreed to take you on board.'

Walmsley had clearly not expected such a transfer and Drinkwater hoped that he would be appreciative of it. 'I hope,' he added, 'that you are sensible of the honour done you by Admiral Louis. No word of your conduct has been communicated to the *Leopard*. You will join with a clean slate. Do you understand?'

'Sir.'

'Very good. We will transfer you to the cutter as soon as the sea allows a boat to be launched. You may pack your traps.'

Drinkwater stared after the midshipman. He felt he had failed to make an impression on the youth and he feared that Walmsley would

77

see that his sending him to a flagship only indicated his own lack of interest or influence.

It was two days before Walmsley departed, two days in which *Antigone* worked slowly south and west in obedience to her new orders. The formation of Rear-Admiral Louis's squadron had released her from her duties in the Channel and she was sent out to join Cornwallis and the Channel Fleet. Drinkwater greeted this news with mixed feelings. The close contact with the shore would be broken now, the arrival of mail less frequent and he would feel his isolation more. Nor was he very sure of the opinion Cornwallis had formed of him when they had last met. But his puritan soul derived that strange satisfaction from the anticipation of an arduous duty, and in his innermost heart he welcomed the change and the challenge.

It was two days, too, before he found the time to read the newspapers and mail. The most electrifying news for the officers and men of the *Antigone* was that war with Spain seemed imminent. Since the end of the Peace of Amiens 'neutral' Spanish ports had been shamelessly used by French warships. Their crews had enjoyed rights of passage through the country to join and leave their ships, and Spain had done everything to aid and abet her powerful and intimidating neighbour short of an actual declaration of war against Great Britain. Now the new British government had precipitated a crisis by sending out a flying squadron of four frigates to intercept a similar number of Spanish men-o'-war returning from Montevideo with over a million and a quarter in specie. Opposed by equal and not overwhelming force, the Spanish admiral, Don Joseph Bustamente, had defended the honour of his flag and in the ensuing action the Spanish frigate *Mercedes* had blown up with her crew and passengers. Although no immediate declaration of war had come from Madrid, it was hourly anticipated, and Drinkwater immediately calculated that the addition of the Spanish fleet to the French would augment it by over thirty ships of the line. They were superb ships too; one, the *Santissima Trinidad*, had four gun-decks and was the greatest ship in the world.

It was while reflecting on the possible consequences of Mr Pitt's aggressive new policy, and on whether it would enable the French Emperor to attempt invasion, that his eye fell upon another piece of news; a mere snippet of no apparent importance. Thomas Pitt, second Baron Camelford, had been killed in a duel near Holland House. The circumstances of the affair were confused, but what was of interest to

Drinkwater was that there was some veiled and unsubstantiated claims in the less respectable papers that Camelford's death had been engineered by French agents.

PART TWO

Break-Out

'I beg to inform your Lordship that the Port of Toulon has never been blockaded by me: quite the reverse – every opportunity has been offered to the Enemy to put to sea . . .'

NELSON TO THE LORD MAYOR OF LONDON   August 1804

'Sail, do not lose a moment, and with my squadrons reunited enter the Channel. England is ours. We are ready and embarked. Appear for twenty-four hours, and all will be ended.'

NAPOLEON TO ADMIRAL VILLENEUVE   August 1805

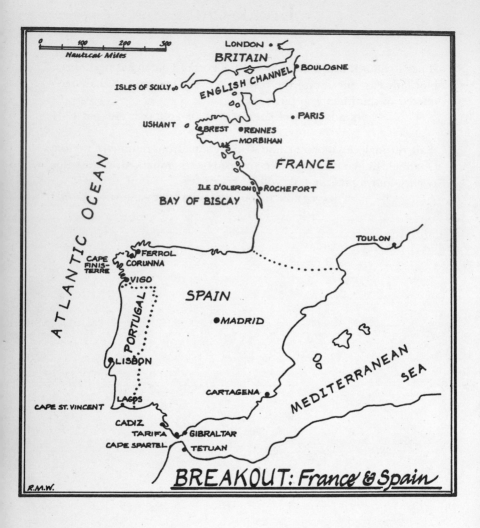

BREAKOUT: *France & Spain*

The Rochefort Squadron

'Signal from Flag, sir.' Midshipman Wickham's cheerful face poking round the door was an effront to Drinkwater's seediness as he woke from a doze.

'Eh? Well? What o'clock is it?'

'Four bells, sir,' Wickham said, then, seeing the captain's apparent look of incomprehension added, 'in the afternoon, sir.'

'Thank you, Mr Wickham' said Drinkwater drily, now fully awake. 'I shall be up directly.'

They had received and acknowledged the signal by the time Drinkwater reached the quarterdeck. Lieutenant Fraser handed him the slate as he touched his hat. Drinkwater had grown to like the ruddy Scotsman with his silent manner and dry humour. Drinkwater read the message scribbled on the slate. Midshipman Wickham was already copying it out into the Signal Log.

'Very well, Mr Fraser, we will close on *Doris* and see if Campbell has any specific orders for us. In the meantime watch the admiral for further signals.'

'Aye, sir.'

Drinkwater eased his right shoulder. Of all the stations to be consigned to during the winter months, the west coast of France with its damp procession of gales was possibly the worst for his wound. He drew the cloak closer around him and began to pace the deck, from the hance to the taffrail, casting an eye across the grey, white-streaked waves that separated him from the rest of the squadron. He watched the half-dozen ships of Rear-Admiral Sir Thomas Graves jockeying into line ahead, their yards braced up on the larboard tack as they began to move away to the north-north-westwards and the shelter of Quiberon Bay where they were to take in stores and water.

The two frigates *Doris* and *Antigone*, being late arrivals at this outpost of the Channel Fleet, were left to watch Rear-Admiral Missiessy's ships anchored off Rochefort, in the shelter of the Basque Roads. Drinkwater turned his attention to the eastwards. On the horizon he could make out the blue blur of the Ile d'Oléron behind which the French squadron was anchored, comfortably secure under the lee of the island, the approach of its mooring blocked by batteries.

He had reconnoitred them several times, sailing *Antigone* under the guns of the French batteries and carrying out manoeuvres between Oléron and the surrounding islands. It was, he admitted to himself a piece of *braggadocio*; but it was good for the men, enabling them to demonstrate before the eyes of the French their abilities. Best of all, it broke the monotony of blockade duty. They had received fire from the land batteries and from the floating battery the enemy had anchored off Oléron which mounted huge heavy mortars and long cannon of the heaviest calibres, together with furnaces for heating shot. Beyond the batteries they had counted the ships of Missiessy's squadron anchored in two neat lines. They appeared so securely moored that their situation seemed permanent, but Drinkwater knew that this was an illusion. There were French squadrons like Missiessy's in all the major French and Spanish ports, joined now, since the declaration of war against Great Britain, by the splendid ships of the Spanish navy. Nor were they entirely supine. Missiessy had sortied in the previous August, only being turned back by the appearance of Vice-Admiral Sir Robert Calder with a stronger force. From the Texel to Toulon the naval forces of the enemy were now united under the imperial eagle of France. Against this mass of shipping the British blockade was maintained unrelentingly. The ships of Keith, Cornwallis, Calder, Collingwood and Nelson watched each of the enemy ports, detaching squadrons like that of Graves's to close up the gaps.

Now that Graves had been driven off his station for want of the very necessaries of life itself, the Rochefort squadron of Missiessy was checked by the rather feeble presence of a pair of 36-gun frigates, *Antigone* and *Doris*.

'*Doris* signalling, sir.'

'Ah, I rather thought she might.' Drinkwater waited patiently while his people did their work and deciphered the numerical signal streaming from *Doris*'s lee yardarms. As senior officer it was up to Campbell of the *Doris* to decide how best to carry out their duties. Drinkwater listened to the dialogue between Wickham and Frey as the import of Campbell's intentions became clear.

'One-two-two.'

'Permission to part company . . .'

'Eight-seven-three.'

'To . . .'

'Seven-six-six.'

'See . . .'

'Two-four-nine.'

84

'Enemy . . . er, "Permission to part company to see enemy", sir.'

'Very well, Mr Frey. Thank you. You may lay me a course, Mr Fraser. Shake out the fore-course, if you please, let us at least give the impression of attending to our duty with alacrity.'

'Verra well, sir.' Fraser grinned back at the captain. He was beginning to like this rather stern Englishman.

Drinkwater woke in the darkness of pre-dawn with the conviction that something was wrong. He listened intently, fully awake, for some sound in the fabric of the ship that would declare its irregularity. There was nothing. They had reduced sail at the onset of the early January darkness and hove-to. Their leeway during the night should have put them between Oléron and the Ile de Ré at dawn, in a perfect position to reconnoitre Missiessy's anchorage with all the daylight of the short January day to beat offshore again. The westerly wind had dropped after sunset and it was inconceivable that their leeway had been excessive, even allowing for the tide.

Then it occurred to him that the reason for his awakening was something entirely different; his shoulder had stopped aching. He smiled to himself in the darkness, stretched luxuriously and rolled over, composing himself for another hour's sleep before duty compelled him to rise. And then suddenly he was wide awake, sitting bolt upright in his cot. An instant later he was feeling for his breeches, stockings and shoes. He stumbled across the cabin in his haste, fumbling for the clean shirt that Mullender should have left. If his shoulder was not aching it meant the air was drier. And if the air was drier it meant only one thing, the wind was hauling to the eastward. He pulled on his coat, wound a muffler around his neck to suppress the quinsy he had felt coming on for several days and, pulling on his cloak, went on deck.

The dozing sentry jerked to attention at this untimely appearance of the captain. As he emerged, Drinkwater knew immediately his instinct was right. Above the tracery of the mastheads the stars were coldly brilliant, the cloudy overcast of yesterday had vanished. A figure detached itself from the group around the binnacle. It was Quilhampton.

'Morning, sir. A change in the weather. Dead calm for the last half-hour and colder.'

'Why did you not call me, Mr Q?' asked Drinkwater with sudden asperity.

'Sir? But sir, your written orders said to call you if the wind freshened . . . I supposed that you were concerned with an increase in our leeway, sir, not . . . not a calm, sir. The ship is quite safe, sir.'

'Damn it, sir, don't patronise me!'

'I beg pardon, sir.' Even in the darkness Quilhampton was obviously crestfallen.

Drinkwater took a turn or two up and down the deck. He realised that the wind had not yet got up, that his apprehensions were not yet fully justified. 'Mr Q!'

'Sir?'

'Forgive my haste, Mr Q.'

'With pleasure, sir. But I assure you, sir, that I would have called you the instant I thought that the ship was in any danger.'

'It is not the ship that concerns me, James. It is the enemy!'

'The enemy, sir?'

'Yes, the enemy. In an hour from now the wind will be easterly and in two hours from now Missiessy, if he's half the man I think him to be, will be ordering his ships to sea. Now d'you understand?'

'Yes . . . yes I do. I'll have the watch cast loose the t'gallants ready to set all sail the moment it's light, sir.'

'That's the spirit. And I'll go below and break my fast. I've a feeling that this will be a long day.'

Over his spartan breakfast of skillygolee, coffee and toast, Drinkwater thought over the idea that had germinated from the seeds sown during his extraordinary conversation with Mr Pitt. He knew that he would not consciously have reasoned a grand strategy for the French by himself, but that game of shuttlecock with ideas at Walmer had produced the only convincing answer to the conundrum of Napoleon's intentions. It was clear that the French would now move their vast armies across the Channel until they had a fleet in the vicinity. Now, with Admiral Ver Huell's Dutch ships joining a Combined Franco–Spanish fleet, the preposterous element of such a grand design was diminishing. Drinkwater did not attempt to unravel the reasoning behind Pitt's deliberate provocation of Spain. It seemed only to undermine the solid foundation of Britain's defence based upon the Channel Fleet off Brest and the understanding that, if the enemy they blockaded escaped, then every British squadron fell back upon the chops of the Channel. In this grand strategy there still remained the factor of the unexpected. Navigationally the mouth of the Channel was difficult to make, particularly when obstructed by an enemy fleet. For the French Commander-in-Chief a passage round

Scotland offered nothing but advantages: prevailing fair winds, a less impeded navigation, the element of surprise and the greater difficulty for the British of watching his movements. In addition the fleets of other nations could be more readily added. Russia, for instance, still not wholly committed to defying the new Emperor of France, perhaps the Danes, and certainly the Dutch. Worst of all was the consideration that the enemy might be in the Strait of Dover while the British waited for them off the Isles of Scilly. And the only place from which to launch such an attack was the West Indies, where the French might rendezvous, blown there by favourable winds to recuperate and revictual from friendly islands.

Nathaniel Drinkwater was not given to flights of wild imagination. He was too aware of the difficulties and dangers that beset every seaman. But during his long years of service intuition and cogent reasoning had served him well. He was reminded of the weary weeks of stalking the Dutch before Camperdown and how conviction of the accuracy of his forebodings had sustained him then. He called Mullender to clear the table and while he waited for the wind to rise he opened his journal, eager to get down this train of logic which had stemmed from some dim perception that lingered from his strange awakening.

8th January, he wrote, and added carefully, aware that he had still not become accustomed to the new year, *1805. Off the Ile d'Oléron in a calm. Woke with great apprehension that the day* ... He paused, scratched out the last word and added: *year is pregnant with great events* ...

'If you are going to record your prophecies,' he muttered to himself, pleased with his improving technique with Elizabeth's pen, 'you might as well make 'em big ones.'

It seems to me that a descent upon the British Isles might best be achieved by the French in first making a rendezvous ...

But he got no further. There was a knock at the cabin door and Midshipman Wickham reappeared.

'Lieutenant Quilhampton's compliments, sir, and the wind's freshening from the east.'

The wind did not keep its early promise. By noon *Antigone* lay becalmed off the Ile d'Oléron, in full view of the French anchorage and with the tide setting her down towards the Basque Road; at one in the afternoon she had been brought to her anchor and Drinkwater was studying the enemy through his glass from the elevation of the mizen top. Beside him little Mr Gillespy was making notes at the captain's dictation.

'The usual force, Mr Gillespy: *Majestueux*, four seventy-fours, the three heavy frigates and two brig-corvettes. Nothing unusual in that, eh?' he said kindly.

'No, sir,' the boy squeaked, somewhat nonplussed at finding himself aloft with the captain. Gillespy had not supposed captains ascended rigging. It did not seem part of their function.

'But what makes today of more than passing interest,' Drinkwater continued, mouthing his words sideways as he continued to stare through the glass, 'is that they are taking aboard stores . . . d'you have that, Mr Gillespy?'

'Stores,' the boy wrote carefully, 'yes, sir.'

'Troops . . .'

'Troops . . . yes, sir.'

'And, Mr Gillespy,' Drinkwater paused. The cloudless sky let sunlight pour down upon the stretch of blue water between the green hills of the island and the main. The brilliantly clear air made his task easy and the sunlight glanced off the dull breeches of cannon. There was no doubt in Drinkwater's mind that Missiessy was going to break out to the West Indies and take back those sugar islands over which Britain and France had been squabbling for two generations. 'Artillery, Mr Gillespy, artillery . . . one "t" and two "ll"'s.'

He closed his glass with a snap and turned his full attention to the boy. He was not so very many years older than his own son, Richard.

'What d'you suppose we'd better do now, eh?'

'Tell the admiral, sir?'

'First class, my boy.' Drinkwater swung himself over the edge of the top and reached for the futtocks with his feet. He began to descend, pausing as his head came level with the deck of the top. Gillespy regarded the captain's apparently detached head with surprise.

'I think, Mr Gillespy, that in the coming months you may see things to tell your grandchildren about.'

Midshipman Gillespy stared at the empty air where the captain's head had just been. He was quite bewildered. The idea of ever having grandchildren had never occurred to him.

The wind freshened again at dusk, settling to a steady breeze and bringing even colder air off the continent. *Antigone* stood offshore in search of *Doris* and, at dawn on the 9th, Drinkwater spoke to Campbell, informing him of the preparations being made by the

French. Two hours later *Antigone* was alone apart from the distant topgallants of *Doris* in the north, as Campbell made off to warn Graves.

'Full and bye, Mr Hill, let us stop up that gap. I mislike those cloud banks building up over the land. We may not be able to stop the Frogs getting out but, by God, we must not lose touch with 'em.'

'Indeed not, sir.'

The wind continued light and steady throughout the day and at dawn on the 10th they were joined by the schooner *Felix* commanded by Lieutenant Richard Bourne, brother of Drinkwater's late lieutenant of the *Melusine*. Bourne announced that he had met Campbell and told him of Graves's whereabouts. Campbell had ordered *Felix* to stand by *Antigone* and act under Drinkwater's directions as a dispatchboat in the event of Graves not turning up in time to catch Missiessy. Having an independent means of communicating such intelligence as he might glean took a great deal of weight off Drinkwater's mind. He had only to hang onto Missiessy's skirts now, and with such a smart ship and a crew tuned to the perfection expected of every British cruiser, he entertained few worries upon that score.

As the day wore on, the wind began to increase from the east and by nightfall was a fresh breeze. Drinkwater stretched out on his cot, wrapped in his cloak, and slept fitfully. An hour before dawn he was awakened and struggled on deck in a rising gale. As daylight grew it revealed a sky grey with lowering cloud. It was bitterly cold. The islands were no longer green, they were grey and dusted with snow. In the east the sky was even more threatening, leaden and greenish. Aloft the watch were shortening down, ready for a whole gale by midmorning. Drinkwater was pleased to see Rogers already on deck.

'Don't like the smell of it, sir.'

'Happen you're right, Sam. What worries me more is what our friends are doing.'

'Sitting Quiberon (he pronounced it 'Key-ber-ron') hoisting in fresh vittals.'

'I ken the Captain means the French,' put in Lieutenant Fraser joining them and reporting the first reef taken in the topsails. Fraser ignored Rogers's jaundiced look.

Drinkwater levelled his glass at the north point of Oléron. 'I do indeed, gentlemen, and here they are!'

The two officers looked round. Beyond the point of the island the white rectangles of topsails were moving as Missiessy's frigates led his squadron to sea.

'Mr Frey!'

'Sir?'

'Make to *Felix*, three-seven-zero.'

Drinkwater ignored Rogers's puzzled frown but heard Fraser mutter in his ear, 'Enemy coming out of port.'

A few minutes later the little schooner was scudding to the north-west with the news for Graves, or Campbell, or whoever else would take alarm from the intelligence.

'Heave the ship to, Mr Rogers. Let us see what these fellows are going to do.' He again raised the glass to his eye and intently studied the approaching enemy. The heavy frigates led out first. Bigger than *Antigone*, though not dissimilar in build, he tried to identify them, calling for Mr Gillespy, his tablet and pencil.

'And clear the ship for action, Mr Rogers. Beat to quarters if you please!'

He ignored the burst of activity, concentrating solely on the enemy. He recognised the *Infatigable*, so similar in name to Pellew's famous frigate. All three frigates seemed to be holding back, not running down upon the solitary *Antigone* as Drinkwater had expected. He could afford to hold his station for a little longer. Ah, there were the little brig-corvettes, exact replicas of the *Bonaparte*. He counted the gun-ports; yes, eight a side, 16-gun corvettes all right. But then came the battleships, with Missiessy's huge three-decked 120-gun flagship, the *Majestueux* in the van. He heard the whistles of surprise from the hands now at their action stations and grinned to himself. This was what they had all been waiting for.

Astern of the *Majestueux* came four 74-gun battleships. All were now making sail as they altered course round the point, and fore-shortened towards *Antigone*. One of the seventy-fours was detaching, moving out of line. He watched intently, sensing that this movement had something to do with himself. As the battleship drew ahead of the others the frigates made sail and within a few minutes all four leading ships were racing towards him, the gale astern of them and great white bones in their teeth. He shut his telescope with a snap and dismissed Gillespy to his action station. Hill and Rogers were staring at him expectantly.

'Hoping to make a prize of us, I believe,' Drinkwater said. 'Put the ship before the wind, Mr Hill.'

The helm came up and *Antigone* turned away. The braces clicked through the blocks as the yards swung on their parrels about the slushed topmasts and the apparent wind over the deck diminished. As

90

the frigate steadied on her course, Drinkwater raised his glass once more.

Led by the seventy-four, the French ships were overhauling them rapidly. Drinkwater looked carefully at the relative angles between them. He longed to know the names and exact force of each of his antagonists and felt a sudden thrill after all the long months of waiting and worrying. For Drinkwater such circumstances were the mainspring of his being. The high excitement of handling an instrument as complex, as deadly, yet as vulnerable as a ship of war, in a gale of wind and with a superior enemy to windward, placed demands upon him that acted like a drug. For his father and brother the love of horseflesh and speed had provided the anodyne to the frustrations and disappointments of life; but for him only this spartan and perilous existence would do. This was the austere drudgery of his duty transformed into a dangerous art.

He looked astern once more. Beyond the advancing French division the remaining French ships had disappeared. A great curtain of snow was bearing down upon them, threatening to obscure everything.

The Snowstorm

Drinkwater stepped forward and held out his hand for Rogers's speaking trumpet. As *Antigone* scudded before the wind he could make himself understood with little difficulty.

'D'you hear, there! Pay attention to all my orders and execute them promptly. No one shall fire until I order it. All guns are to double shot and load canister on ball. All gun-captains to see their pieces aimed before they fire. I want perfect silence at all times. Any man in breach of this will have a check shirt.' He paused to let his words sink in. An excited cheer or shout might transform his intended audacity into foolhardiness. 'Very well, let us show these shore-squatting Frogs what happens to 'em when they come to sea. Lieutenant Quilhampton!'

'Sir?'

'Abandon your guns for the moment, Mr Q. I want you on the fo'c's'le head listening. If you hear anything, indicate with your arm the direction of the noise as you do when signalling the anchor cable coming home.'

'Aye, aye, sir.'

Drinkwater turned to the sailing master. 'Well, Mr Hill, take a bearing of that French seventy-four and the instant the snow shuts him from view, heave the ship to. In the meantime try and lay us in his track.'

Hill turned away and peered over the taffrail, returning to the binnacle to order an alteration of course to the north. Drinkwater also turned to watch the approaching French. He was only just in time to catch a glimpse of them before they vanished. They were well clear of the land now, catching the full fury of the gale and feeling the effects of carrying too much canvas in their eagerness to overtake *Antigone*. Then they were gone, hidden behind a white streaked curtain of snow that second by second seemed to cut off the edge of their world in its silent approach.

'Now, Hill! Now!'

'Down helm! Main-braces there! Leggo and haul!' *Antigone* began to turn back into the wind. As men hauled in on the fore and mizen braces to keep the frigate sailing on a bowline, the main-yards were backed against the wind, opposing the action of the other masts and checking her, so she lay in wait for the oncoming French. *Antigone* turned his attention to Quilhampton who had clambered up into the knightheads and had one ear cocked into the wind. *Antigone* bucked in the rising sea, her way checked and every man standing silent at his post.

' 'Tis a wonderful thing, discipline,' he heard Hill mutter to Rogers, and the first lieutenant replied with characteristic enthusiasm, 'Aye, for diabolical purposes!' And then the snow began to fall upon the deck.

'Keep the decks wet with sea-water, Mr Rogers. Get the firemen to attend to it.' He had not thought of the dangers of slush. Men losing their footing would imperil the success of his enterprise and wreak havoc when they opened fire. The snow seemed to deaden all noise so that the ship rose and fell like a ghost as minute succeeded minute. Drinkwater walked forward to the starboard hance. He wondered what the odds were upon them being run down. Even if they were, he consoled himself, mastering the feeling of rising panic that always preceeded action, they would seriously jeopardise *Missiessy's* escape and the Admiralty would approve of that.

'Sir!' Quilhampton's voice hissed with urgent sibilance and he looked up to see the lieutenant's iron hook pointing off to starboard. For an instant Drinkwater hesitated, his mind uncertain. Then he heard shouting, the creak of rigging and the hiss of a bow wave. The shouting was not urgent, they themselves were undetected, but on board the Frenchman petty officers were lambasting an unpractised crew. And then he saw the ship, looking huge and black, the white patches of her sails invisible in the snow.

'Main-braces!' he hissed with violent urgency. 'Up helm!'

Drinkwater had no alternative but to risk being raked by the Frenchman's broadside. If the crew of the enemy battleship were at their guns, a single discharge would cripple the British frigate. But he hoped fervently that they would not see *Antigone* in so unexpected a place; that the novelty of being at sea would distract their attention inboard where, he knew, a certain amount of confusion was inevitable after so long a period at anchor. Besides, he could not risk losing control of his ship by attempting to tack from a standing start. Hove-to with no forward motion, *Antigone* would jib at passing through the wind and probably be caught 'in irons'.

A group of marines were at the spanker brails, hauling in the big after-sail as *Antigone* turned, gathering way and answering her helm.

At the knightheads Quilhampton's raised arm indicated he still had contact with the enemy. They steadied the ship dead before the wind. Drinkwater went forward to stand beside Quilhampton and listen. The frigate was scending in the following sea and Drinkwater knew the wind, already at gale force, had not finished rising. If he was to achieve anything it would have to be soon. He strained his ears to hear. Above the creak of *Antigone*'s fabric and the hiss and surge of her bow-wave he caught the muffled sound of orders, orders passed loudly and with some urgency as though the giver of those instructions was anxious, and the recipients slow to comprehend. There were a few words he recognised: '*Vite! Vite!*' and '*Allez!*' and the obscenity '*Jean-Foutre!*' of some egalitarian officer in the throes of frustration. And then suddenly he saw the flat surface of the huge stern with its twin rows of stern windows looming through the snow. Drinkwater raced aft.

'Stand by larbowlines! Give her the main course!'

Then they could all see the enemy as a sudden rent in the snow opened up a tiny circle of sea. The gun-captains were frantically spiking their guns round to aim on the bow and Drinkwater looked up to see an officer on the battleship's quarter. He was waving his hat at them and shouting something.

'By God, he thinks we're one of his own frigates come too close!'

Drinkwater watched the relative angles between the two ships. There was a great flogging and rattle of blocks as the main clew-garnets were let run and the waisters hauled down the tacks and sheets of the main-course. The relative angle began to open and someone on the French battleship realised his mistake.

He heard someone scream '*Merde!*' and ordered *Antigone*'s course altered to starboard. Standing by the larboard hance he screwed up one eye.

'Fire!'

The blast and roar of the guns rolled over them, the thunderous climax of Drinkwater's mad enterprise. The yellow flashes from the cannon muzzles were unnaturally bright in the gloom as the snow closed round them once again. He caught a glimpse of the enemy's name in large gilt roman script across her stern: *Magnanime*.

The smoke from the guns hung in the air, drifting forward slowly then suddenly gone, whipped away. The gunners were swabbing, reloading and hauling out, holding up their hands when they were ready. The sound of enemy guns barked out of the obscurity and they were alone again, shut into their own tiny world, and the snow was

94

falling thicker than ever.

'Fire!' yelled Rogers and the second broadside was discharged into the swirling wraiths of white. *Antigone*'s deck took a sudden cant as her stern lifted and she drove violently forward. Down went her bow, burying itself to the knightheads, a great cushion of white water foaming up around her.

'Too much canvas, sir!' yelled Hill. Drinkwater nodded.

'Secure the guns and shorten down!'

It took the combined efforts of fifty men to furl the mainsail. The huge, unreefed sail, set to carry them alongside the *Magnanime*, threatened to throw them off the yard as they struggled. In the end Lieutenant Fraser went aloft and the great sail was tamed and the process repeated with the fore-course. At the end of an hour's labour *Antigone* had hauled her yards round and lay on the starboard tack, her topsails hard reefed and her topgallant masts sent down as the gale became a storm and Drinkwater edged her north to report the break-out of Missiessy and the fact that he had lost contact with the enemy in the snow and violent weather.

Antigone was able to hold her new course for less than an hour. Laughing and chaffing each other, the watch below had been piped down when they were called again. Drinkwater regained the deck to find the wind chopping rapidly round, throwing up a high, breaking and confused sea that threw the ship over and broke on board in solid green water. For perhaps fifteen minutes the wind dropped, almost to a calm while the snow continued to fall. The ship failed to answer her helm as she lost way. The men milled about in the waist and the officers stood apprehensive as they tried to gauge the new direction from which the wind would blow. A few drops of rain fell, mingled with wet snow flakes.

'Sou'wester!' Hill and Drinkwater shouted together. 'Stand by! Man the braces!'

It came with the unimaginable violence that only seamen experience. The squall hit *Antigone* like a gigantic fist, laying her sails aback, tearing the fore-topsail clean from its bolt ropes and away to leeward like a lost handkerchief. The frigate lay over under the air pressure in her top-hamper and water bubbled in through her closed gun-ports. From below came the crash and clatter of the mess kids and coppers on the galley stove, together with a ripe torrent of abuse hurled at the elements by the cook and his suddenly eloquent mates.

'Lee braces, there!' Look lively my lads! Aloft and secure that raffle!'

95

With a thunderous crack and a tremble that could be felt through-out the ship the main-topmast sprang at the instant the main-topsail also blew out of its bolt ropes, and then the first violent spasm of the squall was past and the wind steadied, blowing at a screaming pitch as they struggled to bring the bucking ship under control again.

The gale blew for several days. The rain gave way to mist and the mist, on the morning of the 15th, eventually cleared. On the horizon to the north Drinkwater and Hill recognised the outline of the Ile d'Yeu and debated their next move. *Felix* must by now have com-municated the news of Missiessy's break-out to Graves, in which case Graves would have withdrawn towards Cornwallis off Ushant. But supposing something had happened to Bourne and the *Felix*? After such an easterly wind Graves would be worried that Missiessy had gone, and gone at a moment when, through sheer necessity, his own back had been turned. Graves would have returned to Rochefort and might be waiting there now, unable to get close inshore to see into the Basque Road, for fear of the continuing gale catching him on a lee shore.

'He'd be locking the stable door after the horse had gone,' said Hill reflectively.

'Quite so,' replied Drinkwater. 'And we could fetch the Ile de Ré on one tack under close-reefed topsails to clarify the situation. If Graves is not there we will have lost but a day in getting to Cornwallis. Very well,' Drinkwater made up his mind, clapped his hand over his hat and fought to keep his footing on the tilting deck. 'Course south-east, let us look into the Basque Road and see if Graves has regained station.'

On the morning of the 16th they found Graves off the Ile d'Oléron having just been informed by the *Felix* of Missiessy's departure. In his search for the admiral, Bourne had also run across the French squadron heading north. During a long morning of interminable flag hoists it was established that this encounter had occurred after Drinkwater's brush with the enemy and therefore established that Missiessy's task was probably to cause trouble in Ireland. This theory was lent particular force by Drinkwater's report that troops were embarked. It was a tried strategy of the French government and the signalling system was not capable of conveying Drinkwater's theory about the West Indies. In truth, on that particular morning, with the practical difficulties in handling the ship and attending to the admiral, Drinkwater himself was not over-confident that he was right. Besides, there was other news that permeated the squadron during that blustery morning, news more closely touching themselves. In getting into Quiberon Bay to warn Graves, the *Doris* had found the admiral already gone. Struggling seawards again, *Doris* had struck a rock and, after great exertions by Campbell and his people, had foundered. *Felix* had taken off her crew and all were safe, but the loss of so fine a frigate and the escape of Missiessy cast a shadow over the morale of the squadron. Afterwards Drinkwater was to remember that morning as the first of weeks of professional frustration; when it seemed that providence had awarded its laurels to the Imperial eagle of France, that despite the best endeavours of the Royal Navy, the weeks of weary and remorseless blockade, the personal hardships of every man-jack and boy in the British fleet, their efforts were to come to naught.

But for the time being Graves's squadron had problems of its own. The morning of signalling had thrown them to leeward and in the afternoon they were unable to beat out of the bay and compelled to anchor. When at last the weather moderated, Graves reported to Cornwallis, only to find Sir William in ailing health, having himself been driven from his station to shelter in Torbay. For a while the ships exchanged news and gossip. Cornwallis was said to have requested replacement, while it was known that Admiral Latouche-Tréville had died at Toulon and been replaced by Admiral Villeneuve, the only French flag-officer to have escaped from Nelson's devastating attack in Aboukir Bay. Of what had happened to Missiessy no one was quite sure, but it was certain that he had not gone to Ireland. A few weeks later it was common knowledge that he had arrived at Martinique in the West Indies.

The Look-Out Frigate

'Well, Mr Gillespy, you seem to be making some progress.' Drinkwater closed the boy's journal. 'Your aunt would be pleased, I'm sure,' he added wryly, thinking of the garrulous Mistress MacEwan. 'I have some hopes of you making a sea-officer.'

'Thank you, sir.' The boy looked pleased. He had come out of his shell since the departure of Walmsley, and Drinkwater knew that Frey had done much to protect him from the unimaginative and over-bearing Glencross. He also knew that James Quilhampton kept a close eye on the boy, ever mindful of Gillespy's relationship with Catriona MacEwan; while Lieutenant Fraser lost no opportunity to encourage a fellow Scot among the bear-pit of Sassenachs that made up the bulk of the midshipmen's berth. He was aware that he had been staring at the boy for too long and smiled.

'I trust you are quite happy?' he asked, remembering again how this boy reminded him of his own son. He should not care for Richard Madoc to go to sea with a man who did not take some interest in him.

'Oh yes, sir.'

'Mmmm.' The removal of Walmsley's influence charged that short affirmative with great significance. Drinkwater remembered his own life in the cockpit. It had not been happy.

'Very well, Mr Gillespy. Cut along now, cully.'

The boy turned away, his hat tucked under his arm, the small dirk in its gleaming brass scabbard bouncing on his hip. The pity of his youth and circumstance hit Drinkwater like a blow. The boy's account of the action with the *Magnanime* read with all the fervent patriotism of youth. There was much employment of unworthy epithets. The *Frogs* had *run from the devastating* (spelt wrongly) *thunder of our glorious cannon*. It was the language of London pamphleteers, a style that argued a superiority of ability Drinkwater did not like to see in one so young. It was not Gillespy's fault, of course; he was subject to the influence of his time. But Drinkwater had suffered enough reverses in his career to know the folly of under-estimation.

The *Magnanime* had been commanded by Captain Allemand, he had discovered, one of the foremost French naval officers. It was too easy to assume that because the major part of their fleets was blockaded in harbour they were not competent seamen. With Missiessy's squadron at sea, several hundred Frenchmen would be learning fast, to augment the considerable number of French cruisers already out. Drinkwater sighed, rose and poured himself a glass of blackstrap. He was at a loss to know why he was so worried. There were captains and admirals senior to him whose responsibilities far exceeded his own. All he had to do was to patrol his cruising area, one of a cloud of frigates on the look-out for any enemy movements, who linked the major units of the British fleet, ready to pass news, to pursue or strike at enemy cruisers, and hold the Atlantic seaboard of France and Spain under a constant vigilance.

It was all very well, Drinkwater ruminated, in theory. But the practicalities were different as the events of January had shown. To the east the French Empire was under the direction of a single man. Every major military and naval station was in contact with Napoleon, whose policy could be quickly disseminated by interior lines of communication. No such factors operated in Great Britain's favour. Britain was standing on the defensive. She had no army to speak of and what she had of one was either policing the raw new industrial towns of the Midlands or preparing to go overseas on some madcap expedition to the east under Sir James Craig. Her government was shaky and the First Lord of the Admiralty, Lord Melville, was to be impeached for corruption. Her dispersed fleets were without quick communication, every admiral striving to do his best but displaying that fatal weakness of disagreement and dislike that often ruined the ambitions of the mighty. Orde, off Cadiz, hated Nelson, off Toulon, and the sentiment was returned with interest. Missiessy at sea was bad enough (and Drinkwater still smarted from a sense of failure to keep contact with the French, despite the weather at the time), but the spectre of more French battleships at sea worried every cruiser commander. With that thought he poured a second glass of wine. He doubted Ganteaume would get out of Brest, but Gourdon might give Calder the slip at Ferrol, and Villeneuve might easily get past Nelson with his slack and provocative methods. And that still left the Spanish out of the equation. They had ships at Cartagena and Cadiz, fine ships too . . .

His train of thought was interrupted by a knock at the cabin door. 'Enter!'

Rogers came in followed by Mr Lallo. There was enough in the expressions on their faces to know that they brought bad news. 'What is it, gentlemen?'

'It's Waller, sir . . .'

'He had a bad fit this morning, sir,' put in Lallo, 'I had confined him to a strait-jacket, sir, but he got loose, persuaded some accomplice to let him go.' Lallo paused.

'And?'

'He went straight to the galley, sir, picked up a knife and slashed both his wrists. He was dead by the time I'd got to him.'

'Good God.' A silence hung in the cabin. Drinkwater thought of Waller defying him at Nagtoralik Bay and of how far he had fallen. 'Who let him go?'

'One of his damned whale-men, I shouldn't wonder,' said Rogers.

'Yes. That is likely. I suppose he may still have commanded some influence over them. There is little likelihood that we will discover who did it, Mr Lallo.'

The surgeon shrugged. 'No, sir. Well he's dead now and fit only for the sail-maker to attend.'

'You had better see to it, Mr Rogers.'

It was one of the ironies of the naval service, Drinkwater thought as he stood by the pinrail where the fore-sheet was belayed, that a man killed honourably in battle might be hurriedly shoved through a gun-port to avoid incommoding his mates as they plied their murderous trade, while a man whose death was as ignominious as Waller's, was attended by all the formal pomp of the Anglican liturgy. Casting his eyes over *Antigone*'s assembled crew, the double irony hit him that only a few would be even vaguely familiar with his words. The half-dozen negroes, three Arabs and sixty Irishmen might even resent their being forced to witness a rite that, in Waller's case, might be considered blasphemous. He doubted any of the others, the Swede, Norwegians, three renegade Dutchmen and Russians, understood the words. Nevertheless he ploughed on, raising his voice as he read from Elizabeth's father's Prayer Book.

'We therefore commit . . .' he nodded at the burial party who raised the board upon which Waller's corpse lay stiffly sewn into his hammock under the ensign, 'his body to the deep . . .'

The prayer finished he closed the book and put his hat on. The officers followed suit. 'Square away, Mr Rogers, let us continue with our duties.'

He turned away and walked along the gangway as the main-yards were hauled, and was in the act of descending the companionway when he was halted by the masthead look-out.

'Deck there! Sail-ho! Broad on the lee quarter!'

Drinkwater shoved the Prayer Book in his tail-pocket and pulled out his Dolland pocket glass. It was a frigate coming up hand over fist from the southward, carrying every stitch of canvas the steady breeze allowed. Even at a distance they could see bunting streaming to leeward.

'She's British, anyway.' Of that there could be little doubt and within half an hour a boat danced across the water towards them.

'Boat ahoy!'

'*Fisgard*!' came the reply, and Drinkwater nodded to his first lieutenant.

'Side-party, Mr Rogers.' He turned to Frey who was consulting his lists.

'Captain Lord Mark Kerr, sir.'

'Bloody hell,' muttered Rogers as he called out the marine guard and the white-gloved side-boys to rig their fancy baize-covered man-ropes. Captain Lord Kerr hauled himself energetically over the rail and seized Drinkwater's hand.

'Drinkwater ain't it?'

'Indeed sir,' said Drinkwater, meeting his lordship as an equal upon his own quarterdeck.

'The damnedest thing, Drinkwater. Villeneuve's out!'

'*What?*'

Kerr nodded. 'I was refitting in Gib when he passed the Strait. I got out as soon as I could; sent my second luff up the Med to tell Nelson . . .'

'You mean Nelson wasn't in pursuit?' Drinkwater interrupted.

Kerr shook his head. 'No sign of him. I reckon he's off to the east again, just like the year one . . .'

'East. Good God he should be going west. Doesn't he know Missiessy's at Martinique waiting for him?'

'The devil he is!' exclaimed Kerr, digesting this news. 'I doubt Nelson knows of it. By God, that makes my haste the more necessary!'

'What about Orde, for God's sake?'

'He was victualling off Cadiz. Fell back when Villeneuve approached.'

'God's bones!'

Kerr came to a decision. In the circumstances it did not seem to matter which was the senior officer, they were both of one mind. 'I'm bound to let Calder know off Ferrol, and then to Cornwallis off Ushant. I daresay Billy-go-tight will send me on to the Admiralty.'

'Billy's ashore, now. Been relieved by Lord Gardner,' interrupted Drinkwater. 'And what d'you want me to do? Cruise down towards the Strait and hope that Nelson comes west?'

Kerr nodded, already turning towards the rail. 'First rate, Drinkwater. He must realise his mistake soon, even if my lieutenant ain't caught up with him. The sooner Nelson knows that Missiessy's out as well, the sooner we might stop this rot from spreading.' He held out his hand and relaxed for an instant. 'When I think how we've striven to maintain this damned blockade, only to have it blown wide open by a minute's ill-fortune!'

'My sentiments exactly. Good luck!' Drinkwater waved his hastening visitor over the side. Something of the urgency of Kerr's news had communicated itself to the ship, for *Antigone* was under way to the southward even before Kerr had reached *Fisgard*.

As soon as Drinkwater had satisfied himself that *Antigone* set every inch of canvas she was capable of carrying, he called Rogers and Hill below, spreading his charts on the table before him. He outlined the situation and the import of his news struck home.

'By God,' said Rogers, 'the Frogs could outflank us!' Drinkwater suppressed a smile. The very idea that they could be bested by a handful of impudent, frog-eating 'mounseers' seemed to strike Rogers with some force. His lack of imagination was, Drinkwater reflected, typical of his type. Hill, on the other hand, was more ruminative.

'You say Nelson's gone east, sir, chasing the idea of a French threat to India again?'

'Something of that order, Mr Hill.'

'While in reality the West India interests will already be howling for Pitt's blood. Who's in the West Indies at the moment? Cochrane?'

'And Dacres, with no more than a dozen of the line between them,' added Rogers.

'If Missiessy and Villeneuve combine with whatever cruisers the French have already got out there, I believe that we may be in for a thin time. Meanwhile we have to edge down to the Strait. What strikes me as paramount is our need to tell Nelson what is happening. I dare not enter the Med for fear of missing him, so we must keep station off Cape Spartel until Nelson appears. He may then close on the Channel in good time if the French have to re-cross the Atlantic. If Gardner holds the Channel and Nelson cruises off the Orkneys, we may yet stop 'em.'

'If not,' said Hill staring down at the chart, 'then God help us all.'

'Amen to that,' said Drinkwater.

They did not meet Orde but five days later they found his sloop *Beagle* cruising off Cape Spartel, having observed the passage of Villeneuve's fleet and now lying in wait for Nelson. From *Beagle* Drinkwater learned that Villeneuve had been reinforced by Spanish ships from Cadiz under Admiral Gravina and that *Beagle* had lost contact when the Combined Fleet headed west.

'I knew it!' Drinkwater had muttered to himself when he learned this. He promptly ordered *Beagle* to rejoin Orde who was, he thought, falling back on the Channel to reinforce Lord Gardener. As *Beagle*'s sails disappeared over the horizon to the north and the Atlas Mountains rose blue in the haze to the east, Drinkwater remarked to Quilhampton and Fraser:

'There is nothing more we can do, gentlemen, until his lordship arrives.'

During the first week of May the wind blew westerly through the Strait of Gibraltar, foul for Nelson slipping out into the Atlantic. Drinkwater decided to take advantage of it and enter the Strait. He was extremely anxious about the passage of time as day succeeded day and Nelson failed to appear. If there was no news of Nelson at Gibraltar, he reasoned, he could wait there and still catch his lordship. In addition Gibraltar might have news carried overland, despite the hostility of the Spanish.

Off Tarifa they spoke to a Swedish merchant ship which had just left Gibraltar. There was no news of Nelson but much of a diplomatic nature. Russia was again the ally of Great Britain and Austria was dallying with Britain's overtures. However, there was an even more disturbing rumour that Admiral Ganteaume had sailed from Brest. That evening the wind fell light, then swung slowly into the east. At dawn the following day the topgallants of a fleet were to be seen, and at last Drinkwater breakfasted in the great cabin of *Victory*, in company with Lord Nelson.

It was a hurried meal. Drinkwater told Nelson all he knew, invited to share the admiral's confidence as much for the news he brought as for the high regard Nelson held him in after his assistance at the battle of Copenhagen.

'My dear Drinkwater, I have been in almost perpetual darkness as Hardy here will tell you. I had for some time considered the West Indies a likely rendezvous for the fleets of France and Spain. Would to God I had had some news. I have been *four months*, Drinkwater, without a word. *Four months* with nothing from the Admiralty. They tell me Melville is out of office . . . My God, I hoped for news before now.' The admiral turned to his flag-captain. 'How far d'you think he's gone, Hardy?'

'Villeneuve, my Lord?'

'Who else, for God's sake!'

Hardy seemed unmoved by his lordship's bile and raised his eyebrows reflectively, demonstrating a stolidity that contrasted oddly with the little admiral's feverish anxiety. 'He has a month's start. Even the French can cross the Atlantic in a month.'

'A month. The capture of Jamaica would be a blow which Bonaparte would be happy to give us!'

'Do you follow him there, my Lord?' Drinkwater asked.

'I had marked the Toulon Fleet for my own game, Captain; you say Orde has fallen back from Cadiz?'

'It seems so, my Lord.'

'Then Gardner will not greatly benefit from my ships.' He paused in thought, then appeared to make up his mind. He suddenly smiled, his expression flooded with resolution. He whipped the napkin from his lap and flung it down on the table, like a gauntlet.

'They're *our* game, Hardy, damn it. Perhaps none of us would wish exactly for a West India trip; but the call of our country is far superior to any consideration of self. Let us try and bag Villeneuve before he does too much damage, eh gentlemen?'

'And the Mediterranean, my Lord?' asked Hardy.

'Sir Richard Bickerton, Tom, we'll leave him behind to guard the empty stable and watch Salcedo's Dons in Cartagena.' Nelson raised his coffee cup and they toasted the enterprise.

'You may keep us company to Cadiz, Captain, I shall look in there and see what Orde is about before I sail west.'

Orde was not off Cadiz, but his storeships were, and Nelson plundered them freely in Lagos Bay. Then intelligence reached the British fleet from Admiral Donald Campbell in the Portuguese Navy that confirmed Drinkwater's information. Campbell also brought the news that a British military expedition with a very weak escort under Admiral Knight was leaving Lisbon, bound into the Mediterranean. Nelson therefore ordered his foulest-bottomed battleship, the *Royal Sovereign*, together with the frigate *Antigone*, to see the fleet of transports clear of the Strait of Gibraltar.

Thus it was with something of a sense of anti-climax and of

belonging to a mere side-show that *Antigone*'s log for the evening of 11th May 1805 read: *Bore away in company R-Ad Knight's convoy. Cape St Vincent NW by N distant 7 leagues. Parted company Lord Nelson. Lord Nelson's fleet chasing to the westward.*

Calder's Action

'Fog, sir.'

'So I see.' Captain Drinkwater nodded to Lieutenant Quilhampton as he came on deck and stared round the horizon. The calm weather of the last few days had now turned cooler; what had first been a haze had thickened to mist and now to fog. 'Take the topsails off her, Mr Q. No point in chafing the gear to pieces.' So, her sails furled and her rigging dripping, *Antigone* lay like a log upon the vast expanse of the Atlantic which heaved gently to a low ground swell that told of a distant wind but only seemed to emphasise their own immobility.

Captain and third lieutenant fell to a companionable pacing of the deck, discussing the internal details of the ship.

'Purser reported another rotten cask of pork, sir.'

'From the batch shipped aboard off Ushant?'

'Yes, sir.'

'That makes seven.' Drinkwater cursed inwardly. He had been delighted to have been victualled and watered off Ushant after returning from the Strait of Gibraltar and Admiral Knight's convoy. Lord Gardner had been particular to ensure that all the cruising frigates were kept well stocked, but if they found many more bad casks of meat then his lordship's concern might be misplaced.

'I was just wondering, sir,' said Quilhampton conversationally, 'whether I'd rather be here than off Cadiz with Collingwood. Which station offers the best chance of action?'

'Difficult to say, James,' said Drinkwater, dropping their usual professional formality. 'When Gardner detached Collingwood to blockade Cadiz it was because he thought that Villeneuve and Gravina might have already returned there. When the report proved false, Collingwood sent two battleships west to reinforce Nelson and returned us to Calder. Opinion seems to incline towards keeping as many ships to the westward of the Bay of Biscay as possible. Prowse of *Sirius* told me the other day that both Calder and the Ushant squadron have virtually raised their separate blockades and are edging westwards in the hope of catching Villeneuve.'

'D'you think it will affect us, sir?'

Drinkwater shrugged. 'Not if my theory is right. Villeneuve will head more to the north and pass round Scotland. Besides, we don't know if Nelson caught up with him. Perhaps there has already been a battle in the West Indies.' He paused. 'What is it, James?'

Quilhampton frowned. 'I thought I heard . . . no, it's nothing. Wait! There it is again!'

Both men paused. As they listened the creaking of *Antigone*'s gear seemed preternaturally loud. 'Gunfire!'

'Wait!' Drinkwater laid his hand on Quilhampton's arm. 'Wait and listen.' Both men leaned over the rail, to catch the sound nearer the water, unobstructed by the noises of the ship. The single concussion came again, followed at intervals by others. 'Those are minute guns, James! And since we know the whereabouts of Calder . . .'

'Villeneuve?'

'Or Nelson, perhaps. But we must assume the worst. My theory is wrong if you are right. And they have a wind. Perhaps we will too in an hour.'

He looked aloft at the pendant flying from the mainmast head. It was already beginning to lift a trifle. Drinkwater crossed the deck and stared into the binnacle. The compass card oscillated gently but showed clearly that the breeze was coming from the west.

'You know, James, that report we had that Ganteaume got out of Brest proved false.'

'Yes, sir.'

'Well, perhaps Villeneuve is coming back to spring Ganteaume from the Goulet and *then* make his descent upon the Strait of Dover.'

'Possibly, sir,' replied Quilhampton, unwilling to argue, and aware that Drinkwater must be allowed his prerogative. In Quilhampton's youthful opinion the Frogs were not capable of that kind of thing.

Drinkwater knew of the young officer's scepticism and said, 'Lord Barham, has the same opinion of the French as myself, Mr Q, otherwise he would not have gone to all the trouble of ensuring they were intercepted.'

Thus mildly rebuked, Quilhampton realised his minutes of intimacy with the captain were over. While Drinkwater considered what to do until the breeze gave them steerage way, Quilhampton considered that, as far as second lieutenants were concerned, it did not seem to matter if Lord Melville or Lord Barham were in charge of the Admiralty; the lot of serving officers was still a wretched one.

The breeze came from the west at mid-morning. Setting all sail, Drinkwater pressed *Antigone* to the east-north-east. Then, at six bells

107

in the forenoon watch there was a brief lifting of the visibility. To the north-west they made out the pale square of sails over the shapes of hulls, while to the north-east they saw Calder's look-out ship, *Defiance*. Both *Antigone* and *Defiance* threw out the signal for an enemy fleet in sight and fired guns. Drinkwater knew that Calder could not be far away. Immediately upon making his signal, Captain Durham of the *Defiance* turned his ship away, squaring her yards before the wind and retiring on the main body of the fleet. Taking his cue, Drinkwater ordered studding sails set and attempted to cross the enemy's van and rejoin his own admiral. Shortly after this the fog closed in again, although the breeze held and Drinkwater cleared the frigate for action.

'We seem destined to go into battle blind, Sam,' he said to the first lieutenant as Rogers took his post on the quarterdeck. 'Snow in January and bloody fog in July and this could be the decisive battle of the war, for God's sake!'

Rogers grunted his agreement. 'Only the poxy French could conjure up a bloody fog at a moment like this.'

Drinkwater grinned at Roger's prejudice. 'It could be providence, Sam. What does the Bible say about God chastising those he loves best?'

'Damned if I know, sir, but a fleet action seems imminent and we're going to miss it because of fog!'

Drinkwater felt a spark of sympathy for Rogers. Distinguishing himself in such an action was Roger's only hope of further advancement.

'Look, sir!' Another momentary lifting of the fog showed the French much nearer to them now, crossing their bows and holding a steadier breeze than reached *Antigone*.

'We shall be cut off, damn it,' muttered Drinkwater, suddenly realising that he might very well be fighting for his life within an hour. He turned on Rogers. 'Sam, serve the men something at their stations. Get food and grog into them. You have twenty minutes.'

It proved to be a very long twenty minutes to Drinkwater. In fact it stretched to an hour, then two. Drinkwater had seen no signals from Calder and had only a vague idea of the admiral's position. All he did know was that the French fleet lay between *Antigone* and the British line-of-battle ships. At about one in the afternoon the fog rolled back to become a mist, thickening from time to time in denser patches, so that they might see three-quarters of a mile one minute and a ship's length ahead the next. Into this enlarged visible circle the dim and sinister shapes of a battle-line emerged, led by the 80-gun *Argonauta*, flying the red and gold of Castile.

'It *is* the Combined Fleet, by God,' Drinkwater muttered as he saw the colours of Spain alternating with the tricolour of France. He spun *Antigone* to starboard, holding her just out of gunshot as she picked up the stronger breeze that had carried the enemy thus far.

A vague shape to the north westward looked for a little like the topsails of a frigate and Drinkwater hoped it was *Sirius*. At six bells in the afternoon watch he decided to shorten sail, hauled his yards and swung north, crossing the Spanish line a mile ahead of the leading ship which was flying an admiral's flag. Rogers was looking at him expectantly. At extreme range it seemed a ridiculous thing to do but he nodded his permission. Rogers walked the line of the larboard battery, checking and sighting each gun, doing what he was best at.

As he reached the aftermost gun he straightened up. 'Fire!'

Antigone shook as the guns recoiled amid the smoke of their discharge and their crews swabbed, loaded and rammed home. She trembled as the heavy carriages were hauled out through the open ports again and their muzzles belched fire and iron at the long-awaited enemy. As the smoke from the second broadside cleared they were rewarded by an astonishing sight. Little damage seemed to have been inflicted upon the enemy at the extremity of their range, but the Combined Fleet was heaving to.

'Probably thinks that Calder's just behind us out of sight,' Rogers put in, rubbing his hands with glee.

Drinkwater wore *Antigone* round and immediately the yards were squared they made out the shapes of two frigates on their larboard bow, dim, ghostly vessels close-hauled as they approached from the east.

'The private signal, Mr Frey, and look lively!' He did not want to be shot at as he retreated ahead of the French, and already he recognised *Sirius* with her emerald-green rail.

The colours of flags clarified as the ships closed and Drinkwater turned *Antigone* to larboard to come up on *Sirius*'s quarter. The second British frigate, *Égyptienne*, loomed astern. Drinkwater saw Prowse step up on the rail with a speaking trumpet.

'Heard gunfire, Drinkwater. Was that you?'

'Yes! The Combined Fleet is just to windward of us!'

'Form line astern of the *Égyptienne*. Calder wants us to reconnoitre!'

'Aye, aye!' Drinkwater jumped down from the mizen chains. 'Back the mizen tops'l, Mr Hill. Fall in line astern of the *Égyptienne*.'

Drinkwater watched *Sirius* disappear into a fog patch and the second frigate ghosted past. For one glorious moment at about seven bells in the afternoon the fog lifted and the mist rolled back, giving both fleets a glimpse of each other. Astern of the three westward-heading British frigates, the British fleet of fifteen ships-of-the-line was standing south-south-west on the starboard tack, their topgallants set above topsails, but with their courses clewed up. From Sir Robert Calder's 98-gun flagship, the *Prince of Wales*, flew the signal to engage the enemy. This was repeated from the masthead of his second in command, Rear-Admiral Stirling, on board the *Glory*.

To the southward of the three frigates the Combined Fleet straggled in a long line of twenty ships and a few distant frigates. Since they had hove to, they had adjusted their course, edging away from the British frigates which, in order to hold the wind, were also diverging to the north-west. Prowse made the signal to tack and *Sirius* began to ease round on the enemy rear. She was holding the fluky wind better than either *Antigone* or *Égyptienne*. A few minutes later the mist closed down again. Drinkwater set his courses in an attempt to catch up with *Sirius* and lost contact with the *Égyptienne*. He heard gunfire to the south and then the sound of a heavier cannonade to the south-east. Next to him Rogers was beside himself with impatience and frustration.

'God damn it, God damn it,' he muttered, grinding the fist of one hand into the palm of the other.

'For God's sake relax, Sam. You'll have apoplexy else.'

'This is agony, sir . . .'

'Steer for the guns, Mr Hill.' It was agonising for Drinkwater too. But whereas all Rogers had to do was wait for a target to present itself, Drinkwater worried about the presence of other ships, dreading a collision. Ahead of them the noise of cannon-fire was growing louder and more persistent. Then, once again, the fog rolled back, revealing broad on their larboard bow the shape of a battleship. This time the enemy were ready for them.

The roar of forty cannon fired in a ragged broadside split the air. The black hull of the 80-gun vessel towered over them as Rogers roared, 'Fire!'

Antigone's puny broadside rattled and thudded against the stranger's hull as they saw the red and yellow of Spain and an admiral's flag at her mainmasthead. The wind of the battleship's broadside passed them like a tornado but most of the shot whistled overhead, parting ropes and holing sails. One casualty occurred in the main-top and the main-mast was wounded by two balls, but the *Antigone* escaped the worst effects of such a storm of iron. As the great ship vanished in the mist Drinkwater read her name across the stern: *Argonauta*.

Then there were other ships passing them, the *Terrible* and *America*, both disdaining to fire on a frigate, and Drinkwater realised that the Combined Fleet had tacked and were standing north. In the confusion he wondered what on earth Calder was doing, and whether the British admiral had observed this movement. Then the outbreak of a general cannonade told him that the two fleets were still in contact, and the sudden appearance of spouts of water near them convinced him that the British fleet were just beyond the line of the enemy and that *Antigone* was in the line of fire of the British guns.

A little after five in the afternoon they made contact again with the *Sirius*. Both frigates then hauled round and stood towards the gun-fire. Once they caught a glimpse of the action and, from what could be discerned, the two fleets were engaged in a confusing mêlée.

'I don't know what the devil to make of it, damned if I do,' remarked Hill tensely, his tone expressing the frustration they all felt. *Antigone* continued to edge down in the mist until darkness came, although the gunfire continued for some time afterwards.

'What in God Almighty's name are we doing?' asked Rogers, looking helplessly round the quarterdeck.

'Why nothing, Mr Rogers,' said Hill, who was finding the first lieutenant's constant moaning a trifle tedious. To windward of the group of officers Captain Drinkwater studied the situation, privately as mystified as his officers. On the day following the action the weather had remained hazy and the two fleets had manoeuvred in sight of each other. Both had been inactive, as though licking their wounds. After the utter confusion of the 22nd, the British were pleased to find themselves masters of two Spanish prizes. It was also clear that they had badly damaged several more. However, the British ships *Windsor Castle* and *Malta* were themselves in poor condition and preparing to detach for England and a dockyard.

The wind had held, the Combined Fleet remained with the advantage of the weather gauge, and Calder waited for Villeneuve to attack. But the allied commander hesitated.

'All I've had to do today,' remarked Rogers in one of his peevish outbursts, 'is report another three casks of pork as being rotten! I ask you, is that the kind of work fit for a King's sea-officer?'

Although the question had been rhetorical it had brought forth a *sotto voce* comment from Midshipman Glencross for which the young man had been sent to the foremasthead to cool his heels and guard his tongue. As Drinkwater had written in his journal, the last days had been *inconclusive if our task is to annihilate the enemy*. And today, it seemed, was to be worse. The wind had shifted at dawn and every ship in the British fleet hourly expected Calder to form his line, station his frigates to windward for the repeating of his signals, and to bear down upon the enemy. As hour after hour passed and the wind increased slowly to a fresh breeze and then to a near gale, nothing happened. Villeneuve's fleet edged away to the north. By six o'clock in the evening the Combined Fleet was out of sight.

'Well,' remarked Lieutenant Fraser as he took over the deck and the hands were at last stood down from their quarters, 'at least we stopped them getting into Ferrol, but it's no' cricket we're playing. I wonder what they'll think o'this in London?'

The Fog of War

'Dear God, how many more?'

'Best part of the ground tier, sir, plus a dozen other casks among the batch shipped aboard off Ushant. I'd guess some of that pork was pickled back in the American War.'

Drinkwater sighed. Rogers might be exaggerating, but then again it was equally possible that he was not. 'If we ain't careful, Sam, we'll be obliged to request stores; just at the moment that would be intolerable. Apart from anything else we must wait on this rendezvous a day or two more.'

'D'you think there's going to be a battle then? After that farting match last week? There's a rumour that Calder is going to be called home to face a court-martial,' Rogers said, a note of irreverent glee in his voice.

'I'm damned if I know where these infernal rumours start,' Drinkwater said sharply. 'You should know better than believe 'em.'

Rogers shrugged. 'Well, it's not my problem, sir, whereas these casks of rotten pork are.'

'Damn it!' Drinkwater rose, his chair squeaking backwards with the violence of his movement. 'Damn it! D'you know Sam,' he said, unlocking the spirit case and pouring two glasses of rum, 'I've never felt so uncomfortable before. That business the other day was shameful. We should never have let the French get away unmolested. God knows what'll come of it . . . we don't know where the devil they are now. The only ray of hope is that Calder has joined forces with Gardner or Cornwallis if he's back on station, and that Nelson's rejoined 'em from the West Indies. With that concentration off Ushant, at least the Channel will be secure, but it is the uncertainty of matters that unsettles me.'

Rogers nodded his agreement. 'Worse than a damned fog.'

'But you want to know about the pork,' Drinkwater sighed. 'How many weeks can we last out at the present rate?'

Rogers shrugged, considered for a moment and said, 'Ten, possibly eleven.'

'Very well. I'll see what I can do about securing some from another ship in due course.'

'Beg pardon, sir, but what are *our* orders?'

'Well, we are to sit tight here on Calder's rendezvous for a week. *Aeolus* and *Phoenix* are within a hundred miles of us, with the seventy-four *Dragon* not so far. We are intended to observe Ferrol,' Drinkwater opened one of the charts that lay, almost permanently now, upon his table top. He laid his finger on a spot a hundred miles north-north-west of Cape Finisterre, 'The four of us are holding Calder's old post between us while he retires on the Channel Fleet in case Villeneuve makes his expected push for the Channel.'

'And if Villeneuve obliges and the Channel Fleet does no better than Calder did t'other day, then I'd say Boney had a better than even chance of getting his own way in the Dover Strait.'

'I doubt if Cornwallis would let him . . .'

'But you said yourself, sir, that Cornwallis might not yet be back at sea. What's Gardner's fighting temper?'

'We'll have little enough to worry about if Nelson's back . . .'

'But maybe he isn't. And even Nelson could be fooled by a fog. 'Tis high summer, just what the bloody French want. I reckon they'd be across in a week.'

Drinkwater fell silent. He was not of sufficiently different an opinion to contradict Rogers. He poured them each another glass.

'To be candid, Sam, things look pretty black.'

'Like the Earl of Hell's riding boots.'

No such strategic considerations preoccupied James Quilhampton as, for the duration of his watch and in the absence of the captain, he paced the weather side of the quarterdeck. His mind was far from the cares of the ship, daydreaming away his four hours on deck as *Antigone* rode the blue waters of the Atlantic under easy sail. He was wholly given to considering his circumstances in so far as they were affected by Miss Catriona MacEwan. From time to time, as he walked up and down, his right hand would clasp the stump of his left arm and he would curse the iron hook that he wore in place of a left hand. Although he possessed several alternatives, including one made for him on the bomb-vessel *Virago* that had been painted and was a tolerable likeness to the real thing, he felt that such a disfigurement was unlikely to enable him to secure the young woman as his wife. He cursed his luck. The wound that had seemed such an honourable mark in his boyhood now struck him for what it really was, a part of him that was gone for ever, its absence making him abnormal, abominable. How foolish it now seemed to consider it in any other

114

way. The pride with which he had borne home his iron hook now appeared ridiculous. He had seen the pity in Catriona's eyes together with the disgust. As he recollected the circumstances it seemed that her revulsion had over-ridden her pity. He was maimed; there was no other way to look at the matter. Certainly that harridan of an aunt would point out James Quilhampton had no prospects, no expectations, no fortune and no left hand!

But she had been undeniably pleasant to him, surely. He pondered the matter, turning over the events of their brief acquaintanceship, recollecting the substance of her half-dozen letters that led him to suppose she, at least, viewed his friendship if not his suit with some favour. Reasoning thus he raised himself out of his despondency only to slump back into it when he considered the uncertainty of his fate. He was in such a brown study that the quartermater of the watch had to call his attention to the masthead's hail.

'Deck! Deck there!'

'Eh? What? What is it?'

'Eight sail to the norrard, sir!'

'What d'you make of 'em?'

'Clean torps'ls, sir, Frenchmen!'

'Pass word for the captain!' Quilhampton shouted, scrambling up on the rail with the watch glass and jamming himself against the mizen shrouds. Within minutes Drinkwater was beside him.

'Where away, Mr Q?'

'I can't see them from the deck, sir . . . wait! One, two . . . six . . . eight, sir. Eight sail and they are French!'

Drinkwater levelled his own glass and studied the newcomers as they sailed south, tier after tier of sails lifting over the horizon until he could see the bulk of their hulls and the white water foaming under their bows as they manoeuvred into line abreast.

'Casting a net to catch us,' he said, adding, 'six of the line and two frigates to match or better us.' In the prevailing westerly breeze escape to the north was impossible. But the enemy squadron was sailing south, for the Spanish coast, the Straits of Gibraltar or the Mediterranean itself. Which? And why south if the main strength of the Combined Fleet had gone north? Perhaps it had not; perhaps Villeneuve had got past the cordon of British frigates and into Ferrol or Corunna, or back into the Mediterranean. Perhaps this detachment of ships was part of Villeneuve's fleet, an advance division sent out to capture the British frigates that were Barham's eyes and ears. Perhaps, perhaps, perhaps. God only knew what the truth was.

Drinkwater suddenly knew one thing for certain: he had seen at least one of the approaching ships before. The scarlet strake that swept aft from her figurehead was uncommon. She was Allemand's *Magnanime*, and there too was the big *Majestueux*. It was the Rochefort Squadron, back from the West Indies and now heading south!

'Mr Rogers!'

'Sir?'

'Make sail!' Drinkwater closed his glass with a snap. 'Starboard tack, stuns'ls aloft and alow, course sou' by east!'

'Aye, aye, sir!'

'Mr Quilhampton!'

'Sir?'

'A good man aloft with a glass. I want to know the exact progress of this chase and I don't want to lose M'sieur Allemand a second time.'

He fell to pacing the deck, occasionally turning and looking astern at the enemy whose approach had been slowed by *Antigone*'s increase in sail. The British frigate would run south ahead of the French squadron. It was not Drinkwater's business to engage a superior enemy, nor to risk capture. It was his task to determine whither M. Allemand was bound and for what reason. It was also necessary to let Collingwood, off Cadiz, know that a powerful enemy division was at sea and cruising on his lines of communication.

Drinkwater could not be expected to have more than the sketchiest notion of the true state of affairs during the last week of July and the first fortnight in August. But his professional observations and deductions were vital in guiding his mind to its decisions and, like half a dozen fellow cruiser captains, he played his part in those eventful weeks. Unknown to Drinkwater and after the action with Calder's fleet, Villeneuve had gone to Vigo Bay to land his wounded and refit his damaged ships. From Vigo he had coasted to Ferrol where the fast British seventy-four *Dragon* had spotted his ships at anchor. More French and Spanish ships had joined his fleet and he sailed from Ferrol on 13 August, being sighted by the *Iris* whose captain concluded from the Combined Fleet's westerly course that it was attempting a junction with the Rochefort Squadron before turning north. However, events turned out otherwise, for the wind was foul for the Channel. Villeneuve missed Allemand, encountered what he thought was part of a strong British force but was in fact *Dragon* and some frigates, swung south and arrived off Cape St Vincent on the 18th. Breaking up a small British convoy and forcing aside Vice-Admiral

Collingwood's few ships, Villeneuve's Combined Fleet of thirty-six men-of-war passed into the safety of the anchorage behind the Mole of Cadiz. That evening Collingwood's token force resumed its blockade.

Drinkwater had tenaciously hung on to Allemand's flying squadron, running ahead of his frigates as the French commodore edged eastwards and then, apparently abandoning the half-hearted chasing off of the British cruiser, turning away for Vigo Bay. As soon as Drinkwater ascertained the French commander's intentions he made all sail to the south, arriving off Cadiz twenty-four hours after Villeneuve. He called away his barge and put off to HMS *Dreadnought*, Collingwood's flagship, to report the presence of the Rochefort ships at Vigo, expecting Collingwood's despatches for the Channel immediately.

Instead the dour Northumbrian looked up from his desk, his serious face apparently unmoved by Drinkwater's news.

'Have you looked into Cadiz, Captain Drinkwater? No? I thought not.' Collingwood sighed, as though weary beyond endurance. 'Villeneuve's whole fleet passed into the Grand Road yesterday . . .'

'I am too late then, sir.'

'With the chief news, yes.' Collingwood did not smile, but the tone of his tired voice was kindly.

'And my orders?'

'I have four ships of the line here, Captain, to blockade thirty to forty enemy men of war. You will remain with us.'

'Very well, sir.' Drinkwater turned to go.

'Oh, Captain . . .'

'Sir?'

'From your actions you appear an officer of energy. I should be pleased to see your frigate close inshore.'

Drinkwater acknowledged the vice-admiral's veiled compliment gravely. In the weeks to come he was to learn that this had been praise indeed.

Nelson

'The tower of San Sebastian bearing south-a-half-west, sir.' Hill straightened up from the pelorus vanes.

'Very well!' Drinkwater closed his Dolland glass with a snap, pocketed it and jumped down from the carronade slide. He took a look over Gillespy's shoulder as the boy's pencil dotted his final full stop.

'You make a most proficient secretary, Mr Gillespy,' he said, patting the boy's shoulder in a paternal gesture that spoke of his high spirits. He turned to the first lieutenant. 'Wear ship, Sam!'

'Aye, aye, sir. Sail trimmers, stand by!'

Antigone's company were at their quarters, the frigate cleared for action as she took her daily look into Cadiz harbour. The hills of Spain almost surrounded them, green and brown, spreading from the town of Rota to the north, to the extremity of the Mole of Cadiz, that long barrier which separated the anchorage of the Combined Fleets of France and Spain from the watching and waiting British. From *Antigone*'s quarterdeck the long mole had fore-shortened and disappeared behind the white buildings of the town of Cadiz which terminated in the tower of San Sebastian. The tower had fallen abaft their beam and ahead of them the islets of Los Cochinos, Las Puercas, El Diamante and La Galera barred their passage. Beyond the islets, beneath the distant blue-green summit of the Chiclana hill, the black mass of the Combined Fleet lay, safely at anchor.

Drinkwater turned to Midshipman Frey, busy with paint-box and paper at the rail. 'You will have to finish now, Mr Frey.' He looked from the masts of the enemy to the hurried watercolour executed by the midshipman. 'You do justice to the effects of the sunshine on the water.'

'Thank you, sir.' Frey and Gillespy exchanged glances. The captain was very complimentary this morning.

'Ready to wear, sir,' reported Rogers.

Drinkwater, his hands behind his back, drew a lungful of air. 'Very well, Sam. See to it.' He felt unusually expansive this bright morning, deriving an enormous sense of satisfaction from his advanced post almost under the very guns of Cadiz itself. He knew that *Antigone* had joined the fleet at a fortuitous moment and that Collingwood was desperately short of frigates. As soon as the admiral had seen Villeneuve into Cadiz he had sent off his fastest frigate, the *Euryalus*, commanded by one of the best cruiser captains in the navy, the Honourable Henry Blackwood. Blackwood was to inform Cornwallis off Ushant, and then Barham at the Admiralty in London. The departure of *Euryalus* left Collingwood with only one other frigate and the bomb-vessel *Hydra* until Drinkwater's arrival with *Antigone*. Their present task, although not so very different from their duties of the last eighteen months, seemed more crucial. There was an inescapable sense of expectancy in the fleet off southern Spain. Among the captains of the line-of-battleships cruising offshore this manifested itself in frustration. Collingwood was not an expansive man. His orders to his fleet were curt. The ship's commanders were forbidden to visit each other, there was to be no dining together, no gossip; just the remorseless business of forming line, wearing, tacking and, from time to time, running for Gibraltar or Tetuan for water, meat and other necessaries.

But close up to the entrance of Cadiz, Drinkwater was blissfully unconcerned. He had no desire to exchange stations, for it was here, opinion held, that an action would soon occur. He was not sure whence came these rumours. There was some extraordinary communication between the ships of a fleet that made even the Admiralty telegraph seem slow. Collingwood had been reinforced by the ships of Admiral Bickerton which Nelson had left in the Mediterranean when he chased the Toulon Fleet to the West Indies. Bickerton, his health in ruins, had gone home, but his ships had brought rumour from east of Gibraltar, while the regular logistical communication with Gibraltar ensured that news from Spain gradually permeated the fleet. It was a curious thing, reflected Drinkwater, as *Antigone* completed her turn and the after-sail was reset, that what began in a fleet as rumour was often borne out as fact a few days or weeks later.

'Ship's on the starboard tack, sir,' reported Rogers.

'Very well.' Drinkwater crossed the deck and watched the white walls of Cadiz slowly open out on the larboard beam, exposing the long mole to the south as the frigate beat out of Cadiz bay.

'Mr Frey, make ready the signal for "The enemy has topgallant masts hoisted and yards crossed".'

'Aye, aye, sir.'

Drinkwater idly watched Lieutenant Mount parading his marines for their daily inspection. He was reluctant to go below and break his mood by a change of scenery. Instead he continued his walk. They knew here, off Cadiz, that Pitt's alienation of Spain had been countered by the acquisition of Austria as an ally, and that there was word of a Russian and Austrian army taking the field. He learned also that the commander of the Rochefort Squadron that had so lately pursued him had been Commodore Allemand, promoted after the departure of Missiessy for Paris. What had become of Allemand now, no one seemed certain.

Drinkwater crossed the deck and began pacing the windward side, deep in thought. There was only one cloud on the horizon and that was their dwindling provisions. They had found more pork rotten, a quantity of flour and dried peas spoiled, and the purser and Rogers were reminding him daily of their increasingly desperate need to revictual. Despite Bickerton's ships, Collingwood was still outnumbered. He had hoped that events would have come to some sort of crux before now, but it seemed that Villeneuve delayed as long as possible in Cadiz. All coastal trade had ceased since Collingwood had detached a couple of small cruisers to halt it in an effort to starve Villeneuve out, and much of the business of supplying Cadiz with food was being carried out in Danish ships. It was known that things inside the town were becoming desperate: there seemed little love lost between the French and Spaniards and it was even rumoured that a few Frenchmen had been found murdered in the streets.

'Main fleet's in sight, sir,' reported Quilhampton, breaking his train of thought and forcing him to concentrate upon the matter in hand. He nodded at Frey.

'Very well. Mr Frey, you may make the signal.'

The rolled-up flags rose off the deck and were hoisted swiftly on the lee flag-halliards. The signal yeoman jerked the ropes and the flags broke out, streaming gaily to leeward and informing Collingwood of the latest moves of Villeneuve.

'Deck there! Vessels to the north . . .'

They watched the approach of the strangers with interest as they stood away from the *Dreadnought*. Collingwood threw out no signals for their interception and they were identified as more reinforcements for the British squadron securing Villeneuve in Cadiz, reinforcements from Ushant under Vice-Admiral Calder.

'Well, Sam,' remarked Drinkwater, 'that's one rumour that is untrue.'

'What's that, sir?'

'You said that Calder was going to be court-martialled and here he is as large as life.'

'Oh well, I suppose that shuts the door on Villeneuve then.'

'I wonder,' mused Drinkwater.

My dearest husband, Drinkwater read, Elizabeth's two-month-old letter having found its way to him via one of Calder's ships: *I have much to tell and you will want to know the news of the war first. We are in a fever here and have been for months. The French Invasion is expected hourly and the town is regularly filled with the militia and yeomanry which, from the noise they make, intend to behave most valiantly, but of which I hold no very great expectations. We hear horrid tales of the French. Billie has taught us all how to load and fire a blunderbuss and I can assure you that should they come they will find the house as stoutly defended as a handful of women and a legless boy can make it. The children thrive on the excitement, Richard particularly, he is much affected by the sight of any uniform . . .*

You will have heard of the Coalition with Austria. Much is expected of it, though I know not what to think at the moment. We are constantly disturbed by the passage of post-chaises and couriers on the Portsmouth Road that the turmoil makes it impossible to judge the true state of affairs and indeed to know whether anyone is capable of doing so . . .

There was much more, and with it newspapers and other gossip that had percolated through the officers' correspondence to the gunroom. There had been a movement by the Brest fleet under Ganteaume which had engaged British ships off Point St Matthew and seemed to have followed some direct instruction of the Emperor Napoleon's. It was conjectured that a similar order had gone out to Villeneuve, but the accuracy of this was uncertain.

The news was already old. He felt his own fears for his family abating. The uncertainty of the last months was gone. Whatever French intentions were, it was clear that the two main fleets of the enemy were secured, the one in Brest, the other in Cadiz. This time the doors of the stables were double-bolted with the horses inside.

'Beg pardon, sir, but Mr Fraser says to tell you that *Euryalus* is approaching.'

'*Euryalus?*' Drinkwater looked up from the log-book in astonishment at Midshipman Wickham. 'Are you certain?'

'I believe so, sir.'

'Oh.' He exchanged glances with Hill. 'We are superceded, Mr Hill.'

'Yes,' Hill replied flatly.

'Very well, Mr Wickham, I'll be up directly.' He signed the log and handed it back to the sailing master.

Half an hour later Drinkwater received a letter borne by a courteous lieutenant from the *Euryalus*. He read it on deck:

> Euryalus
> *Off Cadiz*
> *27th September 1805*
>
> Dear Drinkwater,
>
> *I am indebted to you for so ably holding the forward post off San Sebastian. However I am ordered by Vice-Ad. Collingwood to direct you to relinquish the station to myself and to proceed to Gibraltar where you will be able to make good the deficiency in your stores. You are particularly to acquaint General Fox of the fact that Lord Nelson is arriving shortly to take command of His Majesty's ships and vessels before Cadiz, and it is his Lordship's particular desire that his arrival is attended with no ceremony and the news is kept from Admiral Decrès as long as possible.*
>
> *May good fortune attend your endeavours. Lose not a moment.*
>
> Henry Blackwood.

Drinkwater looked at the lieutenant. 'Tell Captain Blackwood that I understand his instructions . . . Does he think that Decrès commands at Cadiz?'

The lieutenant nodded. 'Yes, sir. Captain Blackwood has come directly from London. Lord Nelson is no more than a day behind us in *Victory* . . .'

'But Decrès, Lieutenant, why him and not Villeneuve?'

'I believe, sir, there were reports in London that Napoleon is replacing Villeneuve, sir. Admiral Decrès was named as his successor.'

Drinkwater frowned. 'But Decrès is Minister of Marine. Does this mean the game is not yet played out?'

'Reports from Paris indicate His Imperial Majesty still has plans for his fleets, although I believe the French have decamped from Boulogne.'

'Good Lord. Very well, Lieutenant, we must be about our business. My duty to Captain Blackwood.'

'So,' muttered Drinkwater to himself as he watched the *Euryalus*'s boat clear the ship's side, 'the horse may yet kick the stable door down.'

'Port, Captain Drinkwater?'

'Thank you, sir.' Drinkwater unstoppered the decanter and poured the dark wine into his gleaming crystal glass. Despite the war the Governor of Gibraltar, General Fox, kept an impressive table. He had dined to excess. He passed the decanter to the infantry colonel next to him.

'So,' said the Governor, 'Nelson does not want us to advertise his arrival to the Dons, eh?'

'That would seem to be his intention, sir.'

'It would frighten Villeneuve. I suppose Nelson wants to entice them out for a fight, eh?'

'I think that would be Lord Nelson's intention, General, yes.' He remembered his conversation with Pitt all those months ago.

'Let's hope he doesn't damn well lose 'em this time then.' There was an embarrassed silence round the table.

'Is Villeneuve still in command at Cadiz, sir?' Drinkwater asked, breaking the silence. 'There was, I believe, a report that Napoleon had replaced him.'

Fox exchanged glances with the port admiral, Rear-Admiral Knight. 'We have not heard anything of the kind, though if Boney wants anything done he'd be well advised to do so.'

'The fleet is pleased to have Nelson out, I daresay,' put in Knight.

'Yes, Sir John. I believe his arrival will electrify the whole squadron.'

'Collingwood's a fine fellow,' said Fox, 'but a better bishop than an admiral. Pass the damn thing, John.'

Sir John Knight had his fist clamped round the neck of the decanter, withholding it from the Governor to signal his displeasure at having a fellow admiral discussed before a junior captain.

'Vice-Admiral Collingwood is highly regarded, sir,' Drinkwater remarked loyally, disliking such silly gossip about a man who was wearing himself out in his country's service. Fox grunted and Drinkwater considered that his contradiction of a General Officer might have been injudicious. Knight rescued him.

'I believe you will be able to sail and rejoin the fleet by noon tomorrow, Drinkwater.'

'I hope so, Sir John.'

'Well you may reassure Lord Nelson that he has only to intimate his desire to us and we shall regard it as a command. At this important juncture in the war it is essential that we all co-operate . . .'

·   ·   ·

123

'A magnificent sight is it not? May I congratulate you on being made post, sir.'

'Thank you . . . I er, forgive me, your face is familiar . . .'

'Quilliam, sir, John Quilliam. We met before Copenhagen . . .'

'On board *Amazon* . . . I recollect it now. You are still awaiting your step?'

'Yes. But resigned to my fate. To be first lieutenant of *Victory* is a better berth than many. Come, sir, his Lordship will see you at once and does not like to be kept waiting.'

Drinkwater followed Quilliam across *Victory*'s immaculate quarter-deck, beneath the row of fire-buckets with their royal cipher and into the lobby outside Lord Nelson's cabin. A minute later he was making his report to the Commander-in-Chief and delivering Sir John Knight's documents to him. The little admiral greeted him cordially. The wide, mobile mouth smiled enthusiastically, though the skin of his face seemed transparent with fatigue. But the single eye glittered with that intensity that Drinkwater had noted before Copenhagen.

'And you say it is still Villeneuve that commands at Cadiz, Captain?'

'I have learned nothing positive to the contrary, my Lord, but you well know the state of news.'

'Indeed I do.' Nelson paused and reflected a moment. 'Captain Drinkwater, I am obliged to you. I am reorganising my fleet. Rear-Admiral Louis is here, in the *Canopus* and I am attaching you to his squadron which is to leave to victual in Gibraltar. I know that you have come from there and I wish that you should station your frigate to the eastward of The Rock. I apprehend that Salcedo may break out from Cartagena and I am in my usual desperation for want of frigates.'

The order came like a blow to Drinkwater and his face must have shown something of his disappointment. 'My dear Drinkwater, I have no other means of keeping the fleet complete in provisions and water, but by this means. You may return with Louis but I cannot afford to have him cut off from my main body.'

Drinkwater subdued his disappointment. 'I understand perfectly, my Lord,' he said.

Nelson came round the table to escort Drinkwater to the door with his customary civility and in a gesture that made intimates of all his subordinates.

'We *shall* have a battle, Drinkwater. I *know* it. I *feel* it. And we shall all do our duty to the greater glory of our King and Country!'

And Drinkwater was unaccountably moved by the sincere conviction of this vehement little speech.

Drinkwater looked astern. The sails of Rear-Admiral Louis's squadron were purple against the sunset. Drinkwater wondered if Lord Walmsley had transferred from the *Leopard* with the rear-admiral. He did not greatly care. What he felt most strongly was a sense of anti-climax, and he felt it was common throughout all of Louis's squadron. He crossed the deck and looked at the log.

Thursday 3rd October 1805. 6 p.m. Bore up for the Straits of Gibraltar in company Canopus, *Rear-Ad.* Louis, Queen, Spencer, Zealous *and* Tigre *Wind westerly strong breeze. At sunset handed t'gallants.*

'Very well, Mr Fraser, call me if you are in any doubt whatsoever.'

'Aye, aye, sir.' From his tone Fraser sounded depressed too.

Chapter 16   3–14 October 1805

Tarifa

'It's a ship's launch, sir.'

'I believe you to be right, Mr Hill. Very well, back the mizen topsail until she comes up.'

The knot of curious officers waited impatiently. For over a week *Antigone* had cruised east of Gibraltar, half hoping and half fearing that Salcedo would try and effect a juncture with Villeneuve. The only thing that could satisfy them would be orders to return to Cadiz. Was that what the launch brought them?

'There's a lieutenant aboard, sir,' observed Fraser. 'Aye, and a wee midshipman.'

The launch lowered its mainsail and rounded under *Antigone*'s stern. A moment later a young lieutenant scrambled over the rail and touched his hat to Drinkwater.

'Captain Drinkwater?'

'Yes. You have brought us orders?'

The officer held out a sealed packet which Drinkwater took and retired with to his cabin. In a fever of impatience he opened the packet. A covering letter from Louis instructed him to comply with the enclosed orders and wished him every success in his 'new appointment'. Mystified, he tore open Nelson's letter.

Victory
Off Cadiz
10th October 1805

My Dear Drinkwater,

I am sensible of the very great services rendered by you before Copenhagen and the knowledge that you were exposed to, and suffered from, the subsequent attack on Boulogne. It is your name that I call to mind at this time. Poor Sir Robert Calder has been called home to stand trial for his actions in July last. I cannot find it in me to send him in a frigate and am depriving the fleet of the Prince of Wales *to do honour to him. Brown of the* Ajax *and Letchmere of the* Thunderer *are also to go home as witnesses and it is imperative I have experienced captains in these ships. Leave your first lieutenant in command. Louis has instructions to transfer a lieutenant from one of his ships. You may bring one of your own, together with two midshipmen, but no more. These orders will come by the*

126

*Entreprenante cutter, but she has orders to return immediately. Therefore hire
a barca longa and join* Thunderer *without delay.*

Nelson and Brontë

'God bless my soul!' He was to transfer immediately into a seventy-
four! 'How damnably providential!' he muttered, then recalled himself. He would be compelled to leave most of his effects . . .

'Mullender!' He began bawling orders. 'Rogers! Pass word for the
first lieutenant!' He sat down and wrote out a temporary commission
for Rogers, interrupting his writing to shout additional wants to his
steward. Then he shouted for Tregembo and sent him off with a
bewildering series of orders without an explanation.

Rogers knocked and entered.

'Come in, Sam. I am writing out your orders. You are to take
command. This lieutenant is staying with you. I am transferring to
Thunderer. You may send over my traps when you rejoin the fleet . . .
Hey! Tregembo! Pass word for my coxswain, damn it! Ah, Tregembo,
there you are. Tell Mr Q and Midshipmen Frey and Gillespy to pack
their dunnage . . . oh, yes, and you too . . . Sam, set course immediately for Gibraltar. Take that damned launch in tow. . . Come,
Sam, bustle! Bustle!' He shooed the first lieutenant out of the cabin.
Rogers's mouth gaped, but Drinkwater took little notice. He was
trying to think of all the essential things he would need, amazed at
what he seemed to have accumulated in eighteen months' residence.

'Mullender! God damn it, where is the fellow?'

He would take Frey because he was useful, and Gillespy out of pity.
He could not leave the child to endure Rogers's rough tongue. James
Quilhampton he would have to take. If he did not he doubted if
Quilhampton, like Tregembo, would ever forgive him the omission.

Antigone hove to off Europa Point and Drinkwater and his party
transferred to the launch. The midshipman in command of the boat
hoisted the lugsails and set his course for Gibraltar. Drinkwater
looked back to see the hands swarming aloft.

'God bless my soul!' he said again. The cheer carried to him over
the water and he stood up and doffed his hat. An hour later, still much
moved by the sudden change in his circumstances, he stood before
Louis.

'Sorry to lose you, Drinkwater, but I wish you well. I am fearful
that my ships will miss the battle and I told Lord Nelson so, but . . .'
the admiral shrugged his shoulders. 'No matter. I have hired a local

lugger to take you down the coast. It is all that is available but the passage will not be long and you will not wish to delay for something more comfortable, eh?'

'Indeed not, sir. I am obliged to you for your consideration.'

By that evening, in a fresh westerly breeze, the *barca longa* was beating out of Gibraltar Bay. Below, in what passed for a cabin, Drinkwater prepared to sleep in company with Quilhampton and his two midshipmen.

'We must make the best of it, gentlemen,' he said, but he need not have worried. The events of the day had tired him and, shorn for a time of the responsibilities of command, he fell into a deep sleep.

He was awakened by a sharp noise and a sudden shouting. Against the side of the lugger something heavy bumped.

'By God!' he shouted, throwing his legs clear of the bunk, 'there's something alongside!' In the darkness he heard Quilhampton wake. 'For God's sake, James, there's something wrong!' The unmistakable sound of a scuffle was going on overhead and suddenly it fell quiet. Drinkwater had tightened the belt of his breeches and had picked up a pistol when the hatch from the deck above was thrown back and the grey light of dawn flooded the mean space.

A moustachioed face peered down at them from behind the barrel of a gun. '*Arriba!*'

Drinkwater lowered his pistol; there was no point in courting death. He scrambled on deck where a swarthy Spaniard twisted the flintlock from his grasp. They were becalmed off the town of Tarifa and the *Guarda Costa* lugger that had put off from the mole lay alongside, her commander and crew in possession of the deck of the *barca longa*. A glance forward revealed Tregembo still struggling beneath three Spaniards. 'Belay that, Tregembo!'

'*Buenos Dias, Capitán.*' A smirking officer greeted his emergence on deck, while behind him Quilhampton and Frey struggled over the hatch-coaming swearing. The master of the *barca longa* was secured by two Spanish seamen and had obviously revealed the nature of his passengers. For a second Drinkwater suspected treachery, but the Gibraltarian shrugged.

'Eet is not my fault, Captain . . . the wind . . . eet go,' he said.

'That's a damned fine excuse.' Drinkwater expelled his breath in a long sigh of resignation. Any form of resistance was clearly too late.

'Wh . . . what is the matter?' Little Gillespy's voice piped as he came on deck behind Frey, rubbing the sleep from his eyes. The

Spanish officer pointed at him, looked at Drinkwater and burst out laughing, exchanging a remark with his men that was obviously obscene.

'We are prisoners, Mr Gillespy,' said Drinkwater bitterly. 'That is what is the matter.'

'Preesoners,' said the Coast Guard officer, testing the word for its aptness, '*si, capitán*, preesoners,' and he burst out laughing again.

Had he not had Quilhampton and Tregembo with him and felt the necessity of bearing their ill-luck with some degree of fortitude in front of the two midshipmen, Drinkwater afterwards thought he might have gone mad that day. As it was he scarcely recollected anything about the ignominious march through the town beyond a memory of curious dark eyes and high walls with overhanging foliage. Even the strange smells were forgotten in the stench of the prison in which the five men were unceremoniously thrown. It was a large stone-flagged room, lined with decomposed straw. A bucket stood, half-full, in a corner and the straw moved from the progress through it of numerous rats. Drinkwater assumed it must be the Bridewell of the local *Alcaid*, emptied for its new inmates.

Conversation between the men was constrained by their respective ranks as much as their circumstances. Tregembo, with customary resource, commenced the murder of the rats while James Quilhampton, knowing the agony through which Drinkwater was going, proved his worth by reassuring the two midshipmen, especially Gillespy, that things would undoubtedly turn out all right.

'There will be a battle soon and Nelson will have hundreds of Spaniards to exchange us for,' he kept saying. 'Now, Mr Gillespy, do you know how many Spanish seamen you are worth, eh? At the present exchange rate you are worth three. What d'you think of that, eh? Three seamen for each of you reefers, four for me as a junior lieutenant, one for Tregembo and fifteen for the captain. So all Nelson has to do is take twenty-six Dagoes and we're free men!'

It went on all day, utterly exhausting Quilhampton, while Drinkwater paced up and down, for they drew back for him, clearing a space as though the cell was a quarterdeck and the free winds of the Atlantic blew over its stinking flagstones. Once or twice he stopped, abstracted, his fists clenched behind his back, his head cocked like one listening, though in reality from his mangled shoulder. They would fall silent then, until he cursed under his breath and went on pacing furiously up and down.

Towards evening, as darkness closed in, the heavy bolts of the door were drawn back and a skin of bitter wine and a few hunks of dark bread were passed in on a wooden platter. But that was all. Darkness fell and the place seemed to stink more than ever. Drinkwater remained standing, wedged into a corner, unable to compose his mind in sleep. But he must have slept, for he woke cramped, as another platter of bread and more raw wine appeared. They broke their fast in silence and an hour later the bolts were drawn back again. The Coast Guard officer beckoned Drinkwater to follow and led him along a passage, up a flight of stone steps and through a heavy wooden door. A strip of carpet along another passage suggested they had left the prison. The officer threw open a further door and Drinkwater entered a large, white-walled room. A window opened onto a courtyard in which he could hear a fountain playing. Leaves of some shrub lifted in the wind. On the opposite wall, over a fireplace, a fan of arms spread out. A table occupied the centre of the room, round which were set several chairs. Two were occupied. In one sat a tall dragoon officer, his dark face slashed by drooping moustaches, his legs encased in high boots. His heavy blue coat was faced with sky-blue and he wore yellow leather gloves. A heavy, curved sabre hung on its long slings beside his chair. He watched Drinkwater through a blue haze of tobacco smoke from the cigar he was smoking.

The other man was older, about sixty, Drinkwater judged, and presumably the *Alcaid* or the *Alcalde*. The Coast Guard officer made some form of introduction and the older man rose, his brown eyes not unkind. He spoke crude English with a heavy accent.

'Good day, Capitán. I am Don Joaquín Alejo Méliton Pérez, *Alcade* of Tarifa. Here', he indicated the still-seated cavalry officer, 'is Don Juan Gonzalez De Urias of His Most Catholic Majesty's Almansa Dragoons. Please to take a seat.'

'Thank you, señor.'

'I too have been prisoner. Of you English. When you are defending Gibraltar under General Elliott.'

'Don Pérez, I protest, my effects . . . my clothes . . .' he grasped his soiled shirt for emphasis, but the old man raised his hand.

'All your clothes and equipments are safe. I ask you here this morning to tell me your name. Don Juan is here coming from Cadiz. He is to take back your name and the ship that you are *capitán* from . . . This you must tell me, please.'

The *Alcalde* picked up a quill and dipped it expectantly in an ink-pot.

'I am Captain Nathaniel Drinkwater, Don Pérez, of His Britannic Majesty's frigate *Antigone* . . .'

At this the hitherto silent De Urias leaned forward. Drinkwater heard the name *Antigone* several times. The two men looked at him with apparently renewed interest.

'Please, you say your name, one time more.'

'Drink-water . . .'

'Eh?' The *Alcalde* looked up, frowned and mimed the act of lifting a glass and sipping from it, '*Agua?*'

Drinkwater nodded. 'Drink-water.'

'*Absurdo!*' laughed the cavalry officer, pulling the piece of paper from the *Alcalde*, then taking his quill and offering them to Drinkwater who wrote the information in capital letters and passed it back.

Don Juan De Urias stared at the letters and pronounced them, looked up at Drinkwater, then thrust himself to his feet. The two men exchanged a few words and the officer turned to go. As he left the room the Coast Guard officer returned and motioned Drinkwater to follow him once again.

He was returned to the cell and it was clear that much speculation had been in progress during his absence.

'Beg pardon, sir,' said Quilhampton, 'but could you tell us if . . .'

'Nothing has happened, gentlemen, beyond an assurance that our clothes are safe and that Cadiz is being informed of our presence here.'

Drinkwater saw Quilhampton's eyes light up. 'Perhaps, sir, that means our release is the nearer . . .'

It was an artificially induced hope that Quilhampton himself knew to be foolish, but the morale of the others should not be allowed to drop.

'Perhaps, Mr Q, perhaps . . .'

They languished in the cell for a further two days and then they were suddenly taken out into a stable yard and offered water and the contents of their chests with which to prepare themselves for a journey, the *Alcade* explained. When they had finished they were more presentable. Drinkwater felt much better and had retrieved his journal from the chest. The *Alcalde* returned, accompanied by Don Juan De Urias.

'Don Juan has come', the *Alcalde* explained, 'to take you to Cadiz. You are known to our ally, *Capitán*.

Drinkwater frowned. Had the French summoned him to Cadiz?

131

'Who knows me, señor?'

Perez addressed a question to De Urias who pulled from the breast of his coat a paper. He unfolded it and held it out to Drinkwater. It was in Spanish but at the bottom the signature was in a different hand.

'Santhonax!'

PART THREE

Battle

'Now, gentlemen, let us do something today which the world may talk of hereafter.'

VICE-ADMIRAL COLLINGWOOD TO HIS OFFICERS,
HMS *Royal Sovereign*, forenoon, 21st October 1805

'The enemy . . . will endeavour to envelop our rear, to break through our line and to direct his ships in groups upon such of ours as he shall have cut off, so as to surround them and defeat them.'

VICE-ADMIRAL VILLENEUVE TO HIS CAPTAINS
Standing Orders given on board the *Bucentaure*,
Toulon Road, 21st December 1804

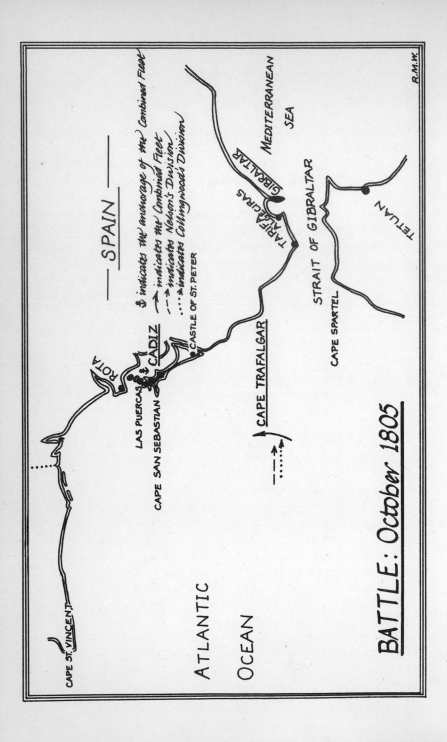

CAPE ST. VINCENT

ATLANTIC

OCEAN

SPAIN

ROTA

CADIZ

LAS PUERCAS

CAPE SAN SEBASTIAN

CASTLE OF ST. PETER

⚓ indicates the anchorage of the Combined Fleet
→ indicates the Combined Fleet
→ indicates Nelson's Division
····→ indicates Collingwood's Division

CAPE TRAFALGAR

MEDITERRANEAN

SEA

GIBRALTAR

TARIFA

ALGECIRAS

STRAIT OF GIBRALTAR

CAPE SPARTEL

TETUAN

R.M.W.

BATTLE: October 1805

Santhonax

Lieutenant Don Juan Gonzalez de Urias of His Most Catholic Majesty's Dragoons of Almansa flicked the stub of a cigar elegantly away with his yellow kid gloves and beckoned two of his troopers. Without a word he indicated the sea-chests of the British and the men lifted them and took them under an archway. Motioning his prisoners to follow, he led them through the arch to the street where a large black carriage awaited them. Dragoons with cocked carbines flanked the door of the carriage and behind them Drinkwater caught sight of the curious faces of children and a wildly barking dog. The five British clambered into the coach, Drinkwater last, in conformance with traditional naval etiquette. Tregembo was muttering continual apologies, feeling awkward and out of place at being in such intimate contact with 'gentlemen'. Drinkwater was compelled to tell him to hold his tongue. Behind them the door slammed shut and the carriage jerked forward. On either side, their gleaming sabres drawn, a score of De Urias's dragoons formed their escort.

For a while they sat in silence and then they were clear of the town, rolling along a coast-road from which the sea could be seen. None of them looked at the orange groves or the cork oaks that grew on the rising ground to the north; they all strove for a glimpse of the blue sea and the distant brown mountains of Africa. The sight of a sail made them miserable as they tried to make out whether it was one of the sloops Collingwood had directed to blockade coastal trade with Cadiz.

'Sir,' said Quilhampton suddenly, 'if we leapt from the coach, we could signal that brig for a boat . . .'

'And have your other hand cut off in the act of waving,' said Drinkwater dismissively. 'No, James. We are prisoners being escorted to Cadiz. For the time being we shall have to submit to our fate.'

This judgement having been pronounced by the captain produced a long and gloomy silence. Drinkwater, however, was pondering their chances. Freedom from the awful cell at Tarifa had revived his spirits. For whatever reason the French wanted them at Cadiz, it was nearer to the British battle-fleet than Tarifa and an opportunity might present itself for them to escape.

'Beg pardon, sir,' put in Quilhampton.

'Yes, James?'

'Did you say "Santhonax", sir, when were were in the stable yard? Is that the same cove that we took prisoner at Al Mukhra?'

'I believe so, yes.'

'I remember him. He escaped off the Cape . . . D'you remember him, Tregembo?'

'Aye, zur, I do. The Cap'n and I know him from away back.' Tregembo's eyes met those of Drinkwater and the old Cornishman subsided into silence.

Piqued by this air of mystery, Frey asked, 'Who is he sir?'

Drinkwater considered; it would do no harm to tell them. Besides, they had time to kill, the jolting of the coach was wearisome, and it is always the balm of slaves and prisoners to tell stories.

'He is a French officer of considerable merit, Mr Frey. A man of the stamp of, say, Captain Blackwood. He was, a long time ago, a spy, sent into England to foment mutiny among the fleet at the Nore. He used a lugger to cross the Channel and we chased him, I recollect, Tregembo. He shot part of our mast down . . .'

'That's right, zur,' added Tregembo turning on the junior officers, 'but we was only in a little cutter, the *Kestrel*, twelve pop-guns. We had 'im in the end though, zur.' Tregembo grinned.

'Aye. At Camperdown,' mused Drinkwater, calling into his mind's eye that other bloody October day eight years earlier.

'At Camperdown, sir? There were French ships at Camperdown?' asked Frey puzzled.

'No, Mr Frey. Santhonax was sent from Paris to stir the Dutch fleet to activity. I believe him to have been instrumental in forcing Admiral De Winter to sail from the Texel. Tregembo and I were still in the *Kestrel*, cruising off the place, one of Duncan's look-outs. When the Dutch came out Santhonax had an armed yacht at his disposal. We fought and took her, and Santhonax was locked up in Maidstone Gaol.' Drinkwater sighed. It all seemed so long ago and there was the disturbing image of the beautiful Hortense swimming into his mind. He recollected himself; that was no part of what he wanted to tell his juniors about Santhonax.

'Unfortunately,' he went on, 'whilst transferring Santhonax to the hulks at Portsmouth, much as we are travelling now . . .'

'He escaped,' broke in Quilhampton, 'just as we might . . .'

'He spoke unaccented and near perfect English, James,' countered Drinkwater tolerantly, ignoring Quilhampton's exasperation. 'How

136

good is your Spanish, eh?'

'I take your point, sir, and beg your pardon.'

Drinkwater smiled. 'No matter. But that is not the end of the story, for Mr Quilhampton and I next encountered Edouard Santhonax when he commanded our own frigate *Antigone* in the Red Sea. He was in the act of re-storing her after careening and we took her one night, in a cutting-out expedition, and brought both him and his frigate out together from the Sharm Al Mukhra. Most of the guns were still ashore and we were caught in the Indian Ocean by a French cruiser from Mauritius. We managed to fight her off but in the engagement Santhonax contrived to escape by diving overboard and swimming to his fellow countryman's ship. We were saved by the timely arrived of the *Telemachus*, twenty-eight, commanded by an old messmate of mine.'

'And that was the last time you saw him, sir?'

'Yes. But not the last time I heard of him. After Napoleon extricated himself from Egypt and returned from Paris a number of officers that had done him singular services were rewarded. Santhonax was one of them. He transferred, I believe, to the army, not unknown in the French and Spanish services,' he said in a didactic aside for the information of the two young midshipmen who sat wide-eyed at the Captain's tale, 'who often refer to their fleets as "armies" and their admirals as "captains-general". Now, I suppose, he has recognised my name and summoned me to Cadiz.'

'I think he may want information from you, sir,' said Quilhampton seriously.

'Very probably, Mr Q. We shall have to decide what to tell him, eh?'

'Sir,' said Gillespy frowning.

'Yes, Mr Gillespy?'

'It is a very strange story, sir. I mean the coincidences . . . almost as if you are fated to meet . . . if you see what I mean, sir.'

Drinkwater smiled at the boy who had flushed scarlet at expressing this fantasy.

'So I have often felt, Mr Gillespy; but in truth it is not so very remarkable. Consider, at the time Tregembo, Mr Q and I were fighting this fellow in the Red Sea, Sir Sydney Smith was stiffening the defences of Acre and thwarting Boney's plans in the east. A little later Sir Sydney fell into Bonaparte's hands during a boat operation off Havre, along with poor Captain Wright, and the pair of them spent two years in The Temple prison in Paris,' he paused, remembering

137

Camelford's revelations about the connection of Santhonax with the supposed suicide. 'The two of them escaped and Wright was put in command of the sloop-of-war *Vinejo*, only to be captured in a calm by gunboats in the Morbihan after a gallant defence. He was returned to the Temple . . .'

'Where Bonaparte had him murdered,' put in Quilhampton.

Drinkwater ignored the interruption. Poor Quilhampton was more edgy than he had been a few days earlier. Presumably the strain of playing Dutch uncle to this pair of boys had told on his nerves. 'Very probably,' he said, 'but I think the events not dissimilar to my own encounters with Santhonax; a sort of personal antagonism within the war. It may be fate, or destiny, or simply coincidence.' Or witchcraft, he wanted to add, remembering again the auburn hair of Hortense Santhonax.

Silence fell again as the coach rocked and swayed over the unmade road and the dragoons jingled alongside. From time to time De Urias would ride up abreast of the window and peer in. After several hours they stopped at a roadside *taverna* where a change of horses awaited them. The troopers had a meal from their saddlebags, watered their horses and remounted. For some English gold Drinkwater found in his breeches pocket he was able to buy some cold meat and a little rot-gut wine at an inflated price. The inn-keeper took the money, bit it and, having pocketed the coin, made an obscene gesture at the British.

'We are not popular,' observed Quilhampton drily, with a lordly indifference that persuaded Drinkwater he was recovering his spirits after the morning's peevishness. They dozed intermittently, aware that as the coast-road swung north the distant sea had become wave-flecked under a fresh westerly breeze. Drinkwater was awakened by Quilhampton from one of these states of semi-consciousness that was neither sleep nor wakefulness but a kind of limbo into which his mind and spirit seemed to take refuge after the long, unremitting months of duty and the hopelessness of captivity.

'Sir, wake up and look, sir.'

From the window he realised they were headed almost north, running across the mouth of a bay. To the west he could see distant grey squares, the topsails of Nelson's look-out ships, keeping contact with the main fleet out of sight over the horizon to the westward. The thought made him turn to his companions.

'Gentlemen, I must caution you against divulging any information to our enemy. They are likely to question us all, individually. You have nothing to fear,' he said to young Gillespy. 'You simply state that you were a midshipman on your first voyage and know nothing.' He regretted the paternal impulse that had made the child his note-taker. 'You may say I was an old curmudgeon, Mr Gillespy, and that I told you nothing. Midshipmen are apt to hold that opinion of their seniors.' He smiled and the boy smiled uncertainly back. At least he could rely upon Frey and Quilhampton.

They crossed the back of a hill that fell to a headland whereon stood a tall stone observation tower. A picket of *Guarda Costa* horses and men were nearby and they turned and holloaed at the coach and its escort as it swept past.

'I recognise where we are,' said Drinkwater suddenly. 'That is Cape Trafalgar. Have we changed horses again?'

'Twice while you were dozing, sir.'

'Good God!' It was already late afternoon and the sun was westering behind great banks of cloud. On their right, above the orange and olive groves, Drinkwater caught sight of the Chiclana hill. They crossed a river and passed through a small town.

'Look sir, soldiers!' said Frey a little later as the coach slowed. They could hear De Urias shouting commands and swearing. Drinkwater looked out of the window but the nearest trooper gestured for him to pull his head in; he was not permitted to stare. The coach increased speed again and they were jolting through a bivouac of soldiers. Drinkwater recognised the bell-topped shakoes of French infantry and noted the numerals '67' and '16'. Someone saw his face and raised a shout: *'Hey, Voilà Anglais . . . !'*

The cooking fires of the two battalions drew astern as they began to go downhill and then they pulled up. Drinkwater saw water on either side of them before a dragoon opened each door and the window blinds were drawn. The trooper said something to them in Spanish from which they gathered that any attempt to see any more would be met by a stern measure. The doors were slammed and, in darkness, they resumed the last miles of their journey from Tarifa, aware that the coach was traversing the long mole of Cadiz.

They were hurried into their new place of incarceration. The building seemed to be some kind of a barracks and they were taken into a bare corridor and marched swiftly along it. Two negligent French sentries made a small concession to De Urias's rank as they halted by a door. A turnkey appeared, the door was unlocked and the two midshipmen, Tregembo and Quilhampton were motioned to enter. De Urias restrained Drinkwater whose quick glance inside the cell revealed it as marginally cleaner than the hole at Tarifa, but still unsuitable for the accommodation of officers.

'Lieutenant, I protest; the usages of war do not condemn officers doing their duty to kennels fit for malefactors!'

It was clear that the protest, which could not have failed to be understood by the Spanish officer, fell on deaf ears. As the turnkey locked the door De Urias motioned Drinkwater to follow him again. They emerged into a courtyard covered by a scrap of grey sky. The wind was still in the west, Drinkwater noted. As they crossed the square he saw a pair of horses with rich shabraques being held by an orderly outside a double door beneath a colonnade. The door was flanked by two sentries. Drinkwater's eye spotted the grenadier badges and the regimental number '67' again. They passed through the door. A group of officers were lounging about a table. One, in full dress, stood up from where he half sat on the end of the heavy table.

'Ah,' he said, smiling almost cordially, *'le capitaine anglais. Bienvenu à Cadiz!'* The officer bowed from the waist, his gaudy shako tucked under his arm. *'Je suis Lieutenant Leroux, Le Soixante-septième Régiment de Ligne.'*

'Bravo, Leroux!' There was an ironic laugh from his fellow officers which Leroux ignored. He twirled a moustache. *'Allez, Capitaine . . .'*

Ignoring De Urias, Drinkwater followed the insouciant Leroux up a flight of stairs and to a door at the end of another corridor. At the door Leroux paused and Drinkwater was reminded of a midshipman preparing to enter the cabin of an irascible captain. Leroux coughed, knocked and turned his ear to the door. Then he opened it, crashed to attention and announced Drinkwater. He stood aside and Drinkwater entered the room.

A tall, curly-haired officer rose from the table at which he had been writing. His dark and handsome features were disfigured by a broad, puckered scar which dragged down the corner of his left eye and split his cheek. His eyes met those of Drinkwater.

'So, Captain,' he said in flawless English, 'we meet again . . .' He indicated a chair, dismissed Leroux and sat down, his hand rubbing his jaw, his eyes fastened on his prisoner. For a moment or two Drinkwater thought the intelligence reports might have been wrong – Santhonax wore an elaborate, gold-embroidered uniform that was more naval than military – but he was soon made aware of Santhonax's status and the reason for Leroux's deference.

'I recollect you reminded me that it was the fortune of war that I was your prisoner when we last had the pleasure of meeting.' Santhonax's tone was heavily ironic. Drinkwater said nothing. 'I believe the more apt English expression to be "a turning of tables", eh?'

Santhonax rose and went to a cabinet on which a decanter and glasses stood in a campaign case. He filled two glasses and handed one to Drinkwater.

Drinkwater hesitated.

'It is good cognac, Captain Drinkwater.'

'Thank you.'

'Good. We have known each other too long to be hostile. I see you too have been wounded . . .'

Santhonax inclined his head in an imitative gesture, indicating Drinkwater's mangled shoulder.

'A shell wound, *m'sieur*, received off Boulogne and added to the scars you gave me yourself.'

'*Touché.*' Santhonax paused and sipped his cognac, never taking his eyes off Drinkwater, as though weighing him up. 'Not "*m'sieur*", Captain, but *Colonel, Colonel* and *Aide-de-Camp* to His Imperial Majesty.'

'My congratulations,' Drinkwater said drily.

'And you are to be congratulated too, I believe. You have been commanding the frigate *Antigone*.' He paused, he had commanded her himself once. 'That is something else we have in common. She was a fine ship.'

'She *is* a fine ship, Colonel.'

'Yes. I watched her wear off San Sebastian a week or two ago. You and Blackwood of the *Euryalus* are well known to us.'

'You are no longer in the naval service, Colonel,' said Drinkwater attempting to steer the conversation. 'Could that be because it has no future?'

The barb went home and Drinkwater saw the ice in Santhonax's eyes. But the former agent was a master of self-control. 'Not at all, Captain. As you see from my present appointment, I have not severed my connections with the navy.'

'It occurs to me, however, that you may still be a spy . . .' He was watching Santhonax closely. That fine movement, no more than a flicker of the muscles that controlled the pupils of his eyes, was perceptible to the vigilant Drinkwater. There was no doubt that Santhonax was in Cadiz at the behest of his Imperial master. As an aide-de-camp Santhonax would be allowed the privileges of reporting direct to Napoleon. Even the Commander-in-Chief of the Combined

Fleet, Vice-Admiral Villeneuve, would have to report to Paris through the Minister of Marine, Decrès.

Santhonax attempted to divert the conversation. 'You are still suspiciously minded, Captain Drinkwater, I see. There is little work for a spy here. The Combined Fleets of France and Spain are not as useless as you English would sometimes like to assume. They have twice crossed the Atlantic, ravaging the sugar islands off the West Indies, recovered British possessions in the islands and fought an engagement with the British fleet . . .'

'In which with overwhelming force you managed to lose two ships . . .'

'In which the *Spanish* managed to lose two ships, Captain, and following which the British admiral is being tried for failure to do his utmost. I recall the last time this occurred it was found necessary to shoot him . . .'

Drinkwater mastered the anger mounting in him. Losing his temper would do no good. Besides, an idea was forming in his head. At that moment it was no more than a flash of inspiration, an intuition of opportunity, and it was laid aside in the need to mollify. He remained silent.

Santhonax seemed to relax. He sat back in his chair, although he still regarded Drinkwater with those unwavering eyes.

'Tell me, Captain, when you took *Antigone*, did you discover a portrait of my wife?'

'I did.'

'And . . . what became of it?'

'I kept it. You might have had it back had you not so unceremoniously left us off the Cape. It was removed from its stretcher, rolled up, and is still on board the *Antigone*. If I was to be liberated I should send it back to you as a mark of my gratitude.'

Santhonax barked a short laugh. 'Ha! But you were not on board *Antigone* when the Spanish *Guarda Costa* took you, were you, Captain? Where *were* you going?'

'It would be no trouble to send for the canvas, Colonel, most of my effects remain on board . . .'

'I asked', broke in Santhonax, his eyes hardening again, 'where you were going?'

'I was transferring to another ship, Colonel, the *Thunderer*, seventy-four.'

Santhonax raised one ironic eyebrow. 'Another promotion, eh? What a pity you were asleep the other morning. Our ally's vigilance has deprived Nelson of a captain.'

Drinkwater kept his temper and again remained silent.

'Tell me, Captain, is it correct that Admiral Louis's squadron is in Gibraltar?'

The idea sparked within Drinkwater again. Santhonax's intention was almost certainly similar to that when he had exerted pressure on de Winter in the autumn of '97. He was an aggressive French imperialist, known to be Bonapartist and a familiar of Napoleon's. Surely it was the French Emperor's intention that the Combined Fleet should sail? Even with those reports that Napoleon had broken up the camp at Boulogne, every indication was that he wanted the fleet of Villeneuve at sea. It was clear that Santhonax's question was loaded. The French were not certain about Louis, not absolutely certain, although the movements of British ships were reported to them regularly from Algeçiras. Santhonax wanted extra confirmation, perhaps as added information with which to cajole Villeneuve as he had so successfully worked on de Winter.

And if Napoleon wanted Villeneuve at sea, so too did Nelson!

Anything, therefore, that smoothed Villeneuve's passage to sea was assisting that aim and, if he consciously aided the schemes of Napoleon, at least he had the satisfaction of knowing that the fleet that lay over the horizon to the west was equally anxious for the same result.

'Come, Captain,' urged Santhonax, 'we know that there are British line of battle ships in Gibraltar. Are they Louis's?'

'Yes.' Drinkwater answered monosyllabically, as though reluctant to reply.

'Which ships?'

Drinkwater said nothing. 'It is not a difficult matter to ascertain, Captain, and the information may make the stay of you and your friends', Santhonax paused to lend the threat weight, 'a little pleasanter by your co-operation.'

Drinkwater sighed, as though resigning himself to his fate. He endeavoured to appear crestfallen. '*Canopus, Queen, Spencer, Tigre* and *Zealous.*'

'Ah, a ninety-eight, an eighty and three seventy-fours . . .'

'You are well informed, Colonel Santhonax.' Santhonax ignored the ironic compliment.

'And Calder, he has gone back to England in a frigate?'

'No, he has gone back to England in a battleship, the *Prince of Wales*; and the *Donegal* was to go to Gibraltar to join Louis.'

'You have been most informative, Captain.'

Drinkwater shrugged with the disdain he felt Santhonax would expect, and added, 'It is still a British fleet, Colonel . . .' He deliberately left the sentence unfinished.

'There is nothing to alarm us in the sight of a British fleet, Captain. Your seventy-fours have barely five hundred men on board, they are worn out by a two years' cruise; you are no braver than us, indeed you have infinitely less motive to fight well, less love of country. You can manoeuvre well, but we have also had sea-experience. I am confident, Captain Drinkwater, that we are about to see the end of an era for you and a glorious new era for the Imperial Navy.'

Drinkwater thought at first Santhonax was rehearsing some argument that he would later put to Villeneuve, but there was something sincere in the speech. The guard was down, this was the soul of the man, a revealed intimacy born out of the long years of antagonism.

'Time will tell, Colonel.'

Santhonax rose. 'Oh yes indeed, Captain, time will tell, time and the abilities of your Admiral Nelson.'

The Spectre of Nelson

Drinkwater woke refreshed after a good night's sleep. He had been led from his interview with Santhonax to an upper room, presumably an officer's quarters within the barracks, which was sparsely, though adequately furnished, and served a plain meal of cold meat, fruit and wine. He had later been asked for and given his parole. When this formality had been completed his sea-chest was brought in by an orderly and he was returned his sword. He was refused leave to see the others but assured that they were quite comfortable.

For a long while he had lain awake, staring at a few stars that showed through the window and listening to the sounds of Cadiz; the barking of dogs, the calls of sentries, the periodic ringing of a convent bell and the sad playing of a distant guitar. He went over and over the interview with Santhonax, trying to see more in it than a mere exchange of words, and certain that his instinct was right and that Santhonax was there, in Cadiz, to force Villeneuve to sea. Eventually he had slept.

With the new day came this strange feeling of cheerfulness and he drew himself up in bed, a sudden thought occurring to him. He had been groping towards a conclusion the previous night, but he had been tired, his mind clogged by all the events of the day. Now, he began to perceive something very clearly. He had grasped Santhonax's purpose all right, but only half of its import. Santhonax's last remark, his sneering contempt for Nelson, was the key. He knew that few of the French admirals were contemptuous of Nelson, least of all Villeneuve who had escaped the terrible *débâcle* of Abukir Bay. But Santhonax would not sneer contemptuously without good cause; he had impugned Nelson's abilities, not his character. In what way was Nelson's ability defective?

And then he recalled his own complaint to Pitt. It was not a defect so much as a calculated risk, but it had twice cost Nelson dearly. Nelson's blockade out of sight of land had allowed Brueys to slip out of Toulon to Egypt, and Villeneuve to slip out of Toulon to the West Indies. Now, although he had Blackwood up at the very gates of Cadiz, it might happen again. If the wind went easterly the Combined Fleet could get out of Cadiz and would not run into Nelson unless it continued west. But at this time of the year the wind would soon swing to the west, giving the Combined Fleet a clear run through the Straits of Gibraltar. Nelson was fifty miles west of Cadiz. He might catch up, but then again he might not! And Napoleon was supposed to have decamped his army from Boulogne. They had not gone west, so they too must be marching east! Of course! Drinkwater leapt from the bed and began pacing the little room: Austria had joined the coalition and a small British expeditionary force under General Craig had gone east, he himself had escorted it through the Gut! The ideas came to him thick and fast now, facts, rumours, all evidence of a complete reversal of Napoleon's intentions but no less lethal. Craig would be cut off, British supremacy in the Mediterranean destroyed. *That* was why Ganteaume had not broken out of Brest. He could tie half the Royal Navy down there. And *that* was why Allemand had come no further south. He could not break through Nelson's fleet to reinforce Villeneuve but, by God, he could still keep 'em all guessing! And last, the very man whom Nelson had sent *Antigone* to guard against cutting Louis off in Gibraltar, Admiral Salcedo at Cartagena, had no need to sail west. He could simply wait until Villeneuve came past! It was a brilliant deception and ensured that British eyes were concentrated on the Channel.

Drinkwater ceased pacing, his mind seeing everything with a wonderful clarity. He felt a cold tingle run the length of his spine. 'God's bones,' he muttered, 'now what the devil do I do?'

His plan of the previous evening seemed knocked awry. If he added reasons persuading Santhonax that urging Villeneuve to sail was advantageous to Nelson, would Nelson miss the Combined Fleet? If, on the other hand, Villeneuve was left alone, would Nelson simply blockade him or would he attempt an attack? The long Mole of Cadiz could be cut off by the marines of the fleet and a thousand seamen, the anchorage shelled by bomb-vessels.

'This is the very horns of a dilemma,' he muttered, running his fingers through his hair. His thoughts were abruptly interrupted when the door of his room opened and Tregembo entered with hot shaving water. The sight cheered Drinkwater.

'Good morning, zur,' the old Cornishman rasped.

'God bless my soul, Tregembo, you're a welcome sight!'

'Aye, zur. I was passed word to attend 'ee, zur, and here I am.' Tregembo jerked his head and Drinkwater caught sight of the orderly just outside.

'Are you and the others all right?'

Tregembo nodded and fussed around the room, unrolling Drinkwater's housewife and stropping the razor.

'Aye, zur. All's as well as we can expect, considering . . .'

'No talk!' The orderly appeared in the doorway.

Drinkwater drew himself up. 'Be silent!' he commanded, 'I shall address my servant if I so wish, and desire him to convey my compliments to my officers.' Drinkwater fixed the orderly with his most baleful quarterdeck glare and went on, as though still addressing the French soldier, 'and to let 'em know I believe that things will not remain static for long. D'you hear me, sir?' Drinkwater turned away and caught Tregembo's eye.

'Not remain static long,' the Cornishman muttered, 'aye, aye, zur.' He handed Drinkwater the lathered shaving brush. They exchanged glances of comprehension and Tregembo left the room. Behind him the orderly slammed the door and turned the key noisily in the lock.

The silly incident left Drinkwater in a good enough humour to shave without cutting himself and the normality of the little routine caused him to reflect upon his own stupidity. It was quite ridiculous of him to suppose that he, a prisoner, could have the slightest influence on events. The best he could hope for was that those events might possibly provide him with an opportunity to effect an escape. At least he had Tregembo as a go-between; that was certainly better than nothing.

All day Drinkwater sat or paced in the tiny room. Towards evening he was taken down to walk in the courtyard, seeing little of his surroundings but enjoying half an hour in the company of Quilhampton and the two midshipmen.

'How are you faring, James?'

'Oh, well enough, sir, well enough. A little down-hearted I fear, but we'll manage. And you, sir? Did you see Santhonax?'

'Yes. Did you?'

'No, sir. By the way, I trust you have no objections, but our gaolers have allowed Tregembo to look after us. I hope you don't mind us poaching your coxswain, sir.'

'No,' said Drinkwater, brightening, 'matter of fact it might be a help. He can keep up communications between us. Have you learned anything useful?'

'Not much. From the way those French soldiers behave when a Spanish officer's about there's not much love lost between 'em.'

Drinkwater remembered the negligence of the two sentries in

acknowledging De Urias. 'Good point, James.' He ought to have noticed that himself.

'And I believe there has been an epidemic in Andalucia recently, some sort of fever, and as a consequence there's a shortage of food. Cadiz is like a place under seige.'

'Good God! How d'you know that?'

Quilhampton shrugged. 'This and that, sir. Listening to the guards chatter. You can pick up some of the sense. I thought something of the kind must have happened as we came through the countryside yesterday. Not too many people in the fields, lot of young women and children . . . oh, I don't know, sir . . . just a feeling.'

'By heaven, James, that's well argued. I had not even noticed a single field.'

Quilhampton smiled thinly. 'We ain't too well liked, sir, I'm afraid. "Perfidious Albion" and all that.' He was suddenly serious and stopped strolling. He turned and said, 'D'you think we're going to get out, sir? I mean before the war's over or we're taken to France.'

Drinkwater managed a confident smile. 'D'you know, James, that an admiral is worth four post-captains on exchange. How many lieutenants d'you think that is, eh? By God, we'll be worth our weight in gold! After the battle they'll be queueing up to exchange us for admiral this and commodore that.' He patted Quilhampton's arm. 'Brace up, James, and keep up the spirits of those two reefers.'

'Oh, Frey's all right; he's as tough as a fore-tack despite appearances to the contrary. It's Gillespy I'm worried about. Poor boy cried last night. I think he thought I was asleep . . .'

'Poor little devil. Would it help if I had a word with him?'

'Yes, I think so. Tell him how many admirals there will be to exchange after the battle.'

Drinkwater turned but Quilhampton said, 'Sir . . . sir, do you think there's going to *be* a battle?'

'Damn sure, James,' Drinkwater replied. And for that instant, remembering Nelson's conviction, he was irrationally certain of the fact.

It is very curious, Drinkwater wrote in his journal, *to sit and write these words as a prisoner. I am far from being resigned to my fate but while I can still hear the call of gulls and can hear the distant noise of the sea which cannot be very far from my little window, I have not yet sunk into that despond that men who have been imprisoned say comes upon one. God grant that such a torpor is long in coming or fate releases me from this mischance . . .*

He stopped writing and looked at his pen. Elizabeth's pen. He closed his journal quickly and got up, falling to a violent pacing of the floor in an effort to drive from his mind all thoughts of Elizabeth or his children. He must not give way to that; that was the way to despair.

He was saved from further agony by the opening of his door. A strange officer in the uniform of the Imperial Navy stood behind the orderly. He spoke English.

'*Capitaine* Drinkwater? Good evening. I am Lieutenant René Guillet of the *Bucentaure*. Will you 'ave the kindness to follow me. It would be advisable that you bring your 'at.'

'This is a formal occasion?'

'*Oui.*'

Drinkwater was led into the same room in which he had been interviewed by Santhonax. Santhonax was there again, but standing. Sitting at the table signing documents was another man. After a short interval he looked up and studied the prisoner. Then he stood up and walked round the table, addressing a few words to Guillet who came smartly forward, collected the papers and placed them in a leather satchel. The strange man was tall and thin with an intelligent face. He wore a white-powdered wig over his high forehead. His nose was straight and his mouth well made and small. He had a firm chin, although his jowls were heavy. Drinkwater judged him to be much the same age as himself. He wore a long-skirted blue uniform coat with a high collar and corduroy pantaloons of a greenish colour, with wide stripes of gold. His feet were thrust into elegant black half-boots of the type favoured by hussars and light cavalry. Across his waist there looped a gold watch-chain from which depended a heavy gold seal.

'Introduce us, Colonel.' His voice sounded tired, but his English, although heavily accented, was good.

Santhonax stepped forward. 'Captain Nathaniel Drinkwater of the Royal Navy, formerly commander of His Britannic Majesty's frigate *Antigone* . . .'

'Ahhh . . . *Antigone* . . .' said the stranger knowingly.

'On his way to take command of the *Thunderer*,' Santhonax's voice was ironic 'but taken prisoner *en route*.' He turned to Drinkwater, 'May I present Vice-Admiral Villeneuve, Commander-in-Chief of the Combined Squadrons of His Imperial and Royal Majesty Napoleon, Emperor of the French and of his Most Catholic Majesty King Ferdinand of Spain.'

The two men exchanged bows. 'Please sit down, Captain.' Villeneuve indicated a chair and returned behind the table where he sat, leaned forward with his elbows on the table and passed his hands over his face before resting his chin upon the tips of his fingers.

'Colonel Santhonax has told me much about you. Your frigate has made as much of a name for itself as *Euryalus*.'

'You do me too much honour, sir.'

'They are both good ships. The one was copied from the French, the other captured.'

'That is so, sir.'

'Colonel Santhonax also tells me you informed him that Nelson commands the British squadron off Cadiz. Is this true?'

Drinkwater frowned. He had said no such thing. He looked at Santhonax who was still standing and smiling, the candle-light and his scar giving the smile the quality of a grimace.

'You did not deny it when I said he was with the British fleet,' Santhonax explained. Drinkwater felt annoyed with himself for being so easily trapped, but he reflected that perhaps Santhonax had given away more. In any case, it was pointless to deny it. It seemed that Villeneuve would assume the worst, and if the worst was Nelson, then no harm was done. He nodded.

'Nelson *is* in command, sir,' he said.

He heard Villeneuve sigh and felt he had reasoned correctly.

The French admiral seemed abstracted for a second and Santhonax coughed.

'And several ships have gone to Gibraltar?' the admiral asked.

'Yes, sir.'

'Where is the *Superb*?' asked Villeneuve. 'She had gone to England for repair, no?'

'She had not rejoined the fleet when I left it, sir.' Drinkwater felt a quickening of his pulse. All Villeneuve's questions emphasised his desire to hear that Nelson's fleet was weakened by dispersal.

The admiral nodded. 'Very well, Captain, thank you.' He rang a little bell and Guillet reappeared. Drinkwater rose and bowed to the admiral who was turning towards Santhonax, but Santhonax ignored Villeneuve.

'Captain Drinkwater!'

Drinkwater turned. 'Yes?'

'I am leaving . . . to rejoin the Emperor tonight. You will send the picture to the Rue Victoire will you not . . . when you return to your ship?' Santhonax was sneering at him. Drinkwater remembered Camelford's words: 'Shoot 'em both!'

'When I rejoin my ship . . .'

The two men stared at each other for a second. 'Until the next time, *au revoir.*'

Walking from the room Drinkwater heard a suppressed confrontation between the two men. As the door closed behind him he heard Santhonax quite clearly mention '*Le spectre de Nelson . . .*'

Tregembo's brief visit the next morning disclosed little. 'They've got their t'gallants up, zur. Frogs and Dagoes all awaiting the order, zur . . . and pleased the Frogs'll be to go.'

'There's nothing new about that, Tregembo, they're always getting ready to go. It's the goin' they ain't so good at,' Drinkwater replied, lathering his face. 'But how the hell d'you know all this, eh?'

'There are Bretons in the guardroom, zur. I unnerstand 'em. Their talk, like the Kurnowic it is, zur . . .'

'Ahhh, of course.' Drinkwater smiled as he took the stropped razor from Tregembo, recalling Tregembo's smuggling past and the trips made to Brittany to evade the excise duty of His Majesty King George III. 'Keep your spirits up, Tregembo, and tell Mr Q the same.'

'Aye, zur. Mr Gillespy ain't too good, zur, by the bye . . .'

'No talk!' The orderly, red-faced with fury, shoved Tregembo towards the door.

'Very well,' acknowedged Drinkwater. 'But there's very little I can do about it,' he muttered as, once again, the door slammed and he was left alone with his thoughts.

Meat and wine arrived at midday. He walked with the others after the hour of *siesta*, finding Quilhampton downcast and Gillespy in poor spirits. Today it seemed as if Frey was bearing the burden of cheering his fellow prisoners. At sunset a silent Tregembo brought him bread, cheese and wine. As the shadows darkened in the tiny room, Drinkwater found his own morale dropping. In the end it became irresistible not to think of his family and the 'blue-devils' settled on his weary mind. He did not bother to light his candle but climbed into the bed and tried to sleep. A convent bell tolled away the hours but he had fallen asleep when his door was opened. He woke with a start and lay staring into the pitch-darkness. He felt suddenly fearful, remembering Wright's death in the Temple. He reached for his sword.

'Get dressed please, *Capitaine.*'

'Guillet?'

'Please to 'urry, *m'sieur.*'

'What the devil d'you want?'

'Please, *Capitaine.* I 'ave my orders. Dress and come quickly with no noise.' Guillet was anxious about something. Fumbling in the dark Drinkwater found his clothes and his sword. Guillet must have seen the slight gleam of the scabbard mountings. 'Not your sword, *Capitaine . . .*'

Drinkwater left it on his bed and followed Guillet into the corridor. At the door of the guardroom Guillet collected a cloak and handed it to Drinkwater. Drinkwater threw the heavy garment over his shoulders.

'*Allez . . .*'

They crossed the courtyard and, with Guillet taking his arm, passed the sentry into the street. 'Please, *Capitaine*, do not make to escape. I have a loaded pistol and orders to shoot you.'

'Whose orders? Colonel Santhonax's? Do not forget, Lieutenant Guillet, that I have given my parole.' Drinkwater's anger was unfeigned and Guillet fell silent. Was it Santhonax's purpose to have him murdered in an alleyway?

They were walking down a gentle hill, the cobbled roadway descending in low steps, the blank walls of houses broken from time to time by dimly perceived wrought-iron gates opening onto courtyards. He could see the black gleam of water ahead and they emerged onto a quay. Drinkwater smelt decaying fish and a row of gulls, disturbed by the two officers, flapped away over the harbour. Guillet hurried him to a flight of stone steps. Drinkwater looked down at the waiting boat and the oars held upright by its crew. The lieutenant ordered him down the steps. He scrambled down, pushed by Guillet and sat in the stern-sheets. The bow was shoved off, the oars were lowered and bit into the water. The chilly night air was unbelievably reviving.

A mad scheme occurred to him of over-powering Guillet, seizing his pistol and forcing the boat's crew to pull him out to *Euryalus*. But what would become of Quilhampton and the others? The French, who had treated them reasonably so far, might not continue to do so if he escaped. In any case the plan was preposterous. The lift of the boat, as the water chuckled under the bow and the oars knocked gently against the thole pins, evoked a whole string of emotional responses. The thought that Santhonax was ruthless enough to have him murdered was cold comfort. Yet Guillet seemed to be pursuing orders of a less extreme nature. Nevertheless Drinkwater acknowledged the fact that, removed from his frigate, he was as impotent as an ant underfoot.

The boat was pulled out into the *Grande Rade*, among the huge hulls and towering masts of the Combined Fleet. Periodically a sentry or a

152

guard-boat challenged them and Guillet answered with the night's countersign. A huge hull reared over them. Even in the gloom Drinkwater could see it was painted entirely black. He guessed her to be Spanish. Then, beyond her, he saw the even bigger bulk of a mighty ship. He could make out the greyer shade of lighter paint along her gun-deck. He counted four of these and was aware that he was looking at the greatest fighting ship in the world, the Spanish *navio Santissima Trinidad*.

He was still staring at her as the oarsmen eased their stroke. He looked round as they ran under the stern of a smaller ship. From the double line of lighted stern windows she revealed herself as a two-decker. The light from the windows made reading her name difficult, but he saw enough to guess the rest.

Bucentaure.

Guillet had brought him, in comparative secrecy, to Villeneuve's flagship.

Villeneuve

Vice-Admiral Pierre Charles Jean Baptiste Silvestre de Villeneuve sat alone in the great cabin of the *Bucentaure*. He stared at the miniature of his wife. He had painted it himself and it was not so much her likeness that he was looking at, as the remembrance of her as she had been on the day he had done it. He sighed resignedly and slipped the enamel disc in the pocket of his waistcoat. His eye fell upon the letter lying on the table before him. It was dated a few days earlier and written by an old friend from Bayonne.

My dear friend,

I write to tell you news that will not please you but which you may otherwise not learn until it is brought to you by one who will not be welcome. I learned today that our Imperial master has despatched Admiral Rosily to Cadiz to take over the command from you. My old friend, I know you as undoubtedly the most accomplished officer and the most able tactician, whatever people may say, that the navy possesses. I recall to you the honour of the flag of our country . . .

Vice-Admiral Villeneuve picked up the letter and, holding it by a corner, burnt it in the candelabra that stood upon the table. The ash floated down upon the polished wood and lay upon Admiral Gravina's latest daily report of the readiness of the Spanish Fleet. Of all his flag-officers Gravina was the only one upon whom he could wholly rely. They were both of the nobility; they understood one another. Villeneuve clenched his fist and brought it down on the table top. It was on Gravina that would fall the responsibility of his own answer to defeating the tactics of Nelson. But he might yet avoid a battle with Nelson . . .

The knock at the cabin door recalled him to the present. '*Entrez!*'

Lieutenant Guillet, accompanied by the officer of the watch, Lieutenant Fournier, announced the English prisoner. The two stood aside as Drinkwater entered the brilliantly lit cabin from the gloom of the gun-deck with its rows of occupied hammocks.

The two officers exchanged glances and Fournier addressed a question to the admiral. Villeneuve seemed irritated and Drinkwater heard his own name and the word 'parole'. The two withdrew with a scarcely concealed show of reluctance.

'Please sit, Captain Drinkwater,' said Villeneuve indicating a chair. 'Do you also find young men always know best?' he smiled engagingly and, despite their strange meeting, Drinkwater warmed to the man. He was aware once again that the two of them were of an age. He smiled back.

'It is a universal condition, Your Excellency.'

'Tell me, Captain. What would British officers be doing in our circumstances?' Villeneuve poured two glasses of wine and handed one to Drinkwater.

Drinkwater took the glass. 'Thank you, sir. Much as we are doing. Taking a glass of wine and a biscuit or two in the evening at anchor, then taking their watch or turning in.'

The two men sat for a while in silence, Drinkwater patiently awaiting disclosure of the reason for this strange rendezvous. Villeneuve seemed to be considering something, but at last he said, 'Colonel Santhonax tells me you are an officer of great experience, Captain Drinkwater. He would not have been pleased that we are talking like this.'

Villeneuve's remark was an opening, Drinkwater saw, a testing of the ground between them. On what he said now would depend how much the enemy admiral confided in him. 'I know Colonel Santhonax to be a spy, Your Excellency. As an aide to your Emperor I assume he enjoys certain privileges of communication with His Majesty.' He paused to lend his words weight, 'I would imagine that could be a grave embarrassment to you, sir, particularly as Colonel Santhonax is not without considerable experience as a seaman. I would say, sir, that he shared something of the prejudices of your young officers.'

'You are very – what is the English word? Shrewd, eh? – Yes, that is it.' Villeneuve smiled again, rather sadly, Drinkwater thought. 'Do you believe in destiny, Captain?'

Drinkwater shrugged. 'Not destiny, sir. Providence, perhaps, but not destiny.'

'Ah, that is because you are not from an ancient family. A Villeneuve died with Roland at the Pass of Roncesvalles; a Villeneuve died in the Holy Land and went to battle with your Coeur-de-Lion, and a Villeneuve led the lances of Aragon with Bayard. I was the ninety-first Villeneuve to be a Knight of Malta and yet I saw the justice of the Revolution, Captain. I think as an Englishman you must find that difficult to understand, eh?'

'Perhaps less than you think, sir. My own fortunes have been the other way. My father was a tenant farmer and I am uncertain of my origins before my grandfather. I would not wholly disapprove of your Revolution . . .'

'But not our Empire, eh, Captain?'

Drinkwater shrugged. 'I do not wish to insult you, sir, but I do not approve of the Emperor's intentions to invade my country.'

Villeneuve was obviously also thinking of Napoleon for he said. 'Do you know what Santhonax is doing, Captain?'

'I imagine he has gone to Paris to report to His Imperial Majesty on the state of the fleet you command. And possibly . . .' he broke off, then, thinking it was worth a gamble, added, 'to tell the Emperor that he has succeeded in persuading you to sail.'

'*Bon Dieu!*' The blood drained from Villeneuve's face. 'H . . . how did you . .?'

Villeneuve hesitated and Drinkwater pressed his advantage. 'As I said, Your Excellency, I know Santhonax for what he is. Did he kill Captain Wright in the Temple?'

The colour had not yet returned to the admiral's face. 'Is that what they say in England? That Santhonax murdered Wright?'

'No, they say he was murdered, but by whom only a few suspect.'

'And you are one of them, I think.'

Drinkwater shrugged again. 'On blockade duty, sir, there is ample time to ponder . . .' he paused seeing the admiral's puzzled look, 'er, to think about things.'

'Ah, yes, I understand. Your navy has a talent for this blockading. It is very tedious, is it not?'

'Very, sir . . .'

'And your ships? They wear out also?'

Drinkwater nodded, 'Yes.'

'And the men?'

Drinkwater held the admiral's gaze. It was no simple matter to convey to a Frenchman, even of Villeneuve's intelligence, the balance of the stubborn tenacity of a national character against a discipline that did not admit weakness. Besides, it was not his intention to appear over-confident. 'They wear out too, sir,' he said smiling.

Looking at the Englishman, Villeneuve noticed his hand go up under his coat to massage his shoulder. 'You have been wounded, Captain?'

'Several times . . .'

'Are you married?'

'Yes. I have two children.'

'I also am married . . . This war; it is a terrible thing.'

'I should not be here, sir, were it not for your Combined Fleet,' Drinkwater said drily.

'Ah, yes . . . the Combined Fleet. What is your opinion of the Combined Fleet, Captain?'

'It is difficult to judge, sir. But I think the ships good, particularly, with respect, the Spanish line-of-battle ships. The French are good seamen, but lack practice; the Spanish . . .' he shrugged again.

'Are beggars and herdsmen, the most part landsmen and soldiers,' Villeneuve said with sudden and unexpected vehemence. He stood up and began to pace with a slow dignity back and forwards between the table and the stern windows with an abstraction that Drinkwater knew to reveal he often did thus. 'And the officers are willing, but inexperienced. One cruise to the West Indies and they think they are masters of the oceans. They are all fire or venom because they think Villeneuve a fool! Do you know why I brought you here tonight, Captain, eh? No? Because it is not possible that I talk freely to my own officers! Only Gravina comprehends my position and he has troubles too many to speak of with his own court and that parvenu Godoy, the "Prince of Peace"!' Villeneuve's contempt filled him with a blazing indignation. 'Oh, yes, Captain, there *is* destiny,' he paused and looked down at Drinkwater, then thrust his pointing arm towards the windows. 'Out on the sea is Nelson and here, here is Villeneuve!' He stabbed his own chest with the same finger. Drinkwater sat quietly as Villeneuve took two more turns across the cabin then calmed himself, refilled the glasses and sat down again.

'How will Nelson attack, Captain?' He paused as Drinkwater protested, then held up his hand. 'It is all right, Captain, I know you to be a man of honour. I will tell you as I told my captains before we left Toulon. He will attack from windward if he can, not in line, but so as to concentrate his ships in groups upon a division of our fleet which he will annihilate with overwhelming force.' He slapped his right hand down flat upon the table making the candles gutter and raising a little whirl of grey ash. 'It was done at Camperdown and he did it to us at Abukir . . .' Again Villeneuve paused and Drinkwater watched him silently. The admiral had escaped from that terrible battle, Napoleon accounting him a lucky man, a man of destiny to be taken up to run at the wheels of the Imperial chariot.

'But it has never been done in the open sea with Nelson in command of a whole fleet,' Villeneuve went on, staring abstractedly into the middle distance. Drinkwater realised he was a sensitive and

157

imaginative man and pitied him his burden. Villeneuve suddenly looked at him. 'That is how it will happen, yes?'

'I think so, sir.'

'If you were me, how would you counter it?'

'I . . . er, I don't know . . . It has never been my business to command a fleet, sir . . .'

Villeneuve's eyes narrowed and Drinkwater suddenly saw that the man did not lack courage, whatever might be said of him. 'When it is time for you to command a fleet, Captain, remember there is always an answer; but what you will lack is the means to do it . . .' He stood up again. 'Had I *your* men in *my* ships, Captain, I would astonish Napoleon!'

The admiral tossed off his second glass and poured a third, offering the wine to Drinkwater.

'Thank you, Your Excellency. But how would you answer this attack?' Drinkwater was professionally curious. It was a bold question, but Villeneuve did not seem to regard it as such and Drinkwater realised the extremity of the French admiral's loneliness and isolation. In any case Drinkwater was a prisoner, his escape from the heart of the Combined Fleet so unlikely that Villeneuve felt safe in using the opportunity to see the reaction to his plan of at least one British officer.

'A squadron of reserve, Captain, a division of my fleet kept detached to weather of my line and composed of my best ships, to reinforce that portion of my fleet which receives – how do you say? – the weight, no . . .'

'The brunt?'

'Yes, the brunt of your attack.'

Drinkwater considered Villeneuve's scheme. It was innovative enough to demonstrate his originality of thought, yet it had its defects.

'What if your enemy attacks the squadron of reserve?'

'Then the fleet tacks to *its* assistance, but I do not think this will happen. Your Nelson will attack the main line.' He smiled wryly and added, 'He may ignore the special division as being a badly manoeuvred part of the general line.'

'And if you are attacked from leeward . . .'

'Then the advantage is even more in our favour, yes.'

'But, Excellency, who have you among your admirals to lead this important division?'

'Only Gravina, Captain, on whom I can absolutely depend.' Villeneuve's face clouded over again. For a moment he had been visualising his counter-stroke to Nelson's attack, seeing the moving ships, hearing the guns and realising his dream: to save the navy of France from humiliation and raise it to the heights to which Suffren had shown it could be elevated. He sighed, obviously very tired.

'So you intend to sail, sir?' Drinkwater asked quietly. 'To offer battle to Nelson?'

'If necessary.' Villeneuve's reply was guarded, cautious, even uncertain. Drinkwater concluded, observing the admiral closely.

'But battle *will* be necessary if you wish to enter the Channel.'

'Perhaps . . .' There was an indifference now; Drinkwater felt the certainty of his earlier deliberations.

'Perhaps you are going to return to the Mediterranean?' he ventured. 'I hear his Imperial Majesty has withdrawn his camp from Boulogne?'

'*Diable!*' Villeneuve had paled again. 'How is this known? Do you know everything that comes to me?'

He rose, very angry and Drinkwater hurriedly added, 'Pardon, Excellency. It was only a guess . . . I, I made a guess . . .'

'A guess!' For a second Villeneuve's face wore a look of astonishment. Then his eyes narrowed a little. 'Santhonax was right, Captain Drinkwater, you are no fool. If I have to fight I will, but I have twice eluded Nelson and . . .' He shrugged, 'perhaps I might do it again.'

Drinkwater relaxed. He had been correct all along in his assumptions. The two men's eyes met. They seemed bound in an intensity of feeling, like the eyes of fencers of equal skill where pure antagonism had given way to respect, and only a superficial enmity prevented friendship. Then one of the fencers moved his blade, a tiny feinting movement designed to suggest a weakness, a concern.

'I think you might,' said Drinkwater in a voice so low that it was not much above a whisper. It was a terrible gamble, Drinkwater knew, yet he conceived it his duty to chance Nelson not missing the Combined Fleet.

For what seemed an age a silence hung in the cabin, then Villeneuve coughed and signalled their intimacy was at an end. 'After this conversation, Captain, I regret that you cannot leave the ship. You have given your parole and I will endeavour to make your stay comfortable.'

Drinkwater opened his mouth to protest. A sudden chilling vision of being on the receiving end of British broadsides overwhelmed him and he felt real terror cause his heart to thump and his face to blanch.

It was Villeneuve's turn to smile: 'You did not believe in destiny,

Captain; remember?' Then he added, 'Santhonax wished that I left you to rot in a Spanish gaol.'

Drinkwater woke confused. After leaving Villeneuve he had been conducted to a small cabin intended for a warrant officer below the water-line on the orlop deck of the *Bucentaure*. A sentry was posted outside and for a long time he lay wide awake thinking over the conversation with Villeneuve, his surroundings both familiar and horribly alien. Eventually he had slept and he woke late, disgruntled, hungry and unable for some seconds to remember where he was. His lack of clothing made him feel irritable and the mephitic air of the unventilated orlop gave him a headache made worse by the strange smells of the French battleship. When he opened his door and asked for food he found the moustached sentry singularly unhelpful.

'I don't want your damned bayonet for my breakfast,' muttered Drinkwater pushing the dully gleaming weapon aside. He pointed to his mouth. '*Manger*,' he said hopefully. The sentry shook his head and Drinkwater retreated into the miserable cabin.

A few minutes later, however, the debonair Guillet appeared, immaculately attired as befitted the junior officer of a flagship, and conducted Drinkwater courteously to the gunroom where a number of the officers were breakfasting. They looked at him curiously and Drinkwater felt ill at ease in clothes in which he had slept. However he took coffee and some biscuit, observing that for a fleet in port the officers' table was sparsely provided. His presence clearly had something of a dampening effect, for within minutes only he and Guillet remained at the table.

'I should be obliged if I could send ashore for my effects, Lieutenant . . . I would like to shave . . .' He mimed the action, at which Guillet held up his hand.

'No, Captain, please it is already that I 'ave sent for your . . .' he motioned over his own clothes, stuck for the right word.

'Thank you, Lieutenant.'

They were not long in coming and they arrived together with Mr Gillespy.

'Good Lord, Mr Gillespy, what the devil do you do here, eh?' The boy remained silent and in the bad light it took Drinkwater a moment to see that he was controlling himself with difficulty. 'Come, sir, I asked you a question . . .'

'P . . . please, sir . . .' He pulled a note from his pocket and held it out. Drinkwater took it and read.

160

Sir,

The boy is much troubled by your absence. Permission has been obtained from our captors that he may join you wherever you have been taken and I have presumed to send him to you, believing this to be the best thing for him. We are well and in good spirits.

It was signed by James Quilhampton. He could hardly have imagined Drinkwater was on board the enemy flagship. 'Lieutenant Guillet . . . please have the kindness to return this midshipman to my lieutenant . . .'

'Oh, no, sir . . . please, please . . .' Drinkwater looked at the boy. His lower lip was trembling, his eyes filled with tears. '*Please*, sir . . .'

'Brace up, Mr Gillespy, pray remember who and where you are.' He paused, allowing the boy to pull himself together, and turned towards Guillet. 'What are your orders regarding this young officer?'

Guillet shrugged. His new duty was becoming irksome and he was regretting his boasted ability to speak English. 'The admiral 'e is a busy man, *Capitaine*. 'E says if the, er, midshipman is necessary to you, then he 'as no objection.'

Drinkwater turned to the boy again. 'Very well, Mr Gillespy, you had better find yourself a corner of the orlop.'

'And now, *Capitaine*, perhaps you will come with me onto the deck, yes?'

Drinkwater was ushered on deck, Guillet brushing aside the boy in his ardour to show the English prisoner the puissant might of the Combined Fleet. Drinkwater emerged on deck, his curiosity aroused, his professional interest fully engaged. He was conducted to the starboard waist and allowed to walk up and down on the gangway in company with Guillet. The lieutenant was unusually expansive and Drinkwater considered he was acting on orders from a higher authority. It was difficult to analyse why Villeneuve should want an enemy officer shown his command. He must know Drinkwater was experienced enough to see its weaknesses as well as its strengths; no seaman could fail to do that.

The deck of the *Bucentaure* was crowded with milling seamen and soldiers as the last of the stores were brought aboard. The last water casks were being filled and there were obvious preparations for sailing being made on deck and in the rigging. Boats were out under the bows of the nearest ships, singling up the cables fastened to the buoys laid in the *Grande Rade*.

'Over there,' said Guillet pointing to a 74-gun two-decker, '*le*

Berwick a prize from the Royal Navy, and there, the *Swiftsure*, also once a ship of your navy,' Guillet smiled, 'and, of course, we also 'ave one other ship of yours to our credit, but we could not bring it with us,' he laughed, 'His Majesty's sloop *Diamond Rock!*'

Guillet seemed to think this a great joke and Drinkwater remembered hearing of Commodore Hood's bold fortifying of the Diamond Rock off Martinique which had been held for some time before the overwhelming force of Villeneuve's fleet was brought to bear on it.

'I heard the garrison fought successive attacks off for nineteen hours without water in a tropical climate, Lieutenant, and that they capitulated upon honourable terms. Is that not so?' Guillet appeared somewhat abashed and Drinkwater changed the subject, 'Who is that extraordinary officer who has just come aboard?'

'Ah, that is *Capitaine* Infernet of the *Intrépide*.' Drinkwater watched a tall, flamboyant officer with a boisterous air climb on deck. ' 'E went to sea a powder monkey,' Guillet went on, 'and 'as escaped death a 'hundred times, even when 'is ship it blows apart. 'E speaks badly but 'e fights well . . .'

'And who is that meeting him?'

'That is my *capitaine*, Jean Jacques Magendie, commandant of the *Bucentaure*.'

'Ah, and that man?' Drinkwater indicated a small, energetic officer with the epaulettes of a *Capitaine de Vaisseau*.

'Ah, that', said Guillet in obvious admiration, 'is *Capitaine* Lucas of the *Redoutable*.'

'You obviously admire him, Lieutenant. Why is that?'

Guillet shrugged. 'He is a man most clever, and 'is crew and ship most, er, 'ow do you say it . . . er, very good?'

'Efficient?'

'*Oui*. That is right: efficient.'

Drinkwater turned away, Infernet was looking at him and he did not wish to draw attention to himself. He stared out over the crowded waters of Cadiz, the great battleships surrounded by small boats. He saw the massive hull of the four-decked Spanish ship *Santissima Trinidad*. 'that is the *Santissima Trinidad*, is it not?' Guillet nodded. 'She is Admiral Gravina's flagship?'

'No,' said Guillet, 'the Captain-General 'as 'is flag aboard the *Principe de Asturias* of one 'undred and twelve guns. The *Santissima Trinidad* flies the flag of Rear-Admiral Don Baltazar Cisneros. The ship moored next to 'er, she is the *Rayo* of one 'undred guns. She may interest you, *Capitaine*; she is commanded by Don Enrique Macdon-

162

nell. 'E is an Irishman who became a Spanish soldier to kill Englishmen. 'E fought in the *Regimento de Hibernia* against you when your American colonies bring their revolution. Later 'e is a sailor and when Gravina called for volunteers, Don Enrique comes to command the *Rayo*.'

'Most interesting. The *Rayo* is newly commissioned then?'

'Yes. And the ship next astern is the *Neptuno*. She is Spanish. We also 'ave the *Neptune*. She is', he looked round, 'there, alongside the *Pluton* . . .'

'We also have our *Neptune*, Lieutenant. She is commanded by Thomas Fremantle. He is rather partial to killing Frenchmen.' Drinkwater smiled. 'We also have our *Swiftsure* . . . but all this is most interesting . . .'

They spent the morning in this manner, talking always about ships and seamen, Drinkwater making mental notes and storing impressions of the final preparations of the Combined Fleet. He had a vague notion that they might be of value, yet was aware that he would find it impossible to pass them to his friends whose topsails, he knew, were visible from only a few feet up *Bucentaure*'s rigging. But what was more curious was the strong conviction he had formed that it was Villeneuve himself who wished him to see all this.

A midday meal was served to Drinkwater in his dark and malodourous cabin. Eating alone he was reminded of his time as a midshipman in the equally stinking orlop of the British frigate *Cyclops*. The thought made him call for Gillespy. The only response was from the sentry, who put a finger to his lips and indicated the boy asleep in a corner of the orlop, curled where one of *Bucentaure*'s massive futtocks met the deck.

Guillet did not reappear in the afternoon and, after lying down for an hour, Drinkwater rose. The ship had become strangely quiet, the disorder of the forenoon was gone. The sentry let him pass and he went on deck, passing a body of men milling in the lower and upper gun-decks. As he emerged into a watery sunshine he was aware of the admiral's flag at the masthead lifting to seawards; an easterly wind had come at last!

On the quarterdeck a reception party which included Captain Magendie, his officers and a military guard was welcoming a short, olive-skinned grandee with a long nose. He courteously swept his hat from his head in acknowlegement of the compliments done him, revealing neatly clubbed hair.

Lieutenant Guillet hurried across the deck and took Drinkwater's arm. 'Please, *Capitaine*, is it not for you to be 'ere now.'

'Who was that man, Lieutenant?' asked Drinkwater suffering himself to be hastened below.

'Don Frederico Gravina. Now, *Capitaine*, please you must go to your cabin and to stay.'

'Why?'

'Why, *Mon Dieu, Capitaine*, the order to sail, it is being made.'

But the Combined Fleet did not sail. At four o'clock in the afternoon of 17th October the easterly wind fell away to a dead calm, and Drinkwater sat in his tiny cabin listening to the details of Mr Gillespy's family.

Nelson's Watch-Dogs

Drinkwater woke with the calling of *Bucentaure*'s ship's company. He was denied the privilege of breakfasting with the officers and it was clear that he was not permitted to leave the hutch of a cabin he had been allocated. Nevertheless he was not required to be locked in, and by sitting in the cabin with a page of his journal before him he amused himself by getting Gillespy to attempt to deduce what was going on above them from the noises they could hear.

To a man who had spent most of his life on board ship this was not difficult, although for Gillespy the task, carried out in such difficult circumstances under the eye of his captain, proved an ordeal. There was a great deal of activity in the dark and stinking orlop deck. Further forward were the damp woollen curtains of the magazine and much of the forenoon was occupied by the bare-foot padding past of the *Bucentaure*'s powder monkeys as they scrambled below for the ready-made cartridges. These were supplied by the gunner and his mates whose disembodied hands appeared with their lethal packages through slits in the curtains. Parties of seamen were carrying up cannon balls from the shot lockers and from time to time a gun-captain came down to argue some technicality with the gunner. The junior officers, or *aspirants*, were also busy, running hither and thither on errands for the lieutenants and other officers.

'What do you remark as the most significant difference, Mr Gillespy, between these fellows and our own, eh?' Drinkwater asked.

'Why . . . I don't know, sir. They make a deal of noise . . .'

Drinkwater looked pleased. 'Exactly so. They are a great deal noisier and many officers would judge 'em as inferior because of that; but remark something else. They are also excited and cheerful. I'd say that, just like our fellows, they're spoiling for a fight, wouldn't you?'

'Yes. I suppose so, sir.' A frown crossed a boy's face. 'Sir?'

'Mmmm?' Drinkwater looked up from his journal.

'What will happen to us, sir, if this ship goes into battle?'

'Well, Mr Gillespy, that's a difficult question. We will not be allowed on deck and so, by the usages of war, will be required to stay here. Now do not look so alarmed. This is the safest place in the ship. Very few shot will penetrate this far and, although the decks above us may be raked, we shall be quite safe. Do not forget that instances of ships actually being sunk by gunfire are rare.

'So, let us examine the hypothesis of a French victory. If this is the case we shall be no worse off, for we may have extra company and that will make things much the merrier. On the other hand, assuming that it is a British victory, which circumstances, I might add, I have not the slightest reason to doubt, then we shall find ourselves liberated. Even if the ship is not taken we shall almost certainly be exchanged. We shall not be the first officers present in an enemy ship when that ship is attacked by our friends.' He smiled as reassuringly as he could. 'Be of good heart, Mr Gillespy. You may well have something to tell your grandchildren ere long.'

Gillespy nodded. 'You said that to me before, sir, when the French squadron got out of Rochefort.'

'Did I? I had forgotten.' The captain took up his pen again and bent over his journal.

This remark made Gillespy realise the great distance that separated them. He found it difficult to relate to this man who had shown him such kindness after the harshness of Lord Walmsley. In his first days on board *Antigone* it had seemed impossible that the captain who stood so sternly immobile on the quarterdeck could actually have children of his own. Gillespy could not imagine him as a father. Then he was made aware from the comments of the crew that Drinkwater had done something rather special in getting them out of Mount's Bay and from that moment the boy made it his business to study him. The attentions paid him by the captain had been repaid by a dog-like devotion. Even captivity had seemed tolerable and not at all frightening in the company of Captain Drinkwater. But bereft of that presence, Gillespy had felt all the terrors conceivable to a lonely and imaginative mind. He had implored Quilhampton to request he be allowed to join the captain. Quilhampton acceded to the boy's request, aware that their captors were in any event likely to separate him and the midshipmen from Drinkwater. In due course Drinkwater would probably be exchanged and Gillespy might have a better chance with the captain. He and Frey would have to rely upon their own resources. James Quilhampton was determined not to remain long in captivity. Let the Combined Fleet sail, as everyone said they would, and he would make an attempt to escape, for the thought of Catriona spurred him on.

Now Gillespy waited patiently for Drinkwater to stop writing notes, watching the men of the *Bucentaure* who messed in the orlop

166

coming below for their midday meal. He listened to their conversation, recognising a word or phrase here and there, and recalling some of the French his Dominie had caned into him in Edinburgh all those months ago.

'I think, sir,' he said after a while in a confidential whisper, 'the wind has failed . . . They are laughing at one of the Spanish officers who must have come on board . . . I cannot make out his name . . . Grav . . . something.'

'Gravina?'

'Yes, yes that is it. Do you know what '*mañana*' means sir, in Spanish?'

'Er, "tomorrow", I believe, Mr Gillespy, why?'

'And "*al mar*" must be something to do with the sea; because that fellow there, with the bright bandana and the ear-rings, he keeps throwing his arm in the air and declaiming "*mañana al mar*".' He frowned again, 'I suppose he's imitating this Spanish officer.'

'That is most perceptive of you, Mr Gillespy. If you are right then Gravina has been aboard and announced "tomorrow to sea".' Drinkwater paused reflectively, 'Let us hope to God that you are right.'

He smiled again, encouraging the boy, yet aware that they might not survive the next few days, that ships might not be easily sunk by gunfire but ordinary fire, if it took them, might blow them apart as it had *L'Orient* at Abukir. Staring at the fire-screens round the entrances to the powder magazines, Drinkwater felt the sweat of pure fear prickle his back. Down here they would be caught like rats in a trap.

Towards evening Lieutenant Guillet came to see them. His neck linen was grubby and he looked tired after an active day, but he was courteous enough to apologise for ignoring them and clearly in optimistic spirits.

'Your duty has the greater call upon you than we do, Lieutenant,' said Drinkwater calmly.

'You are permitted 'alf-an-hour on deck, *Capitaine*. And you also,' he added to Gillespy, 'and then I am to take you to the General.'

Drinkwater saw Gillespy frown. 'Admiral Villeneuve, Mr Gillespy. Recall how I told you the French and Spanish use the terms interchangeably.'

The boy nodded and they followed Guillet on deck. The contrast with the previous day was startling. Amidships *Bucentaure*'s boat had been hoisted on the booms. All the ropes were coiled away on their pins and aloft the robands of the harbour stow had been cast off the sails. A light breeze was again stirring from the eastward. Some of the ships had moved, warped down nearer the islets at the entrance of the harbour. The air of expectancy hanging over the fleet after the exertions of the day was almost tangible. The inactivity would now begin to pray on men's minds, and until the order was given to weigh, every man in that vast armada, some twenty thousand souls, would withdraw inside himself to consult the oracles in his heart as to his future in this world.

Drinkwater felt an odd and quite inexplicable lightness of spirit. Whenever the *Bucentaure* cleared for action he knew he too would be a victim to fear, but for the moment he felt strangely elated. He was no longer in any doubt that in the next day or so there was going to be a battle.

After his exercise period, Drinkwater was taken to Villeneuve's cabin. There was no secrecy about the interview; it was conducted in the presence of several other high-ranking officers among whom Drinkwater recognised Flag-Captain Magendie and Villeneuve's Chief-of-Staff, Captain Prigny. Another officer was in Rear-Admiral's uniform. He wore a silver belt around his waist and an air of permanent exasperation.

'*Contre-Amiral* Magon . . . *Capitaine de frégate* Drinkwater Charles . . .'

Magon bowed imperceptibly and regarded Drinkwater with intense dislike. Drinkwater felt he attracted more than his fair share of malice and was not long in discovering that Magon disapproved of Villeneuve's holding Drinkwater on his flagship. Drinkwater's knowledge of French was poor, but Magon's powers of dramatic and expressive gesture were eloquent.

Villeneuve was mastering his anger and humiliation with difficulty and Drinkwater glimpsed something of the problems he suffered in his tenure of command of the Combined Fleet. Eventually Magon ceased his diatribe, turned in disgust and affected to ignore the rest of the proceedings by staring fixedly out of the stern windows.

'Captain Drinkwater informs me, gentlemen,' Villeneuve said in English, 'that Nelson's attack will be as I outlined to you in my standing orders before leaving Toulon. If you wish to question him further he is at your disposal . . .'

Drinkwater opened his mouth to protest that he had done nothing so dishonourable as to reveal Lord Nelson's plan of attack but, seeing the difficulties Villeneuve was under, he shut his mouth again.

'*Excuse, Capitaine, mais*, er, 'ow are you certain Nelson will make this attack, eh?' Captain Magendie asked. ' 'Ave you seen 'is orders to 'is *escadre?*'

'No, *m'sieur*.' It was beyond his power and the limit of his honour to help Villeneuve now.

A silence hung in the cabin and Drinkwater met Villeneuve's eyes. Whatever his defects as a leader, the man possessed personal courage of a high order. Alone of all his officers. Drinkwater thought. Villeneuve was the one man who knew what lay in wait for them beyond the mole of Cadiz.

Drinkwater woke with a start. The *Bucentaure* was alive with shouts and cries, the squeal of pipes and the *rantan* of a snare drum two decks above. For a second Drinkwater thought the ship was on fire and then he heard, or rather felt through the fabric of the ship, two hundred pairs of feet begin to stamp around the capstan. But it was to be a false alarm, athough when he went on deck that evening there were fewer ships in the road. The wind had again dropped and Guillet was in a bad temper, his exertions of the previous day seemingly for nothing.

'Some of your ships got out, Lieutenant,' remarked Drinkwater, indicating the absence of a few of their neighbours of the previous night.

'Nine, *Capitaine*, now anchored off Rota.'

Drinkwater looked aloft at Villeneuve's flag and then at the sky, unconsciously rubbing his shoulder as he did so. 'You will have an easterly wind in the morning, I think.' He turned to Gillespy. 'What is tomorrow, Mr Gillespy. Sunday, ain't it?'

'Yes, sir, Sunday, the twentieth . . .'

'Well, Mr Gillespy, you must remark it . . . What is that in French, Lieutenant, in your new calendar, eh?'

'*Le vingt-huitième Vendémiare, An Quatorze* . . .'

'What have Nelson's frigates been doing today, Lieutenant? Will you tell us that?'

Guillet grinned. 'Not coming into the 'arbour, *Capitaine*. Yesterday we send boats down to the entrance. Your frigate *Euryalus*, she does not come so close, and today with our ships going to Rota she does not engage.'

'That should not surprise you, Lieutenant Guillet. It is her business to watch.' Drinkwater added drily, 'And Nelson? What of him?'

'We 'ave not seen your Nelson, *Capitaine*,' Guillet's tone was almost sneering.

On his way below, Drinkwater realised that Lieutenant de Vaisseau Guillet did not fear Nelson and that the Combined Fleet would sail with confidence. If Guillet thought that, then it was probable that many of the junior officers thought the same. 'Do you also find,' Villeneuve had asked, 'young men always know best?' Drinkwater re-entered his cabin. He stretched himself on the cot, his hands behind his head, and stared unseeing at the low deck beams above. The strange sense of elation and excitement remained.

The following morning there was no doubt about their departure. Even in the orlop the slap of waves upon the hull indicated a wind, and soon the movement of the deck indicated *Bucentaure* was getting under way. Slowly the slap of waves became a hiss and bubbling rush of water. The angle of heel increased and the whole fabric of the ship responded.

'We're turning,' Drinkwater muttered, as Gillespy came anxiously to his doorway. The two remained immobile, the usual courtesies of the morning forgotten, their eyes staring, unwanted sensors in the gloom of the orlop, while their other faculties told them what was happening. A bump and thump came from forward and above.

'Anchor fished, catted and lashed against the fore-chains . . . We must be . . . yes, starboard tack, 'tis a north-easterly wind then . . . Ah, we're fetching out of the lee of the Mole . . .'

The *Bucentaure* began to pitch, gently at first and then settling down to the regularity of the Atlantic swells as they rolled in from the west.

'We're clear of San Sebastian now,' Drinkwater whispered, trying to visualise the scene. Outside the door the sentry staggered, the movement unfamiliar to him.

Gillespy giggled and Drinkwater grinned at him, as much to see the boy in good spirits as at the lack of sea-legs on the part of the soldier. After about an hour of progress the angle of the deck altered and the ship began a different motion.

'What is it, sir?'

'We are hove-to. Waiting for the other ships to come out.'

Evidence of this hiatus came a few minutes later when men came down to their messes for breakfast. *Bucentaure*'s company had divided into their sea-watches. The battleship was leading the Combined Fleet to sea.

· · ·

170

It was afternoon before they were allowed to emerge from the orlop. Lieutenant Guillet appeared. 'You please to come on deck now, *Capitaine*.' There was the undeniable gleam of triumph in his eyes. 'The Combined Fleet is at sea, and there is no sight of your Nelson.'

Drinkwater ascended the companion ladders through the gun-decks. Men looked at him curiously, sharing the same elation as Guillet. Drinkwater's finely tuned sensibilities could detect high morale when he encountered it. Their worst fears had not material-ised. But what interested him more was the weather when he finally reached the rail in the windward gangway. The wind had gone to the south-west, it was overcast and drizzling.

'*Voila, Capitaine* Drinkwater!' Guillet extended an arm that swept around the *Bucentaure* in a gesture that embraced forty ships, adding with a fierce pride, '*C'est magnifique!*'

The Combined Fleet lumbered to the southward, topsails reefed, yards braced sharp up on the starboard tack, in five columns, the colours of their hulls faded in the drizzle.

'The *Corps de Bataille*,' Guillet indicated proprietorially, pointing ahead, 'it is led by Vice-Admiral de Alava in the *Santa Ana*, we are in the centre and Rear-Admiral Dumanoir commands the rear in the *Formidable* . . .'

'And Gravina?'

'Ah, the Captain-General leads the *Corps de Réserve* with Magon as his support.'

'And you steer south, Lieutenant . . for the Mediterranean I presume.'

Guillet shrugged dismissively, 'Per'aps.'

'And you will be lucky with the wind. I think it will be veering very soon to the north-west.' Drinkwater pointed to a patch of blue sky from which the grey cumulus drew back.

'Where is Nelson, *Capitaine*?' Guillet asked with a grin. 'Eh?'

'When the weather clears, Lieutenant, you may well find out.' Drinkwater fervently hoped he was right.

He was not permitted to see the horizon to windward swept of the drizzle to become sharp and clear against the sudden lightening of the sky. It was four o'clock in the afternoon, as the bells of the battleships sounded their four double-chimes that marked the change of watch, when the wind hauled aft. The limit of the visible horizon extended abruptly many miles to the west. From the mastheads of the French and Spanish men-o'-war the six grey topsails of two British frigates could be seen as they lay hull down over the horizon. They were Nelson's watch-dogs.

It had been dark for several hours when Guillet reappeared, demanding Drinkwater's immediate attendance upon the quarterdeck. Wrapping his cloak around him he followed the French officer, emerging on deck in the dim glow of the binnacle. The wind had freshened a little and ahead of them they could see the battle lanterns of the next ship. Casting a glow over the after-deck, their own lanterns shone, together with Villeneuve's command lantern in the mizen top. These points of light only emphasised the blackness of the night to Drinkwater as he stumbled on the unfamiliar deck. But a few minutes later he could pick out details and see that the great arch of the sky was studded with stars.

'*Capitaine* Drinkwater, *mon amiral . . .*'

'Ah, Captain . . .' Villeneuve addressed him. 'I do not wish to dishonour you, but what do you interpret from those signals to the west?' He held out a night-glass and Drinkwater was aware of his anxiety. It was clearly Villeneuve's besetting sin in the eyes of his subordinates.

He could see nothing at first and then he focused the telescope and saw pin-points of light and the graceful arc of a rocket trail. 'British frigates, signalling, sir.' That much must be obvious to Villeneuve.

But he was saved from further embarrassment by a burst of rockets shooting aloft from the direction of the *Principe de Asturias*. From the sudden flurry of activity and the repetition of the Spanish admiral's name, Drinkwater gathered Gravina was signalling the presence of enemy ships even closer than the two cruisers Drinkwater could see on the horizon. *Bucentaure*'s quarterdeck came to sudden and furious activity. Her own rockets roared skywards in pairs and the order was given to go to general quarters and clear for action. Other admirals in the Combined Fleet set up their night signals. The repeating frigates to leeward joined in a visual spectacle better suited to a victory parade than the escape of a hunted fleet, Drinkwater thought, as he was hustled below.

'*Branle-bas-de-combat!*' officers were roaring at the hatchways and the drummers were beating the *rantan* opening the *Générale*. The *Bucentaure* burst into a noisy and spontaneous life, lent a nightmare quality as her people surged on deck and to their stations in the gun-decks, lowering the bulkheads that obstructed the long batteries of heavy artillery that gleamed dully from the fitful lights of the

172

swinging battle lanterns. Drinkwater did not fight the tide of humanity but waited, observing the activity. The noise was deafening, but otherwise the men knew their places and, although not as fast as the ruthlessly trained crew of a British seventy-four, *Bucentaure*'s eighty cannon were soon ready for action. Drinkwater made his way below.

The messing area of the orlop that formed a tiny square of courtyard outside his and the other warrant officers' cabins had been transformed. A number of chests had been pulled into its centre and covered with a piece of sail. A separate chest supported the instrument cases of the *Bucentaure*'s two surgeons. The senior of these two men, Charles Masson, had treated Drinkwater with some consideration and addressed him in English, which he spoke quite well. Drinkwater had come to like the man and, as he retired to his cabin in search of Gillespy, he nodded at him.

'It has come to the time of battle, then, *m'sieur*?' Masson tested the edge of a curette and looked up at the English captain standing stooped and cock-headed under the low beams.

'Soon, now, I think, M'sieur Masson, soon . . .'

Trafalgar

Nathaniel Drinkwater lay unsleeping through the long October night. He was tormented by the thought of the hours to come, of how he might have been preparing the *Thunderer* for action. Alone, without the necessity of reassuring the now sleeping Gillespy or the disturbance of *Bucentaure*'s people who stood at their quarters throughout the small hours, he reflected on his ill-fortune. Such a mischance as his capture had happened in a trice to sea-officers; it was one of the perils of the profession; but this reflection did not make it any easier to bear as he lay inactive in a borrowed cot aboard the enemy flagship. There was nothing he could do except await the outcome of events.

Even these were by no means certain. Gravina's signals of the previous evening had obviously been those of panic. No British cruisers had come close, but those distant rockets seen by Drinkwater meant that the Combined Fleet was being shadowed. The response of the French and Spanish admirals in throwing out rocket signals themselves had undoubtedly attracted the attention of Blackwood's watch-dogs. Connecting Blackwood's Inshore Squadron with the main fleet, Nelson would have look-out ships at intervals, and these would pass on Blackwood's messages. God grant that Nelson had seen them and that he would come up before Villeneuve slipped through the Gut of Gibraltar and into the Mediterranean.

Drinkwater did not like to contemplate too closely what might happen to himself. He had to summon up all his reserves of fortitude and rehearse for his own comfort all the argument he had put to little Gillespy as guaranteeing their safety. But they did not reassure him. The worst aspect of his plight was his inability to influence events. Never in his life had he been so passive. The sea-service had placed a continual series of demands upon his skill and experience so that, although he was a victim of events, he had always had a chance of fighting back. To perish in the attempt was one thing; to be annihilated without being able to lift a finger struck him as being particularly hard to bear.

Some time in the night the *Bucentaure*'s company were stood down from their stations. Drinkwater heard them come below and his gloom increased. To a man used from boyhood to living on board ship he had no difficulty in gauging their mood. They were grim, filled with a mixture of anxiety and hope. They were also unusually subdued and few settled to sleep. Drinkwater tried to judge the course that the *Bucentaure* was sailing on. He could feel a low ground swell gently lifting and rolling the ship. That would not significantly have altered its direction since he had observed it the previous evening. He felt it coming up almost abeam, but lifting the starboard quarter first: Villeneuve was edging away towards the Strait.

He must have slept, for he was startled by the drums again rappelling the *Générale* and the petty officers crying '*Branle-bas-de-combat!*' at the hatchways. The orlop emptied of men and then others came down, the sinister denizens of this area of perpetual night: Surgeon Masson, his assistants and mates. Shortly after this a light and playful rattle of a snare drum and the tweeting of fifes could be heard. Cries of '*Vive le Commandant!*' and '*Vive l'Empereur!*' were shouted by *Bucentaure*'s company as Villeneuve and his suite toured the ship. A sentry came half-way down the orlop ladder and announced something to the surgeon.

'What is the news, M'sieur Masson?' Drinkwater asked.

'One of our frigates has signalled the enemy is in sight.'

'Ah . . . d'you hear that, Mr Gillespy?'

'Yes, sir.' The boy was pale, but he managed a brave smile. 'Do you think that will be the *Euryalus*, sir, or the main body of the fleet?'

'To be candid, Mr Gillespy, I do not know.'

The boy nodded and swallowed. 'Do you know, sir, that *Euryalus* was slain in a wood when gathering intelligence for the Trojans?'

'No, Mr Gillespy, I'm afraid I did not know that.' The arcane fact surprised Drinkwater and then he reflected that the boy might make a better academic than a sea-officer.

'The Trojans were defeated, sir . . .' Gillespy pointed out, as if seeking some parallel with present events.

'Come, sir, that is no way to talk . . . Why, what of Antigone? Who the devil was she?'

'The daughter of Oedipus and and Jocasta, sir. She buried the body of her brother after her uncle had ordered it to be left exposed and he had her bricked up behind a wall . . .'

'Enough of that, Mr Gillespy.' He fell silent. It was true that his own *Antigone* might as well be bricked up, stuck, as she was, with Louis off Gibraltar. If the Combined Fleet got through the Strait unmolested it would come upon the lone *Antigone* cruising to the eastward watching the eastern horizon for Salcedo! He groaned aloud, 'Oh, God damn it!'

'Are you all right, sir?' Gillespy came forward solicitously, but drew back at the sight of the captain's set face.

'Perfectly, Mr Gillespy,' Drinkwater said grimly, 'I am damning my ill-fortune.'

'I'm hungry, sir,' Gillespy said after a little, but this feeble appeal was lost in a sudden canting of the *Bucentaure*. Drinkwater strained to hear orders on deck but it was impossible as the hull creaked about them and the constant wash of the sea beyond the ship's side shut out any noise from the upper deck.

'We're wearing . . . God damn it, we're wearing, Mr Gillespy . . . yes, yes certainly we are . . . wait . . . see, we're steady again . . .' He gauged the way the hull reacted to the swell. It rolled them from the other side now, the larboard side. They were heading north and the rush of water past the hull was much less than it had been the day before. Either they had reduced sail or the wind had dropped significantly.

'What does it mean, sir?'

'I don't know,' snapped Drinkwater, trying to answer that very question himself. 'Either that Louis has appeared ahead of the Combined Fleet, or that Villeneuve has abandoned his intention and wishes to return to Cadiz . . . in which case I judge that the answer to your question is that our friends have sighted the main body of Lord Nelson's fleet.' As he spoke, Drinkwater's voice increased in strength with mounting conviction.

'By God!' he added, knowing Villeneuve's vacillation, 'that *must* be the explanation.' He smiled at the boy. 'I think you *will* have something to tell your grandchildren, my boy!'

Half an hour later Lieutenant Guillet appeared. He wore full dress uniform and was formally polite.

'*Capitaine* Drinkwater, I am ordered by His Excellency Vice-Admiral Villeneuve to remind you of your parole and the courtesy done you by permitting you to keep your sword. It is also necessary that I ask you that you will do nothing during the action to prejudice this ship. Without these assurances I 'ave orders to confine you in irons.' It was a rehearsed speech and he could see the hand of Magendie as well as the courtliness of Villeneuve.

'Lieutenant Guillet, it would dishonour both myself and my country if I was not to conform to your request. I assure you that both myself and my midshipman will do nothing to interfere with the *Bucentaure*. Will you convey my compliments to His Excellency and I thank you for your kind attentions to us and wish you good fortune in the hours ahead.'

They exchanged bows and Guillet departed. The forenoon dragged on. Drinkwater wrote in his journal and comforted the starving Gillespy. A strange silence hung over the groaning fabric of the warship, permeating down through her decks and hatchways. Even the men awaiting the arrival of the wounded in the orlop talked among themselves in whispers. About mid-morning they heard a muffled shout, drowned immediately in a terrific rumbling sound that startled them after the long and heavy silence.

'Running out the guns,' Drinkwater explained to Gillespy.

'*Captaine*, will you come to the deck at once . . .' It was Guillet, his appearance hurried and breathless.

Drinkwater rose and put on his hat. He turned to Gillespy. 'Remain here, Mr Gillespy. You are in no circumstances to leave the orlop.'

'Aye, aye, sir.'

Drinkwater followed Guillet up through the lower gun-deck. It was flooded by shafts of sunshine coming in through the open gun-ports. Every cannon was run out and the crews squatted expectantly round them, one or two peering through at the approaching British. Lieutenants and *aspirants* paced along their divisions and a murmur ran up and down the guns. Guillet and Drinkwater emerged on deck and Guillet led him directly to where Villeneuve, Magendie and Prigny were staring westwards. His heart beating furiously, Drinkwater followed the direction of their telescopes.

Under a sky of blue and over an almost calm sea furrowed by a ponderous swell from the westward, the British fleet came down on the Combined Fleet in two loose groups, prevented from getting into any regular formation by the lightness of the westerly breeze. Drinkwater looked briefly round him to see the Franco–Spanish ships in almost as much disorder. The decision to wear, though two hours old, had thrown them into a confusion from which it would take them some time to recover. Instead of a single line with the frigates to leeward and Gravina's crucial detachment slightly to weather, the whole armada was a loose crescent, bowed away from the advancing British towards the distant blue outline of Cape Trafalgar on the horizon. The line had vast gaps in it, astern of the *Bucentaure* for instance, and in places the ships had bunched two and three abreast.

177

He turned his attention to the British again at the same time as Villeneuve lowered his glass and noticed his arrival. 'Ah, Captain Drinkwater. I desire your opinion as to the leading ships . . .' He handed Drinkwater his glass.

Drinkwater focused the telescope and the image leapt into the lenses with unbelievable clarity. The two groups of British ships were led by three-deckers. These ships were going to receive the brunt of the fire of several broadsides before they could retaliate and Drinkwater sensed a certain elation amongst the officers on *Bucentaure*'s quarterdeck. They came on like a row of skittles, one behind the other. Knock the end one over and it would take them all down.

As he watched, flags soared up to the mastheads and out to the yardarms of the leading British ships. Between the two groups he could see the frigates *Naiad*, *Euryalus*, *Siruis* and *Phoebe*, a cutter and schooner, standing by to repeat signals or tow a wounded battleship out of the line.

'Well, Captain?' Villeneuve was reminding him he was a prisoner and had been asked a question. He looked again at the leading ships. They had every stitch of sail set, their studding sails winged out on the booms, their slack sheets trailing in the water. The swell made the great ships pitch gently as they came on, their hulls black and yellow barred, their decorated figureheads bright with paintwork. The southern group was further advanced than the northern column. He closed the telescope with a snap.

'The southern column is led by *Royal Soveriegn*, Your Excellency, flagship of Vice-Admiral Collingwood . . .'

'And Nelson?' Villeneuve's eagerness betrayed his anxiety.

'There, sir,' Drinkwater pointed with Villeneuve's telescope, the brass instrument gleaming in the sunshine, 'there is *Victory*, leading the northern column and bearing the flag of Lord Nelson.'

Villeneuve's hand was extended for his glass, but his eyes never left the black and yellow hull of *Victory*. As Drinkwater watched, the ship astern of *Victory* seemed to edge out of line, as if making to overtake. Then he saw her sails shake and she disappeared from view behind the flagship again. 'She seems to be supported by the *Téméraire*,' he added, 'of ninety-eight guns.'

Bucentaure's officers studied the menacing approach of the silent British ships. All along her own decks animated chatter had broken out. He noticed there was no check put to this and the men seemed in high spirits now that action was inevitable. Aware that at any moment he would be ordered below, he again looked round. The gap astern was a yawning invitation to the British, and Drinkwater's practised eye soon reckoned that *Victory* was heading for that gap. Collingwood, he judged, would strike the allied line well astern of the *Bucentaure*, somewhere about the position of the funereal black hull of the Spanish 112-gun *Santa Ana* with her scarlet figurehead of the saint. Ahead of the *Bucentaure* the mighty *Santissima Trinidad*, with her hull of red and white ribbands, seemed to wait placidly for the onslaught of the heretic fleet, a great wooden cross hanging over her stern beneath the red and gold ensign of Spain.

'Nelson attacks as I said he would, Captain,' Villeneuve remarked in English. And added, as his glass raked the following ships crowding down astern of their leaders, 'It is not that Nelson leads, but that every captain thinks *he* is Nelson . . .' Then, in his own tongue and in a tone of anguish he said, '*Où est Gravina?*'

Drinkwater realised the import of the remark, forgotten in the excitement of watching the British fleet approach. By wearing to the northward, Villeneuve had reversed his order of sailing. The van was led by Dumanoir now. Instead of commanding a detached squadron to windward, Gravina was tailing on the end of the immense line. Villeneuve's counterstroke was destroyed!

Drinkwater's eyes met those of the French Commander-in-Chief, then Villeneuve looked away; Magendie was speaking impatiently to him and at that moment smoke belched from a ship well astern of *Bucentaure*. The rolling concussion of a broadside came over the water towards them as white plumes rose around the *Royal Sovereign*. Collingwood had shifted his flag from the sluggish *Dreadnought* to the swift and newly coppered *Royal Sovereign* as soon as she had come out from England. Now that speed carried her into battle ahead of her consorts and her chief. Soon other ships were trying the range along with the *Fougeuex*, smoke and flame belched from the side of the *Santa Ana*, and still the *Royal Sovereign* came on, her guns silent, her defiance expressed by the hoisting of additional colours in her rigging.

Drinkwater turned his attention to the other column. Much nearer now, *Victory* could be seen clearly, her lower fore-sheets trailing in the water as the lightness of the breeze wafted her down on the waiting *Bucentaure*.

Magendie barked something and Guillet tugged at Drinkwater's sleeve. He followed Guillet to the companionway. As he left the deck he heard the bells of several ships strikes the quadruple double ring of noon.

'*Tirez!*'

179

As Drinkwater passed the lower gun-deck, Lieutenant Fournier gave the order to one of *Bucentaure*'s 24-pounder cannon. It rumbled inboard with the recoil after the explosion of discharge, snatching at its breeching while its crew ministered to it, stuffing sponge, cartridge wad and ball into its smoking muzzle. The lieutenant leaned forward, peering through the gun-port to see where the ranging shot had fallen, and Drinkwater knew he was aiming at *Victory*. The first coils of white powder smoke drifted innocently around the beams of the deck above and its acrid smell was pungent.

Drinkwater descended into the orlop and made his way back, where he was greeted by a ring of expectant faces. Masson and his staff as well as Gillespy awaited news from the upper world.

'M'sieur Masson, the allied fleets of France and Spain are being attacked by a British fleet under Lord Nelson . . .'

He heard the name 'Nelson' repeated as men looked at one another, and then all hell broke loose above them.

For the next hours the world was an immensity of noise. The stygian darkness of the orlop, pitifully lit with its faint lanterns whose flames struggled in the foul air, became in its own way an extension of hell. But it was the aural senses that suffered the worst assault. Despite twenty-six years in the Royal Navy, Nathanel Drinkwater had never before experienced the ear-splitting horror of a sustained action in a ship larger than a frigate; never been subjected to the rolling waves of blasting concussion that reverberated in the confined space of a gun-deck and down into the orlop below. The guns belching their lethal projectiles leapt back on their carriages with an increasing eagerness as they heated up. They became like things with a life of their own. The shouts of their captains and the *aspirants* and officers who controlled them became nothing more than howls of servitude as the iron monsters spat smoke, fire and iron into the enemy. The stench of powder permeated the orlop, itself full of shuddering air, its shadows a-tremble from the vibrating lantern hooks as the *Bucentuare* flexed and quivered in response to her own violence. This was the moment for which she had been called into being, to resist force with force and pit iron against iron in a ruthless carnage of cacophonous death.

Initially the men stationed in the orlop had nothing to do. The surgeon and his mates waited for the first of the wounded to come down, the gunner and his staff peered from their shot and powder rooms, waiting for the first of the boys requiring more cartridges and shot. So far *Bucentaure* had shivered only from the discharge of her own guns. In his imagination Drinkwater saw *Victory* looming ever larger as she made for that yawning gap astern of the French flagship. He tried to recall the two ships that were trying to fill it and thought that they should have been the *Neptune* and the Spanish *San Leandro*, but they were both to leeward, he remembered, and only Lucas in the *Redoubtable* was in direct line astern of the *Bucentaure*. Drinkwater felt a sympathy for Villeneuve. Gravina had let him down and now he went almost unsupported into action with a ship heavier than his own. *Bucentaure* was a new ship and *Victory* fifty years old, but the added elevation of her third gun-deck would make her a formidable opponent.

And then Drinkwater heard the most terrible sound of his life. The concussion was felt through the entire body rather than heard with the ears alone, a distant noise above the thunder of *Bucentaure*'s cannon, a strange mixture of sounds that had about it the tinkle of imploding glass and the noise of a million bees driving down wind on the back of a hurricane. The whole of *Bucentaure* trembled, men standing were jerked slightly and the bees were followed by the whoosh and crash, the splintering, jarring shock of impact, as musket balls and double- and triple-shotted guns raked the whole length of the *Bucentaure*. It was over in a few seconds as *Victory* crossed their stern, pouring the pent-up fury of her hitherto silent guns through the *Bucentaure*'s stern galleries and along her gun-decks, knocking men over like ninepins. It took cannon off their carriages too, for above their heads they heard the crash of guns hitting the deck, but by this time the orlop had its own terrible part to play.

As the first wave of that raking broadside receded, Drinkwater released Gillespy whom he found himself clasping protectively. He could not stand idle and tore off his coat as the first wounded were stretched upon the canvas of the operating 'table'.

'Come, Mr Gillespy, come; let us do something in the name of humanity to say we were not idle when brave men did their duty.'

Ghostly pale, Gillespy came forward and held the arm of a man while Masson excised a splinter from his shoulder and shoved him roughly aside. It took four men to hold some of the wounded who were filling the space like a human flood so that for a second Drinkwater imagined they might drown under the press of bloody bodies that seemed to inundate them. Men screamed or whimpered or stared hollow-eyed. Pain robbed them of the last protest as their lives drained out into the stinking bilge beneath them.

'It is important we operate fast,' Masson shouted, the sweat

181

pouring from him as he wiped a smear of blood across his forehead. 'Not him, Captain, he is too much gone . . . this man . . . ah, a leg . . . we must cut here . . .' The knife bit into the flesh, its passage marked by a line of blood, and Masson's practised wrist took the incision right around the limb, inclining the point towards the upper thigh.

'If I am quick, he is in shock . . . see how little his arteries bleed, they have closed, and I can do no more damage than his wound . . .' Masson nodded to the bunch of bleeding rags that had once been a leg. As he spoke his deft fingers tied thread around the blood vessels and then he had picked up his saw, thrust it deep into the mess and quickly cut through the femur. He drew the skin together and swiftly sutured it. 'Do you know, Captain,' he bawled conversationally as he nodded and the wounded man was removed to be replaced by another, 'that the Russians and Prussians simply cut through, tie the ligatures and draw the flesh together, leaving the bone almost at the extremity of the amputation and the skin tight as a drum . . .' Masson glanced at his next patient, caught the eye of his assistant and made a winding motion with one finger. The assistant brought a roll of linen bandage and the great welling wound in the stomach was bound, the white quickly staining red. The man was moved to a corner, to lean against a great futtock and bleed out his life.

Drinkwater looked round. The wooden tubs were full of amputated limbs and still men arrived and were ministered to by Masson as he hacked and sawed, bound and bandaged. The surgeon was awash in blood and the foul air of the orlop was thick with the stink of it. Above their head *Bucentaure* was raked again, and then again at intervals as, following *Victory*, *Téméraire* and then the British *Neptune* crossed her stern.

Another body appeared under the glimmer of the lanterns and Masson looked at his assistant busy amputating the arm of a negro. He called some instructions and then shouted at Drinkwater, 'Assistance, Captain. This one we will have to hold!' Masson tore the blood-soaked shirt off the frail body of the boy, a powder monkey or some such.

'Hold him, Captain! He is fully conscious! They are always difficult!'

The white body arched as Masson began his curettage. 'We may save him, its a fragment from a ball, perhaps it burst when it hit a gun, but it is deep. Hold him!' There was demonic strength in the thin body and it wailed pitifully. Drinkwater looked at the face. It was Gillespy.

'Dear God. . . .' The boy was staring up at him, his eyes huge and dark and filled with tears. Blood seeped from his mouth and Drinkwater was aware that he was biting his lip. Masson's mate had seen it and as Gillespy opened his mouth to scream he rammed a pad of leather into it. Masson wrestled bloodily with the fragment, up to his wrist in the boy's abdomen until Drinkwater found himself shouting at the boy to faint.

'He will not stand the shock . . .' Drinkwater could see Masson was struggling. '*Merde*!' The surgeon shook his head. 'I cannot waste time . . . he is finished . . .'

They dragged Gillespy aside and Drinkwater picked him up. He made for the cot in his cabin, but it was already occupied and, as gently as he could, Drinkwater laid the boy down in a dark corner and knelt beside him.

'There, there, Mr Gillespy . . .' He felt desperately inadequate, unable even to give the midshipman water. He could not understand how it had happened. The boy had been helping them . . . and then, Drinkwater recollected, he had withdrawn, his hand over his mouth as though about to vomit. He looked at Gillespie. He had spat the leather pad out and his mouth moved. Drinkwater bent to hear him.

'The . . . the pain has all gone, sir . . . I went on deck, sir . . . to see for myself. I wanted to see something . . . to tell my grandchildren . . . disobeyed you . . .' Gillespy's voice faded into an incoherent gurgle. Drinkwater knew from the blood that suddenly erupted from his mouth that he was dead.

Another broadside raked *Bucentaure* and Drinkwater laid the body down and straightened up. He was trembling all over, his head was splitting from the noise, the damnable, thunderous, everlasting bloody noise. He stumbled over the recumbent bodies of the wounded and dying. Reaching into the cabin he had occupied, he picked up his sword and made for the ladder of the lower gun-deck. Nobody stopped him and he was suddenly aware that *Bucentaure*'s guns had been silent for some time, that the continued bombardment was the echo in his belaboured head.

The lower gun-deck was a shambles. Swept from end to end by the successive broadsides of British battleships, fully half its guns were dismounted, their carriages smashed. The decks were ploughed up by shot, the furrows lined by spikes of wood like petrified grass. Men writhed or lay still in heaps, their bodies shattered into bloody mounds of flesh, brilliant hued and lit by light flooding in through the pulverised and dismantled stern. Drinkwater could not see a single man on his feet throughout the whole space. He made for the ladder to the upper deck and emerged into a smoke-stifled daylight.

Drinkwater stared around him. *Bucentaure* was dismasted, the stumps of her three masts incongruous, their shattered wreckage hanging all about her decks, over her guns and waist where a vain attempt was being made to get a boat out. A man was shouting from the poop. It was Villeneuve.

'*Le* Bucentaure *a rempli sa tâche: la mienne n'est pas encore achevée.*'

Amidships a lieutenant gestured it was impossible to get a boat in the water. Villeneuve turned away and nodded at a smoke-begrimed man whom Drinkwater realised was Magendie. All together there were only a handful of men on *Bucentaure*'s deck. Magendie waved his arm and shouted something. Drinkwater was aware of the masts and sails of ships all around them, towering over their naked decks, and in the thick grey smoke the brilliant points of fire told where the iron rain still poured into *Bucentaure*. It was quite impossible to tell friend from foe and Drinkwater stood bemused, sheltered by the wreckage of the mainmast which had fallen in a great heap of broken spars and rope and canvas.

A wraith of smoke dragged across *Bucentaure*'s after-deck and Drinkwater saw Villeneuve again. He had been wounded and he stood looking forward over the wreckage of his ship. 'A Villeneuve died with Roland at the Pass of Roncesvalles,' Drinkwater remembered him saying as, behind him, the great tricolour came fluttering down on deck.

Bucentaure had struck her colours.

Surrender and Storm

Drinkwater stood dazed. At times the surrounding smoke cleared and he caught brief glimpses of other ships. On their starboard quarter a British seventy-four was slowly turning – it had been she that had last raked *Bucentaure* – and, to windward, yet another was looming towards them. Beneath his feet the deck rolled and Drinkwater came to his senses, instinct telling him that the swell was building up all the time. He turned. Ahead of them another British battleship was swinging, presumably she too had raked *Bucentaure*, though now she was ranging up to leeward of the *Santissima Trinidad*. And still from the weather side British battleships were coming into action! Drinkwater felt his blood run chill.

'God!' he muttered to himself, 'what a magnificent bloody risk Nelson took!' And he found himself shaking again, his vision blurred, as around the shattered *Bucentaure* the thunder of battle continued to reverberate. Then suddenly a double report sounded from *Bucentaure*'s own cannon. Two guns on the starboard quarter barked a continued defiance at the British ship that had just raked them. Drinkwater saw splinters dance from her hull and an officer point and shout, clearly outraged by such conduct after striking. He saw muzzles run out and the yellow and scarlet stab of flame. The shot tore over his head and, with a crash, what was left of the *Bucentuare*'s foremast came down. The two quarter-guns fell silent.

Drinkwater clambered aft. No one stopped him. Men slumped wounded or exhausted around the guns, their faces drained of expression. *Bucentaure*'s company had been shattered into its individual fragments of humanity. Pain and defeat had done their work: she was incapable of further resistance. He hesitated to climb to the poop. This was not his moment, and yet he wished to offer Villeneuve some comfort. On her after-deck officers were waving white handkerchiefs at the British battleship. He turned away below. It was not his business to accept *Bucentaure*'s surrender. He reached the lower gun-deck. Running forward from aft came a party of British seamen led by two midshipmen.

'Come, Mr Hicks, we've a damned Frog here!'

Drinkwater turned at the familiar voice. The young officer was partially silhouetted against the light from the shattered stern, but his drawn sword gleamed and from the rapidity of his advance Drinkwater took alarm. His hand went to his own hanger, whipping out the blade.

'Stand still, God damn you!' he roared. 'I'm a British officer!'

'Good God!'

Recognition came to the two men at the same time.

'Captain Drinkwater, sir . . . I, er, I beg your pardon . . .'

'Mr Walmsley . . . you and your men can put up your weapons. *Bucentaure* is finished.'

'So I see . . .' Walmsley looked round him, his face draining of colour as his eyes fell on an entire gun crew who had lost their heads. Alongside them lay Lieutenant Guillet. He had been cut in half.

'Oh Christ!' Lord Walmsley put his hand to his mouth and the vomit spurted between his fingers.

'I was a prisoner of the French admiral, gentlemen. I am obliged to you for my liberty,' Drinkwater said, affecting not to notice Walmsley's confusion.

'Midshipman William Hicks, sir, of the *Conqueror*, Captain Israel Pellew.' The second midshipman introduced himself, then turned as more men came aboard led by a marine officer. 'This is Captain James Atcherley, sir, of the same ship.'

The ridiculous little ceremony was performed and the scarlet-coated Atcherley was acquainted with the fact that Captain Drinkwater, despite his coatless appearance and blood-stained shirt, was a British officer.

'Come, sir, I will take you to the admiral.' They clambered onto the upper deck and Drinkwater stood aside to allow Atcherley to precede him onto the poop.

'No, no, it is your task, Captain,' Drinkwater said as Atcherley demured. 'He speaks good English.'

He followed the marine officer. Villeneuve lowered the glass through which he had been studying some distant event and turned towards the knot of British officers.

'To whom have I the honour of surrendering?' Villeneuve asked.

Atcherley stepped forward: 'To Captain Pellew of the *Conqueror*.'

'I am glad to have struck to the fortunate Sir Edward Pellew.'

'It is his brother, sir,' said Atcherley.

'His brother! What! Are there two of them? *Hélas!*'

Atcherley refused the proffered sword. Captain Magendie shrugged. '*Fortune de la guerre*. I am now three times a prisoner of you British.'

186

'I shall secure the ship's magazines, sir,' Atcherley said. 'You shall retain your swords until able to surrender them to someone of sufficient rank –' he turned – 'unless Captain Drinkwater would receive them?'

Drinkwater shook his head. 'No Captain Atcherley. I have in no way contributed to today's work and am bound by my word to Admiral Villeneuve. Do you do as you suggest.' He acknowledged the tiny bow made in his direction by Villeneuve.

'In that case, sir,' said Atcherley, addressing the French officers, 'I should be obliged if you would descend to the boat.' He looked round. The *Conqueror* had disappeared in the smoke, joining in the mêlée round the huge *Santissima Trinidad* that had not yet struck to her many enemies.

'I shall convey you to *Mars*, sir,' he nodded at the next British ship looming up on the quarter. Atcherley turned to Drinkwater. 'Will you come, sir?'

Drinkwater shook his head. 'Not yet, Captain Atcherley. I have some effects to gather up.' He had no desire to witness Villeneuve's final humiliation.

'Very well, sir . . . come, gentlemen . . .'

Villeneuve turned to Drinkwater. 'Captain, we fought well. I hope you will not forget that.'

'Never, sir.' Drinkwater was moved by the nobility of the defeated admiral.

Villeneuve stared at the north. 'Dumanoir wore but then turned away,' he said with quiet resignation. 'See, there, the van is deserting me.' Without another word Villeneuve followed Magendie from the deck.

Drinkwater found himself almost alone upon *Bucentaure*'s poop. A few seamen and petty officers sat or squatted, resting their heads upon their crossed arms in attitudes of dejection. Exhausted, concussed and hungry, they had given up. Drinkwater watched Villeneuve, Magendie and Prigny pulled away to the *Mars* in *Conqueror*'s cutter. Lord Walmsley sat in the stern, his hand on the tiller. Drinkwater leaned on the rail. Despite *Bucentaure*'s surrender the battle still raged about her. He watched Dumanoir's unscathed ships standing away to the north, feeling an immense and traitorous sympathy for the unfortunate Villeneuve. It occurred to him to seek the other part of Villeneuve's miscarried strategy and he looked southward to identify Gravina. But astern the battle continued, a vast milling mêlée of ships, their flanks belching fire and destruction, their masts and yards

187

continuing to fall amid clouds of grey powder smoke. Ahead too, the hounds were closing round the *Santissima Trinidad*, and one of Dumanoir's squadron, the Spanish *Neptuno*, had been cut off and taken. Away to the north a dense column of black smoke billowed up from an unidentifiable ship on fire.

He looked for the British frigates. Astern he could see the schooner *Pickle* and the trim little cutter *Entreprenante*. Then he caught sight of *Euryalus*, obeying the conventions of formal war, her guns unemployed as she towed what Drinkwater thought at first was a prize but then realised was the *Royal Sovereign*, Collingwood's dismasted flagship.

'God's bones,' he muttered to himself, aware that this was a day the like of which he hoped he would never see again. The shattered hulls of ships lay all around, British, French and Spanish. Some still bore their own colours; none that he would see bore the British colours underneath the Spanish or French, although he could distinguish several British prizes. Masts and yards, sails and great heaps of rigging lay over their sides and trailed in the oily water while the whole mass rolled and ground together on the swell that rolled impassively from the west.

'Wind,' he muttered, 'there will be a wind soon,' and the thought sent him below, in search of his few belongings among the shambles.

He found he could retrieve only his journal, coat, hat and glass. He and one of Atcherley's marines brought up the body of Gillespy. Drinkwater wrapped the body in his own cloak and found a couple of shot left in the upper deck garlands. They bound the boy about with loose line and lifted the sad little bundle onto the rail. Had Drinkwater not agreed to Gillespy accompanying him on the *Bucentaure* he would be alive now, listening in Cadiz to the distant thunder of the guns in company with Frey and Quilhampton. The marine took off his shako and Drinkwater recited the familiar words of the Anglican prayer of committal. Then they rolled Gillespy into the water.

'He is in good company,' he murmured to himself, but his voice was drowned in a vast explosion. To the north the ship that had taken fire, the French *Achille*, blew apart as the fire reached her magazine. The blast rolled over the sea and hammered their already wounded ear-drums, bringing with it the first hint of a freshening breeze.

Captain Atcherley's prize crew consisted of less than half a dozen men, besides himself. They had locked the private cabins of Villeneuve and his senior officers, asked for and obtained the parole of

188

those remaining officers capable of posing a threat, and locked the magazines and spirit rooms. Following Drinkwater's advice, some food was found and served out to all, irrespective of nationality. As the battle began to die out around them, Masson came on deck. His clothes were completely soaked in blood, his pale face smudged with gore and drawn with exhaustion.

'Did you notice,' he said to Drinkwater, 'how the raking fire mostly took off men's heads? It is curious, is it not, Captain?'

Drinkwater looked at him, seeing the results of terrible strain. Masson sniffed and said, 'Thank you for your assistance.'

'It was nothing. I could not stand idle.' Drinkwater paused, not wishing to seem to patronise defeated men. 'They were brave men,' he said simply.

Masson nodded. 'That is their only epitaph.' The surgeon slumped down between two guns and within a minute had fallen fast asleep.

Atcherley joined Drinkwater on the poop, watching the last of the fighting.

'My God, they have made a mess of us, by heaven!' exclaimed Atcherley when he saw the damage to the masts of the British ships. 'If the wind gets up we'll be caught on a dead lee shore.'

'I believe it will get up, Captain Atcherley, and we would do well to take some precautions.' Drinkwater was staring through his glass.

'Is that *Victory*? She is a wreck, look . . .' He handed the glass to Atcherley.

'Yes . . . and Collingwood's flag is down from the *Royal Sovereign*'s masthead . . .'

The two men looked at one another. There was little left of *Royal Sovereign*'s masts, but they had seen Collingwood's flag there ten minutes ago, atop the stump of the foremast with a British ensign hoisted to the broken stump of the main. Had Collingwood been killed? And then they saw the blue square go up to the masthead of the *Euryalus*.

'He has shifted his flag to the frigate,' said Atcherley betraying a sense of relief.

'But why?' asked Drinkwater. 'Surely Nelson would not permit that?'

But further conjecture was distracted by a movement to the south-east. They could see ships making sail, running clear of the pall of smoke. Drinkwater trained his glass. He knew the leading vessel; it was Gravina's flagship.

'God's bones!' Drinkwater watched as the *Principe de Asturias* led some ten or eleven ships out of the Allied line, making all possible sail in the direction of Cadiz. The Spanish grandee had finally deserted his chief, Drinkwater thought, not knowing that Gravina lay below with a shattered arm, nor that his second, Rear-Admiral Magon, galled by a dozen musket balls, had finally been cut in two by a round shot. At the time it seemed like the final betrayal of Villeneuve.

Under their stern passed a British launch, commanded by a master's mate and engaged in carrying prize crews about the shattered remnants of the Combined Fleet. Atcherley stared at her as she made her way amongst the floating wreckage of the great ships of three nations that lay wallowing upon the heaving sea.

'Good God, sir, I believe those fellows to be crying!'

Drinkwater levelled his glass on the straining oarsmen. There could be no mistake. He could see awful grimaces upon the faces of several men, and streaked patches where tears had washed the powder soot from their cheeks. 'Good God!'

'Boat 'hoy!' Atcherley hailed.

The elderly master's mate called his men to stop pulling and looked up at the two officers standing under the British ensign hoisted over the French.

'What ship's that?'

'The French admiral, *Bucentaure*,' called Atcherley, proudly adding, 'prize to the *Conqueror*. What is the matter with your men?'

'Matter? Have ye not heard the news?'

'News? What news beyond that of victory?'

'Victory? Ha!' The mate spat over the side. 'Why, Nelson's dead . . . d'you hear? Nelson's dead . . .'

The wind began to rise at sunset when *Conqueror* beat up to reclaim her prize, ranging to weather of her. Pellew sent a boat with a lieutenant and more men to augment Atcherley's pathetic prize crew. Drinkwater scrambled up onto *Bucentaure*'s rail and hailed Pellew.

'Have the kindness, sir, to report Captain Drinkwater as having rejoined the fleet. I was taken off Tarifa and held a prisoner aboard this ship!'

'Ah!' cried Pellew waving his hat in acknowledgement. 'We wondered where you had got to, Drinkwater. Stockham won't be complaining! He drove The *Prince of the Asturias* off the *Revenge*! We've seventeen prizes but lost Lord Nelson!'

'I heard. A bad day for England!'

'Indeed. Will you look after *Bucentaure* then? 'tis coming on to blow!'

'She is much damaged but we shall do our best!'

'Splendid. I shall take you in tow!' Pellew waved his hat and jumped down onto his own deck. His lieutenant, Richard Spear, touched his hat to Drinkwater.

'I have orders to receive a line, sir.'

'Carry on, sir, and be quick about it . . . Who the devil is Stockham, d'you know Mr Atcherley?'

'John Stockham, sir? Yes, he's first luff of the *Thunderer*. He'll get his step in rank for this day's work.'

'I expect so,' said Drinkwater flatly, moving towards the compass in order to determine their position. In the last light of day Cape Trafalgar was a dark smudge on the eastward horizon to leeward.

Astern of the *Conqueror* the *Bucentaure* dragged and snubbed at the hemp cable. The wind backed round to south-south-west and increased to gale force by midnight. British and French alike laboured for two hours to haul an undamaged cable out of the hold and forward, onto an anchor. In the blackness of the howling night they were briefly aware of other ships; of the soaring arcs of rockets signalling distress; of the proximity of wounded leviathans in a similar plight to themselves. But many of these wallowed helplessly untowed, their mastless hulks rolling in the troughs of the seas which quickly built up to roll the broken ships closer to the shallows off the cape. From *Euryalus* Collingwood had thrown out the night signal to wear. Those ships which were able complied, but most simply lay a-hull, broached to and waiting for the dawn.

Short of sleep and starved of adequate food, Drinkwater nevertheless spent the night on deck, directing the labours of his strange crew in their efforts to save the *Bucentaure* from the violence of the gale. Atcherley and Spear deferred to him naturally; the French were familiar with him and he had earned their respect, if not their trust, from his exertions at the side of Masson during the battle. While *Conqueror* inched them to windward, away from the shoals off Cape Trafalgar, they cut away the rigging and wreckage of *Bucentaure*'s masts. But her battered hull continued to ship water which drained to her bilges, sinking her deeper and deeper into the water. Of her huge crew and the many soldiers on board – something not far short of eight hundred men – scarcely ten score were on their feet at the end of the action. Many of these fell exhausted at the pumps.

Daylight revealed a fearful sight. Ahead of them, her reefed topsails straining under the continued violence of the gale that had now become a storm, Pellew's ship tugged and strained at the tow-rope, jerking it tight until the water was squeezed out of the lay of the rope.

191

Bucentaure would move forward and the rope would dip into a wave, then come tight again as she dragged back, jerking the stern of *Conqueror* and making her difficult to handle. But by comparison they were fortunate. There were other ships in tow, British and Allied, all struggling to survive the smashing grey seas as they rolled eastwards, streaked white with spume and driving them inexorably to leeward. Already the unfortunate were amongst the shoals and shallows of the coast.

All day they were witness to this tragedy as men who had escaped the fire of British cannon were dashed to their deaths on the rocks and beaches of the Spanish coast. As darkness came on again the wind began to veer, allowing Pellew to make a more southerly course. But *Bucentaure*'s people were becoming increasingly feeble and their efforts to keep the water from pouring into her largely failed. Spirits rose, however, on the morning of the 23rd, for the wind dropped and the sky cleared a little as it veered into the north-west. Drinkwater was below eating a mess of what passed for porridge when Spear burst in.

'Sir! There are enemy ships under way. They seem to be making some sort of an effort to retake prizes!'

Drinkwater followed the worried officer on deck and trained his glass to the north-east. He could see the blue-green line of the coast and the pale smudge that was Cadiz.

'There, sir!'

'I have them.' He counted the topsails: 'Four line-of-battle ships, five frigates and two brigs!'

Had Gravina remembered his obligation to Villeneuve, Drinkwater wondered? But there were more pressing considerations.

'Get forrard, Mr Spear, and signal *Conqueror* that the enemy is in sight!'

Drinkwater spent the next two hours in considerable anxiety. The strange ships were coming up fast, all apparently undamaged in the battle. He recognised the French *Neptune* and the Spanish *Rayo*.

Spear came scrambling aft with the news that Pellew had seen the approaching enemy and intended casting loose the tow. There was nothing Drinkwater could do except watch *Conqueror* make sail and stand to windward, to join the nine other British warships able to manoeuvre and work themselves between the enemy and the majority of the prizes.

Bucentaure began to roll and wallow to leeward, continuing to ship water. On deck Drinkwater watched the approach of the enemy, the leading ship with a commodore's broad pendant at her masthead. It was not Gravina but one of the more enterprising of the escaped French captains who was leading this bold sortie. The leading ship was a French eighty, and she bore down on *Bucentaure* as the stricken vessel drifted away from the protection of the ten British line-of-battle ships. As she luffed to windward of them they read her name: *Indomptable*.

The appearance of the Franco–Spanish squadron revived the crew of the *Bucentaure*. One of her lieutenants requested that Drinkwater released them from their parole and he had little alternative but to agree. A few moments later, boats from *Indomptable* were alongside and the *Bucentaure*'s lieutenant were representing the impossibility of saving the former French flagship. '*Elle est finie*,' Drinkwater heard him say, and they began to take out of the *Bucentaure* all her crew, including the wounded. For an hour and a half the boats of the *Indomptable* ferried men from the *Bucentaure* with great difficulty. The sea was still running high and damage was done to the boats and to their human cargo. Drinkwater summoned Atcherley and Spear.

'Gentlemen,' he said, 'I believe the French to be abandoning the ship. If we remain we have still an anchor and cable. We might yet keep her a prize. It is only a slender chance, but I do not wish to be retaken prisoner just yet.'

The two officers nodded agreement. 'volunteers only, then,' added Drinkwater as the French lieutenant approached.

'It is now you come to boats, *Capitaine*.'

'*Non, mon ami*. We stay, perhaps we save the ship.'

The lieutenant appeared to consider this for some moments and then shrugged.

'Ver' well. I too will stay.'

So a handful of men remained aboard the *Bucentaure* as the Allied squadron made sail, refusing battle with the ten British ships. Drinkwater watched them hauling off their retaken ships, the Spanish *Neptuno* and the great black bulk of the *Santa Ana*, the latter towed by a brig, scraps of sails and the Spanish ensign re-hoisted on what remained of her masts. Hardly had *Indomptable* taken in her boats than the wind backed suddenly and increased with tremendous strength from the west-south-west. Immediately *Bucentaure*'s leeway increased and as the afternoon wore on the pale smudge of Cadiz grew swiftly larger and more distinct. They could see details: the towers of the partly rebuilt cathedral, the belfry of the Carmelite convent, the lighthouse at San Sebastian and, along the great bight of Cadiz Bay from beyond Rota in the north to the Castle of St Peter to the southward, the wrecked hulks of the Combined Fleet being pounded to matchwood in the breakers.

As they drove inshore, Drinkwater had soundings taken, and at about three in the afternoon he had the anchor let go in a last attempt to save the ship. The fluke bit and *Bucentaure* snubbed round at the extremity of the cable to pitch head to sea as the wind blew again with storm force. They could see the British ships in the offing and around them some of the vessels that had sallied from Cadiz that morning. They had run for the shelter of the harbour as the wind began to blow, but several had not made it and had been forced to anchor like themselves.

Bucentaure's anchor held for an hour before the cable parted. Drinkwater called all her people on deck and they stood helplessly in the waist as the great ship drove again to leeward, beam on to the sea, rolling heavily as ton after ton of water poured on board. The rocks of Cape San Sebastian loomed towards them.

'Call all your men together, Mr Spear,' Drinkwater said quietly as the *Bucentaure* rose on the back of a huge wave. The heavy swell, enlarged by the violence of the storm, increased its height as its forward momentum was sapped by the rising sea-bed. Its lower layers were slowed and its upper surface tore onwards, rolling and toppling with its own instability, bearing the huge bulk of the *Bucentaure* upon its collapsing back.

In a roar of white water, as the spray whipped across her canting deck, the ship struck, her whole hull juddering with the impact. Water foamed all about her, thundering and tearing over the reef beyond the *Bucentaure*. Then it was receding, pouring off the exposed rocks as the trough sucked out and the stricken battleship lolled over. Suddenly she began to lift again as the next breaker took her, a white-flecked avalanche of water that rose above her splintered rail.

'Hold on!' shouted Drinkwater, and the urgency of the cry communicated itself to British and French alike. Then it broke over them, intensely cold, driving the breath from their bodies and tearing them from their handholds. Drinkwater felt the pain in his shoulder muscles as the cold and the strain attacked them. He clung to an eyebolt, holding his breath as the red lights danced before his eyes and his lungs forced him to inhale. He gasped, swallowing water, and then he was in air again and, unbelievably, *Bucentaure* was moving beneath them. He struggled upright and stared about him. Not fifty yards away the little bluff of Cape San Sebastian rushed past. Beneath its lighthouse crowds of people watched the death throes of the ship.

194

Bucentaure had torn free, carried over the reef at a tangent to the little peninsula of the cape. He looked about the deck. There were less men than there had been. God alone knew how many had been swept into the sea by that monstrous wave.

For twenty minutes the ship drifted to leeward, into slightly calmer water. But every moment she sank lower and, half an hour later, had stuck fast upon the Puercas Reef. Drinkwater looked around him, knowing the long travail was over at last. In the dusk, boats were approaching from a French frigate anchored in the *Grande Rade* with the remnants of Gravina's escaped detachment. He turned to Spear and Atcherley. They were both shivering from cold and wet.

'Well, gentlemen, it seems we are not to perish, although we have lost your prize.'

Atcherley nodded. 'In the circumstances, sir, it is enough.' The marine officer looked at the closing boats with resignation.

'I suppose we must be made prisoners now,' said Spear dejectedly.

'Yes, I suppose so,' replied Drinkwater shortly, aware of the dreadful ache in his right shoulder and that beneath his feet *Bucentaure* was going to pieces.

Gibraltar

'Were you received by the Governor-General at Cadiz, Captain?' asked Vice-Admiral Collingwood, leaning from his chair to pat the head of a small terrier by his side.

'The Marquis of Solana granted me several interviews, sir, and treated all the British prize crews with the utmost consideration.'

Collingwood nodded. 'I am very pleased to hear it.' Collingwood's broad Northumbrian accent struck a homely note to Drinkwater's ears after his captivity.

'Your decision to return the Spanish wounded and the expedition with which it was done undoubtedly obtained our release, sir. I must make known my personal thanks to you.'

'It is no matter,' Collingwood said wearily. 'Did you obtain any knowledge of the state of the ships still in Cadiz?'

Drinkwater nodded. 'Yes, sir. Admiral Rosily arrived to find his command reduced to a handful of frigates. Those ships which escaped the action off Trafalgar were almost all destroyed in their attempt to retake the prizes on the twenty-third last. Although they got both the *Neptuno* and *Santa Ana* back into port, both are very badly damaged. However, it cost them the loss of the *Indomptable* which went ashore off Rota and was lost with her company and most of the poor fellows off the *Bucentaure*. The *San Francisco* parted her cables and drove on the rocks at Santa Catalina. As you know, the *Rayo* and *Monarca* were wrecked after their action with *Leviathan* and *Donegal*. I believe Gravina's *Principe de Asturias* to be the only ship of force fit for sea now left in Cadiz.'

'And Gravina? Do you know the state of his health, Captain?'

'Not precisely, sir, but he was severely wounded and it was said that he may yet lose an arm. . . May I ask the fate of Admiral Villeneuve, sir?'

'Villeneuve? Ah, yes, I see from your report that you made his acquaintance while in Cadiz. He was sent home a prisoner in the *Euryalus*. What manner of man did you judge him?'

'Personally courageous, sir, if a little lacking in resolve. But he was a perceptive and able seaman, well fitted to judge the weight of opposition against him. I do not believe he was ever in doubt as to the outcome of an action, although he entertained some hopes of eluding you . . .'

'Eluding us?' Collingwood raised an incredulous eyebrow.

'Yes, sir. And he had devised a method of counter-attacking, for he knew precisely by what method Lord Nelson would make his own attack.'

'How so?'

Drinkwater explained the function of the reserve squadron to bear down upon the spearhead of Nelson's advance.

'A bold plan,' said Collingwood when he had finished, 'and you say Villeneuve had argued the manner of our own attack?'

'Yes, sir. I believe that his fleet might have had more success had the wind been stronger and Gravina been able to hold the weather position.'

'Hmmm. As it was, they put up a stout and gallant defence. Admiral Villeneuve seems a well-bred man and I believe a very good officer. He has nothing in his manner of the offensive vapouring and boasting which we, perhaps too often, attribute to Frenchmen.'

'The Spaniards are less tolerant, sir,' Drinkwater said. 'The French were not well received in Cadiz after the battle. There was bad blood between them before the action. I believe relations were much worse afterwards.'

Collingwood nodded. 'You will have heard that a squadron under Sir Richard Strachan caught Dumanoir's four ships and took them on the third.'

'Then the enemy is utterly beaten,' said Drinkwater, perceiving properly the magnitude of the victory for the first time.

'Carthage is destroyed,' Collingwood said with quiet satisfaction, 'It would have pleased Lord Nelson . . .' The admiral fell silent.

Drinkwater also sat quietly. He did not wish to intrude upon Collingwood's grief for his dead friend. In the few hours he had been at Gibraltar since the *Donegal* landed him from Cadiz, Drinkwater had learned of the grim reaction within the British fleet to the death of Nelson. At first men exhausted with battle had sat and wept, but now the sense of purpose with which the little one-armed admiral had inspired his fleet had been replaced. Instead there was a strange, dry-eyed emotion, affecting all ranks, that prevented any levity or triumphant crowing over a beaten foe. This strange reticence affected Drinkwater now, as he sat in the great cabin of HMS *Queen*, to which Collingwood had shifted his flag, and waited for the new Commander-in-Chief to continue the interview. The little terrier raised its head and licked its master's hand.

'Yes, Captain Drinkwater,' said Collingwood at last, 'we have gained a great victory, but at a terrible cost . . . terrible!' He sighed and then pulled himself together. 'Perhaps we can go home soon . . . eh, Captain, home . . . but not before we've cornered Allemand and blockaded Salcedo in Cartegena, eh? Which brings me to you.' Collingwood paused and referred to some papers on his desk. 'We have lost not only Lord Nelson but several post-captains. I am endeavouring to have the Admiralty make promotions among the most deserving officers; many distinguished themselves. Quilliam, first of the *Victory*, for instance, and Stockham of the *Thunderer* . . .' He fixed his tired eyes upon Drinkwater.

Drinkwater wondered how much of Collingwood's exhaustion was due to his constant battle to placate and oblige people of all stations in his extensive and responsible command. He leaned forward.

'I understand perfectly, sir. Stockham has earned and deserves his captaincy.'

Collingwood smiled. 'Thank you, Captain. No doubt the Admiralty will find him a frigate in due course, but you see my dilemma.'

'Perfectly, sir. I shall be happy to return to the *Antigone*.'

'That will not be possible. I have sent her in quest of Allemand. Louis put a commander into her and, for the moment, you will have to undertake other duties.'

'Very well, sir.' Drinkwater had no time to digest the implications of this news beyond realising that a stranger was using his cabin and that poor Rogers would be put out.

Collingwood continued: 'I am putting you in command of the *Swiftsure*, prize, Captain Drinkwater. It should give you a measure of satisfaction that she was once a British ship of the line. I believe you returned from Cadiz with three other prisoners from your own frigate?'

'Yes, sir, Lieutenant Quilhampton and Midshipman Frey, and my man Tregembo.'

'Very well. They will do for a beginning and I shall arrange for a detachment from the fleet to join you forthwith.' Collingwood paused to consider something. 'We shall have to rename her, Captain Drinkwater. We already have a *Swiftsure*. We shall call her *Irresistible* . . . I will have a commission drawn up for you and until your frigate comes in with news of Allemand you will find your talents in great demand.'

Drinkwater rose. 'It is an apt name, sir,' he said smiling, 'one that I think even our late enemies might have approved . . .' He paused as

Collingwood frowned. 'The Dons were much impressed by the spectacle of British ships continuing the blockade of Cadiz even after the battle. I apprehend the enemy expected us to have suffered too severe a blow.'

'We did, my dear sir, in the loss of our chief, but to have withdrawn the blockade would not have been consistent with his memory.' Collingwood's words of dismissal were poignant with grief for his fallen friend.

Drinkwater sat in the dimly lit cabin of the *Irresistible* and read the sheaf of orders that had come aboard earlier that evening. Outside the battered hulk of the ship, the wind whined in from the Atlantic, moving them gently even within the shelter of the breakwater, so that the shot-torn fabric of the ship groaned abominably. He laid down the formal effusion of praise from both Houses of Parliament that he had been instructed to read to the assembled ship's company tomorrow morning. It was full of the usual pompous Parliamentary cant. There was a notice that Vice-Admiral Collingwood was elevated to the peerage and a list of confirmed promotions that would bring joy to half the ships that crammed Gibraltar Bay, making good the damage inflicted by the Combined Fleet and the great gale.

Drinkwater was acutely conscious that he would not be part of the ritual. He knew that, in his heart, he would live to regret not being instrumental in an event which was epochal. Yet he was far from being alone. Apart from Quilhampton and Frey, there was not a man in Admiral Louis's squadron that was not mortified to have been sitting in Gibraltar Bay when Lord Nelson was dying off Cape Trafalgar. They could not reconcile themselves to their ill-luck. At least, Drinkwater consoled himself, he had been a witness to the battle. It did not occur to him that he had in any way contributed to the saving of a single life by his assisting Masson in the cockpit of the *Bucentaure*. His mind shied away from any contemplation of that terrible place, unwilling to burden itself with the responsibility of poor Gillespy's death. He knew that remorse would eventually compel him to face his part in the boy's fate, but events pressed him too closely in the refitting of *Irresistible* for him to relax yet. Once they sailed, he knew, reaction would set in; for the moment, he was glad to have something constructive to do and to know that neither Quilhampton nor Frey had come to any harm.

A knock at his cabin door broke into his train of thought and he was glad of the interruption. 'Enter!'

Drinkwater looked up from the pool of lamp-light illuminating the litter of papers upon the table.

'Yes. Who is it?' The light from the lamp blinded him to the darkness elsewhere in the cabin. The white patches of a midshipman's collar caught the reflected light and suddenly he saw that it was Lord Walmsley who stepped out of the shadows. Drinkwater frowned. 'What the devil d'you want?' he asked sharply.

'I beg pardon, sir, but may I speak with you?'

Drinkwater stared coldly at the young man. Since his brief, unexpected appearance on the *Bucentaure*, Drinkwater had given Walmsley no further thought.

'Well, Mr Walmsley?'

'I . . . I, er, wished to apologise, sir . . .' Walmsley bit his lip, 'to apologise, sir, and ask if you would accept me back . . .'

Drinkwater studied the midshipman. He sensed, rather than saw, a change in him. Perhaps it was the lamp-light illuminating his face, but he seemed somehow older. Drinkwater knitted his brow, recalling that Walmsley had killed Waller. He dismissed his momentary sympathy.

'I placed you on board *Canopus*, Mr Walmsley, under Rear-Admiral Louis. The next thing I know is that you are on *Conqueror*. Then you come here wearing sack-cloth and ashes. It will not do, sir. No, it really will not do.' Drinkwater leaned forward in dismissal of the midshipman, but Walmsley persisted.

'Sir, I beg you give me a hearing.'

Drinkwater looked up again, sighed and said, 'Go on.'

Walmsley swallowed and Drinkwater saw that his face was devoid of arrogance. He seemed chastened by something.

'Admiral Louis had me transferred, sir. I was put on board *Conqueror* . . .'

'Why?' Drinkwater broke in sharply.

Walmsley hesitated. 'The admiral said . . .'

'Said what?'

Walmsley was trembling, containing himself with a great effort: 'That my character was not fit, sir. That I should be broke like a horse before I could be made a seaman . . .' Walmsley hung his head, unable to go on. A silence filled the cabin.

'How old are you?'

'Nineteen, sir.'

'And Captain Pellew, what was his opinion of you?'

Walmsley mastered his emotion. The confession had clearly cost him a great deal, but it was over now. 'Captain Pellew had given me no marks of his confidence, sir. My present position is not tolerable.'

'And why have you suddenly decided to petition me, sir? Do you consider me to be *easy*?' Drinkwater raised his voice.

'No, sir. But the events of recent weeks have persuaded me that I should better learn my business from you, sir.'

'Do you have a sudden desire to learn your business, Mr Walmsley? I had not noticed your zeal commend you before.'

'No, sir . . . but the events of recent weeks, sir . . . I am . . . I can offer no explanation beyond saying that the battle has had a profound effect upon me. So many good fellows going . . . the sight of so many dead . . .'

It struck Drinkwater that the young man was sincere. He remembered him vomiting over the shambles of the *Bucentaure*'s gun-deck and supposed the battle might have had some redeeming effect upon Walmsley's character. Whether reformed or not, Walmsley watched by a vigilant Drinkwater might be better than Walmsley abusing his rank and privileges with men who had fought with such gallantry off Cape Trafalgar.

'Very well, Mr Walmsley,' Drinkwater reached for a clean sheet of paper, 'I will write to Captain Pellew on your behalf.'

The Martyr of Rennes

'So you finally came home in a frigate?' Lord Dungarth looked at his single dinner guest through a haze of blue tobacco smoke.

'Aye, my Lord, only to miss *Antigone* sent in convoy with the West India fleet, and then go down with the damned marsh ague . . .'

Dungarth looked at Drinkwater's face, cocked at its curious angle and pale from the effects of the recent fever. It had not been the homecoming Drinkwater had dreamed of, but Elizabeth had cosseted him back to full health.

'I have been languishing in bed for six weeks.'

'Well I am glad that you could come in answer to my summons, Nathaniel.' He passed the decanter across the polished table. 'I have a commission for you before you rejoin your ship.'

Drinkwater returned the decanter after refilling his glass. He nodded. 'I am fit enough, my Lord, to be employed on any service. Besides,' he added with his old grin, 'I am obliged to your Lordship . . . personally.'

'Ah, yes. Your brother.' Dungarth blew a reflective ring of tobacco smoke at the ceiling. 'He was at Austerlitz, you know. His report of the confusion on the Pratzen Heights made gloomy reading.'

'God bless my soul . . . at Austerlitz.' The news of Napoleon's great victory over the combined forces of Austria and Russia, following so hard upon the surrender of another Austrian army at Ulm, seemed to have off-set the hard-won achievements of Trafalgar, destroying at a · stroke Pitt's carefully erected alliance of the Third Coalition.

'Aye, Austerlitz. It killed Pitt as surely as Trafalgar killed Nelson.'

Both men remained silent for a moment and Drinkwater thought of the tired young man with the loose stockings.

'It was the one thing Pitt dreaded, you know, a great French victory . . . and at the expense of three armies.' Dungarth shook his head. The victory over the Russo–Austrian army had taken place on the first anniversary of Napoleon's coronation as Emperor and had had all the impact of a fatal blow to British foreign policy. Worn out with responsibility and disappointment, Pitt had died just over a month later.

'I believe,' Dungarth continued with the air of a man choosing his words carefully, 'that Pitt foresaw the destruction of Napoleon himself as the only way to achieve lasting peace in Europe.'

'Is that why he sent Camelford to attempt his murder?'

Dungarth nodded. 'I think so. It was done without approval; a private arrangement. Perhaps Pitt could not face the future if Napoloen destroyed an allied army. Pitt chose badly by selecting Camelford, but I imagine the strength of family obligation seemed enough at the time; besides, Pitt was out of office.' Dungarth sipped his port.

'The attempt was not secret, though. I recall D'Auvergne and Cornwallis both alluding to the fact that something was in the wind,' said Drinkwater, intrigued.

'No, it was not kept secret enough, a fact from which Napoleon has made a great deal of capital. D'Auvergne shipped Camelford into France from Jersey, and Cornwallis knew of the plan, on a private basis, you understand. Billy-go-tight no more likes blockading than does poor Collingwood now left to hold the Mediterranean.' Dungarth refilled his glass.

'Poor Collingwood talked of coming home,' remarked Drinkwater, taking the decanter.

'He will be disappointed, I fear. Pitt was right, I think: almost anything was acceptable to end this damnable war, so that he and Cornwallis and Collingwood and all of us could go home and enjoy an honourable retirement.'

'And Camelford's death,' asked Drinkwater, 'was that an act fomented by French agents?'

Dungarth filled his glass again. 'To be honest I do not know. Camelford was a rake-hell and a philanderer. What he got up to on his own account I have no idea.' Dungarth sipped his port and then changed the subject. 'I understand you met our old friend Santhonax at Cadiz?'

Drinkwater recounted the circumstances of their meeting. 'I suppose that, had Santhonax not recognised my name on the *Guarda Costa* report, I might still be rotting in a cell at Tarifa.'

'Or on your way to a French dépot like Verdun.'

'I was surprised he departed suddenly before the action.'

'I believe he too was at Austerlizt, though on the winning side.' Dungarth's smile was ironic. 'Napoleon recalled several officers from Cadiz. We received reports that they passed through Madrid. I think the Emperor's summons may have saved you from a fate worse than a cell at Tarifa or even Verdun.'

'A fact of which I am profoundly sensible,' Drinkwater replied.

'Now what of this new service, my Lord?'

The ironic look returned to Dungarth's face. 'A duty I think you will not refuse, Nathaniel. I have a post-chaise calling for you in an hour. You are to proceed to Reading and then to Rye where a lugger awaits you.'

'A lugger?'

'A cartel, Nathaniel. You will pick up a prisoner at Reading. He has been exchanged for four post-captains.'

Drinkwater remembered Quilhampton's multiplication table of exchange. He frowned. 'An admiral, my Lord?'

'Precisely, Nathaniel. Vice-Admiral Pierre de Villeneuve. He wishes to avoid Paris and he mentioned you specifically.'

'You are awake, sir?' Drinkwater looked at Villeneuve opposite, his face lit by the flickering oil-lamp set in the chaise's buttoned-velvet side.

Admiral Villeneuve nodded. 'Yes, Captain, I am awake.'

'We do not have far to go now,' said Drinkwater. The pace of the chaise was smooth and fast as it crossed the levels surrounding Rye. A lightening in the east told of coming daylight and Drinkwater was anxious to have his charge below decks before sunrise.

'You are aware that I wish to be landed at Morlaix?' Villeneuve's tone was anxious, even supplicating.

'Indeed yes, sir. I have specific instructions to that effect,' Drinkwater replied tactfully. Then he added, 'You have nothing to fear, sir. I am here to see you safe ashore.'

Villeneuve made as though to speak, then thought better of it. After a silence he asked, 'Have you seen your wife, Captain?'

'Yes.' Drinkwater did not add that he had been prostrated by fever and that Elizabeth had born his delirium with her customary fortitude.

'You are fortunate. I hope that I may soon see my own. If . . .' he began, then again stopped and changed the subject. 'I recall', he said with a firmer tone to his voice, 'that we spoke of destiny. Do you remember?'

'Yes, I do.'

'I was present at the funeral of Lord Nelson, Captain. Do you not think that remarkable?'

'No more than the man whose interment you honoured, sir.'

Villeneuve's sigh was audible. He said something to himself in French. 'Do you think we were disgraced, Captain?'

'No, sir. Lord Nelson's death was proof that you defended your flag

204

to the utmost. I myself was witness to it.'

'It was a terrible responsibility. Not the defeat – I believe victory was earned by you British – but the decision to sail . . . to set honour against safety and to let honour win . . . terrible . . .'

'If it is any consolation, sir, I do not think that Lord Nelson intended leaving you unmolested in Cadiz. I believe it was his intention to attack you in Cadiz itself if necessary.'

Villeneuve smiled sadly. 'That is kind of you, Captain. But the decision to send many brave men to their deaths was mine, and mine alone. I must bear that burden.'

Villeneuve fell silent again and Drinkwater began to pay attention to their appoach to Rye. Then, as the chaise slowed, Villeneuve said suddenly, '*You* played your part, Captain, you and Santhonax and Admiral Rosily who was already coming to replace me . . .'

'*I* sir? How was that?'

But the chaise jerked to a stop, the door was flung open and the opportunity to elaborate lost. They descended onto a strip of wind-swept wooden-piled quay and Drinkwater was occupied with the business of producing his documents and securing his charge aboard the cartel-lugger *Union*. An hour later, as the lugger crossed Rye bar, he went below to find something to eat and renew his talk with Villeneuve. But the French admiral had rolled himself in a cloak and gone to sleep.

They enjoyed a swift passage down Channel, being bought-to twice by small and suspicious British cruisers. They crossed the Channel from the Isle of Wight and raised the Channel Islands where a British frigate challenged them. Drinkwater was able to keep the identity of their passenger secret as he had been ordered and, making certain that he had the passport from the French commissioner for prisoners in London, he ordered the lugger off for the Breton coast and the port of Morlaix. During the passage Villeneuve made no attempt to renew their discussion. The presence of other people, the cramped quarters and the approaching coast of France caused him to withdraw inside himself. Drinkwater respected his desire for his own company. It was after they had raised Cap Frehel and were coasting westwards, that Villeneuve called for pen and paper. When he had finished writing he addressed Drinkwater.

'Captain, I know you to be a man of honour. I admired your ability before you had the misfortune to become a prisoner, when I watched your frigate run up into Cadiz Road. Colonel Santhonax only rein-

forced my opinion of you. You came to me as an example of many . . .
a specimen of the *esprit* of the British fleet . . . everywhere I was
surrounded by suspicion, dislike, lack of co-operation. You understand?'

Drinkwater nodded but remained silent as Villeneuve went on.
'For many years I have felt myself fated, Captain. They called my
escape from Abukir lucky, but,' he shrugged, 'for myself it was
dishonourable. It was necessary that I expiate for that dishonour.
You persuaded me that to fight Nelson, to be beaten by Nelson, would
be no dishonour. I would be fighting men of *your* quality, Captain, and
it is to *you* as one of Nelson's officers that I entrust this paper. Should
anything befall me, Captain, I beg you to make known its contents to
your Admiralty.'

'Your Excellency,' said Drinkwater, much moved by this speech
and unconsciously reverting to the form of address he had used when
this unfortunate man commanded the Combined Fleet, 'I assure you
that you will be landed in perfect safety . . .'

'Of that I too am certain, Captain. But my Imperial master is
unlikely to receive me with the same hospitality shown by my late
enemies. You know he has servants willing to express his displeasure.'

For a moment Drinkwater did not understand, and then he remembered Santhonax, and the allegations of the murder of John Wesley
Wright in the Temple. Drinkwater picked up the letter and thrust it
into his breast pocket. 'I am sure, sir, that you will find happiness with
your wife.'

'It is a strong condemnation of the Emperor Napoleon and of the
impossible demands he has put upon his admirals, captains and
seamen,' said Lord Dungarth as he laid down Villeneuve's paper and
looked at Drinkwater. 'This is dated the sixth of April. He wrote it on
board the cartel?'

'And gave it to me for personal delivery to the Admiralty in the
event of anything untoward occurring to him. He seemed intent on
making his way south to his estate and joining his wife. I cannot
believe he took his own life.'

Dungarth shook his head and picked up another paper from his
desk. It seemed to be in cipher and beneath the queer letters someone
had written a decoding. 'I have received various reports, mainly
public announcements after the post-mortem which, I might add,
was held with indecent haste. Also some gossip from the usual
waterfront sources. He wrote to the Minister of Marine, Decrès, from

206

Morlaix, also to some captains he proposed calling as witnesses at the enquiry he knew would judge his conduct. They were Infernet and Lucas, who had both been lionised by the Emperor at St Cloud. He received no reply, travelled to Rennes and arrived on the seventeenth. Witnesses at the post-morten conveniently said he was depressed. Hardly remarkable, one would have thought. Then, on the morning of the twenty-second of April his body was found with six knife wounds in the heart. The body was undressed, face upwards. One witness said face down, but this conflicting evidence seems to have been ignored. Evidence of suicide was supported by the discovery of a letter to his wife and his telescope and speaking trumpet labelled to Infernet and Lucas. Ah, and the door was locked on the inside . . . that is no very great achievement for a man of Santhonax's abilities . . .'

'Santhonax?'

Dungarth nodded. 'He arrived in town the previous evening, Nathaniel. In view of the fact that he was at the post-mortem, I regard that as a most remarkable coincidence, don't you? And consider: Villeneuve is alleged to have stabbed himself six times in the heart. *Six*, Nathaniel, *six*! Is that consistent with the man you knew, or indeed for any man committing suicide?'

Drinkwater shook his head. 'I think not.'

'No, nor I,' said Dungarth vehemently. 'I wish to God we could pay Santhonax in like coin, by God I do.'

The eyes of both men met. Drinkwater recalled Dungarth passing up an opportunity to shoot both Santhonax and his wife Hortense as Camelford had advised. Perhaps if Camelford had succeeded in his mission neither he, nor Villeneuve, nor little Gillespy would be dead. 'I think Villeneuve anticipated some such end, my Lord,' Drinkwater said solemnly. 'I think he felt it his destiny.'

'Poor devil,' said Dungarth, his hazel eyes glittering intensely. 'Trafalgar notwithstanding, Nathaniel, this damnable war is not yet over.'

'No, not yet.'

'And that bastard Santhonax has yet to get his just deserts . . .'

207

Author's Note

In using the Trafalgar campaign as a basis for a novel I have not consciously meddled with history. All the major events actually took place and many of the characters existed. I have used a novelist's freedom in interpreting the actions of some of these, such as Camelford, who remains an enigma to this day. As for other figures, I have used their written or recorded words or opinions to preserve historical accuracy.

There is no doubt that Napoleon's intention to invade Great Britain some time between 1803 and 1805 was very real indeed. That he swung his army away from the Channel to defeat Austria and Russia does not diminish that intent; it merely illustrates his disillusion with his admirals, an understandable desire to secure his rear after the formation of the Third Coalition, and the strategic adaptability of his genius.

A great deal has been written about Trafalgar and its consequences. Perhaps the most lamentable of these is an improper appreciation of our opponents. It was this reflection that attracted me to the character of Pierre de Villeneuve, the noble turned republican, whose abilities have been entirely eclipsed by the apotheosis of Nelson. It was Villeneuve's prescience that made him the 'coward' his contemporaries took him for. Ten months before the battle, Villeneuve outlined the precise method by which Nelson would attack. Realising this and the comparative qualities of the two fleets, Villeneuve was astute enough to foresee the likely outcome of action, notwithstanding his plan for a counter-attack. Of his personal courage or that of his fleet, there is no doubt. I hope I have done justice to their shades.

None of these assertions detract from the British achievement; quite the contrary. The Battle of Trafalgar remains the completest example of the annihilation of a battlefleet until the Japanese attack on Pearl Harbor. Nevertheless there were grave misgivings about Nelson's ideas of how a blockade ought to be conducted, and these were freely expressed at the time. History vindicated Nelson, but contemporary opinion was not always so kind, and French officers like Santhonax wanted to exploit what was held to be a weakness.

Napoleon always disclaimed any part in the death of John Wesley

Wright and profoundly regretted that of D'Enghien. Between denial and admission lie a number of other mysterious deaths, particularly that of Pierre de Villeneuve. Despite the official verdict of suicide, I find it inconceivable that Villeneuve stabbed his own heart six times and I have laid the blame elsewhere. As to Villeneuve's curious letter of denunciation, one authority states that such a document of unproven origin came to light among the papers of a British diplomat employed at the time. It seemed to me that it might have formed some part of those supplementary revelations of unrecorded history which the adventures of Nathaniel Drinkwater have exposed.

If you have enjoyed this book and would like to receive details of other Walker Adventure titles, please write to:

Adventure Editor
Walker and Company
720 Fifth Avenue
New York, NY 10019